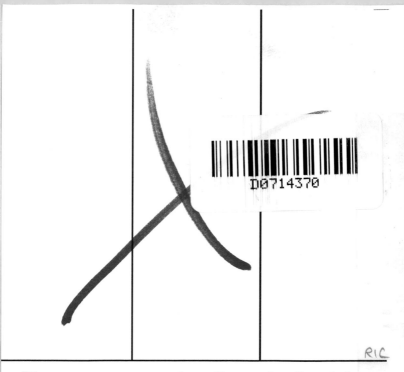

RIC

Please renew or return items by the date shown on your receipt

www.hertfordshire.gov.uk/libraries

Renewals and enquiries: 0300 123 4049

Textphone for hearing or 0300 123 4041
speech impaired users:

L32 11.16

Hertfordshire

530 300 64 6

Also by Colin Falconer

Crime:

Lucifer Falls (First in the DI Charlie George series)
Venom

20th-century fiction:

The Unkillable Kitty O'Kane
Anastasia
My Beautiful Spy
Sleeping with the Enemy
Live for Me
Loving Liberty Levine

For more about Colin Falconer books,
and to subscribe to his newsletter,
please go to colinfalconer.org

COLIN FALCONER

INNOCENCE DIES

CONSTABLE

CONSTABLE

First published in Great Britain in 2019 by Constable
This paperback edition published in 2020 by Constable

A CIP catalogue record for this book
is available from the British Library.

ISBN: 978-1-47212-804-1

Typeset in Sabon by Initial Typesetting Services, Edinburgh
Printed and bound in Great Britain by Clays Ltd, Elcograf S.p.A.

Papers used by Constable are from well-managed forests and
other responsible sources.

Constable
An imprint of
Little, Brown Book Group
Carmelite House
50 Victoria Embankment
London EC4Y 0DZ

An Hachette UK Company
www.hachette.co.uk

www.littlebrown.co.uk

For Jess and Loz

'Hell is empty and the devils are all here.'

The Tempest, *William Shakespeare*

GLOSSARY

ANPR: Automated Number Plate Recognition

Cellebrite: generic name for a portable device used to download digital data from a mobile phone

CPS: Crown Prosecution Service

CS: Crime Scene

FLO: Family Liaison Officer

FME: Forensic Medical Examiner

FONC: Either Charlie's DCI's initials, *or* a term of endearment used by the rest of the squad highlighting certain facets of the DCI's personality

HAT: Homicide Assessment Team

HOLMES: Home Office Large Major Enquiry System

IC3: code used by British police to describe ethnicity

IR: Incident Room

LOC: Loss of consciousness

MAPPA: Multi Agency Public Protection Arrangement

MISPERS: Missing Persons

MIT: Major Incident Team

NPC: National Police Computer

PACE: Police and Criminal Evidence

PNC: Police National Computer

POD:	Police Observation Device
SOCO:	Scenes of Crime Officer
TIE:	Trace, Interview, Eliminate
TOD:	Time of Death
TSG:	Territorial Support Group

CHAPTER ONE

The Nokia default ringtone is a three-second snippet taken from a 1902 guitar solo, 'Gran Vals', by the Spanish musician, Francisco Tárrega, considered one of the greatest classical guitarists of all time. It was sampled, before sampling was even fashionable, from Frédéric Chopin's 1834 waltz 'Grand Valse Brilliante'. The greatest thing about the piece, from the point of view of the executives at Nokia, who decided to use it, was that it was out of copyright.

The musical phrase had quite a different meaning for DI Charlie George; it told him that someone, somewhere, had lost their life through an act of extreme violence.

The Nokia on his bedside table belonged to the Force, regulation issue. He stared at the glow from the LED display in the dark, listened to it buzz and vibrate for a few grim seconds before he reached for it. He had thought about changing the default to something more appropriate for the distress and ugliness he was being summoned to; something already ruined for him. Pre-fucked, as DC Jayden Greene would say.

Kanye West, for instance.

He sat up, had the feeling of being dragged out of a play halfway through. Already the roseate world of his dreams was slipping away; he tried to hold on to it, a hand reaching back in a fast-flowing stream. No, it was gone, not even a few cold details to mull over when he was scraping the frost off his windscreen a few minutes from now. It had been a good dream, with a good woman in it, and Arsenal winning. Nothing at all like reality.

1

He flicked on the bedside lamp, picked up his Oliver Coen Berkeley and peered at it. 2.37. Nice. Come on, Charlie son, pick up the freaking phone. The duty officer isn't going to change his mind and ring someone else. You're on call, mate. Your shout.

'DI George?'

He didn't recognise the voice. Must be the new one, what was her name, Barnes, Barnett? No, Bartlett.

'It's DS Barlow at Essex Street.'

Right, that was it; close.

'Yes, Barlow.'

'Suspected homicide on a disused rail line in Finsbury Park. The HAT team are out there now. An eleven-year-old girl, missing since yesterday evening.'

His first thought: who finds bodies on a railway line in the middle of the night? That was one for the early morning joggers. Well, he supposed he'd find out soon enough. He scribbled down the details for his GPS, wished Barlow a good morning, and hung up.

A dead kid. Oh, great. He felt like he'd swallowed a cup of cold fat. He knew what that was like, too; his old man had made him do it once when he caught him stealing a bit of chicken out of the fridge.

He hated homicides involving kids; something you never got used to, they reckoned, no matter how many years you racked up in the job. 'Orpheus descending into the Underworld,' he said and got out of bed.

He stared at the clothes in his walk-in; he still missed his old place, this was like hanging up his suits in a phone box. He thought about his Corneliani suit, forty quid at a Salvo in Chelsea; the Incotex smart casual trousers, still hadn't worn them; the Marni trainers bought for a tenner at a market stall down the road. But they weren't for jobs like this. He grabbed one of his regulation navy CID suits, ninety quid at TK Maxx, and got dressed.

His car keys were on the bedside table, next to his phone.

He peered down into the street. There was a sheen of ice on the pavement.

He stumbled down the stairs, put on his Stone Island, hurried out of the door and nearly went arse over breakfast down his front steps. There was a high-pitched squeal; it sounded like a stuck pig, scared the bejesus out of him. He fumbled in his jacket for his iPhone, turned on the torch.

'What the fuck,' he said and bent down.

It was a dog, a cocker spaniel by the looks, shivering with cold, all skin and bone like a puppy. No collar on it. It licked his hand, the crafty bugger.

'What are you doing here?' Charlie said. 'Get yourself off home.'

The spaniel scrambled to its feet and trotted inside.

'No, you can't do that. I've got to go to work.'

The little dog sat himself down in his kitchen, half sitting, half leaning against the refrigerator door. He was still shivering, stared at him with its big sad eyes like he expected him to do something about it.

'You're wet,' Charlie said.

He grabbed a towel from the linen cupboard, dried him off as best he could. He went to the cupboard, got an empty beer box, put the towel in it to make a bed. He sorted through the shelves; there was a half-eaten packet of chocolate digestives. No, he'd read somewhere that dogs couldn't have chocolate. It would have to be the Rich Tea. 'Sorry mate, I ate all the custard creams,' he said, scooped the damned thing up under one arm and put it in the box. 'Look at you, you're all ribs, like an underwear model. Doesn't anyone ever feed you?'

Well, now what? He put the box under his arm and went out to the car.

I must be mad, Charlie thought. Who takes a spaniel to a crime scene? 'If you crap in my car,' he said to the dog, 'there'll be two bodies to sort out.' He wondered where the bloody thing had come from; no one in the block had a dog, far as he knew,

3

at least nothing bigger than a terrier. How was he going to find the owner? Facebook, he supposed. The spaniel didn't look as if he was missing anyone in particular, though, the state of him.

He hesitated a moment before getting in his car. But what else was he going to do? He couldn't leave the dog in the flat and he couldn't leave it to freeze on the doorstep.

He clicked the key remote, put the box and the spaniel on the floor on the passenger side. He got out one of the Rich Teas and gave it to him. 'Christ, you inhaled that. Didn't your mother teach you to chew your food?' He gave it another one, same result.

'Here, have the packet, why not,' he said, tossed the biscuits in the box with the spaniel and shut the door. He used the plastic scraper to get the frost off the windscreen, then got behind the wheel and warmed up the engine. He turned on the GPS. Seven minutes to Finsbury Park, according to Mrs Google. He wondered what was waiting for him.

He put the car into gear. He could feel the cocker spaniel looking at him.

'You have the right to remain silent,' he said. 'Use it.'

CHAPTER TWO

Charlie slowed at the police checkpoint, leaned out of the window to show his warrant card to a uniform in a high-viz jacket, and signed in. He parked behind a dark blue Beemer. Christ, the DCI was here. Was it that bad?

The local Bill had cordoned off the high street either side of the railway bridge. He could see the glow of the Crime Scene unit's halogens on the embankment; a nice climb up an icy slope then, that's the way to start a day.

The cocker peered at him over the edge of the box. 'Unless you've got a certificate showing me you're qualified as a sniffer dog, you cannot come to a crime scene,' Charlie said. 'So just sit here and be quiet. Don't eat all the biscuits and, for real, don't crap in my car.'

As he got out, his breath misted on the air. A few moments later it started chucking it down again, the weather gods conspiring to stuff up his crime scene. He went to the boot, got his white coveralls and shoe covers, struggled into them, got a fresh log book, then headed up the embankment. The CS team had set up their blue and white tent about a hundred yards further down the track; only there was no track, it looked as if there hadn't ever been one. He shone his torch around. Everything on the embankment either side was grown over with weeds.

He headed towards the scrum of CS officers, all in their papery white hooded suits and face masks. It looked like a scene from a sci-fi film.

One of them pulled down his mask. 'Morning, Charlie. All right, then?'

'Bit nippy, Jack.'

'This rain's not doing us any favours either.'

'What have you got for me?'

'You'll not be best pleased. Victim's father trampled over everything before we got here, the weather did the rest. The local guvnor's bringing in extra uniforms to do a search.'

'What is this? Thought it was a railway.'

'Meant to be, back when Jesus was a boy, then someone changed their mind. Now the locals use it for dogging and drug deals.'

'It's always good to have a designated area. Lobbying the council for one where I live, next to the skateboard park. What's that over there? Public toilet?'

'Ventilation shaft for the underground. It's all locked up.'

'The tube go under here?'

'Not any more.'

They were moving the body. Two lads from the Forensic Medical Examiner's office had loaded the body bag on to a stretcher and roped some uniforms into helping them carry it back to the bridge. Rain had beaded on the heavy-duty green plastic.

'The FME's been and gone,' Jack said. 'Your guvnor's still here.'

'Brilliant.'

'Good luck,' Jack said.

Inside the tent it was hot from the lights, the slap of the rain all but drowning out the murmur of voices. Two of his Homicide Assessment Team were still there, Ty Gale and Lovejoy. Lovejoy looked a bit green under the lights. He nodded to her. 'OK?'

'Yeah, I'm OK, guv.'

'You don't look OK.'

'Well, dead kids. I've been doing this job long enough, but it still upsets me.'

'That's all right then. Not good to get too cynical. When it stops upsetting you, tell me, and I'll get you transferred to traffic.' He turned to Gale. 'Where's Malik?'

'He's taken the father home.'

'Jack told me the victim's father was here.'

'He was the one that found her, guv.'

'That a fact. Did you get any kind of statement?'

'Got it on my phone. He was quite lucid, which surprised me. Calm. It was a bit odd, like.'

'What's his name?'

'Raymond Okpotu. The victim's name was Mariatu. Her family's from Sierra Leone.'

'That where she was found?' The tent had been put up over and around a clump of brambles. Two SOCOs were still at work, on their hands and knees.

'He said he found her lying right there, face down. She was reported missing . . .' He checked his notes, '. . . at 7.40 p.m. yesterday evening. The 999 call was logged at 12.07 a.m.'

'He went looking for her in the middle of the night and just happened to find her right there.'

'Apparently.'

'The FME say anything?'

'He said he was cold.'

'After you exchanged pleasantries.'

'Massive head wound. Blunt-force trauma.'

'Murder weapon?'

Gale shook his head.

Charlie slapped the log book into Lovejoy's arms. 'That's yours. You can follow me around on this one, see how it's done. Every decision gets written down in there, along with date and time. Anywhere I go, you go. Almost.'

He went back outside; the DCI was talking to someone, they both had their hoods back.

'FONC,' Lovejoy murmured, and she managed to get the tone just right. She was learning fast. 'What's he doing here, guv?'

7

It was four in the morning, chief inspectors didn't get out of bed for just any old dead body. This was the sort of murder that could really bunch the commissioner's pants; was it a hate crime, sex crime, what? Both? This would need a steady hand or the locals would be burning cars and chucking bottles at uniforms in full riot gear. Never mind the crime wave sweeping London, blokes on mopeds with zombie knives. This could turn political.

'Charlie.'

'Guv.'

'This is Inspector David Mansell from Crouch End. This is his borough.'

Charlie shook hands.

'Bad business,' Mansell said. He nodded towards the houses on either side of the embankment, lights blinking on in kitchens and upstairs windows. Word must have got around, people were waking up to police cordons and halogen lights. 'I've called in my entire duty roster to help with the house-to-house. Someone must have seen or heard something.'

'And we appreciate your assistance,' the DCI said to Mansell. 'Will you excuse us a moment? I need to consult with my DI about a private matter.'

Mansell was taken off guard. He raised an eyebrow and nodded. 'Of course. Keep me informed.'

FONC stared at Lovejoy, who was still at Charlie's shoulder. 'It's all right,' Charlie said to her. 'You don't need to log this.'

The DCI waited until she was out of earshot.

'You up for this Charlie?'

'Sir?'

'Well, you've only just come back on the roster. I was hoping to ease you back into things. This is not what I had in mind.'

'It's a murder investigation like any other.'

'No, it isn't. A murder investigation like any other is a gang-banger with a knife in him, not an eleven-year-old Somali schoolgirl.'

8

'She's from Sierra Leone.'

'Whatever. How's your arm?'

'The arm is fine. Even if it wasn't, I don't need my arm to run a murder investigation.'

'It's not your arm I'm worried about.'

'I'll be fine.'

'You'd better be. I want twice-daily briefings. Any major developments, let me know immediately. You know what immediately means, don't you?'

'Within a day or two.'

'Don't be a smartarse.'

'No, sir.'

'I want swift progress.'

He stamped back towards the bridge. Charlie looked at Lovejoy, shivering and wet in her blue coveralls; she suddenly looked very young, too young for this job. He felt that way too, sometimes.

'He's in a good mood,' she said.

'He's under a lot of pressure,' Charlie said. They found the uniforms who had been first response by their patrol car, sheltering from the rain under the bridge. Charlie waited until Mansell had finished debriefing them, then went over.

'You were first responders?' Charlie said. 'What happened?'

The older of the two cops spoke up. 'We got the dispatch while we were on patrol, blue-lighted our way over. When we got here, there was an IC3 standing at the top of the embankment up there, yelling and waving his torch about. We followed him up.'

'Mr Okpotu.'

He checked his notebook. 'That's him. By the time we got up there, he'd run back to the girl's body, picked her up. He was holding her in his arms, wouldn't let go of her.'

'Did he say anything?'

'Said a lot of things, but most of it was in his own lingo, like. He only used English if we asked him a direct question.'

'Did he say where he found her?'

'The bushes where Crime Scene have the tent, that's what he reckoned.'

'And then?'

'We called for back-up, cordoned off the area as best we could, but I mean, all the bleedin' good it would do, he'd already trampled all over it.'

'How did he seem?'

'Matter of fact,' the younger cop said. 'Weren't he, Sarge? You'd think he'd be more upset.'

'Did he say what position she was in when he found her?'

'He said he'd come across her lying face down in the bushes,' the sergeant said. 'She had this . . .' He touched the back of his head. 'Just here. It was a pulpy mess. He had her blood all over him.'

'Was she dressed?'

'He told me her knickers were down around her knees. That was what he said. He'd pulled them up again before we got there.'

'Do you know if there had been an attempt to conceal the body?'

'No. Said she was just lying there.'

'And no sign of a weapon?'

They both shook their heads.

'Thanks fellas.'

They went back to their patrol car. It was raining harder now, rivers of it gurgling as it gushed down the drains. Charlie decided to wait for it to ease up. He turned to Lovejoy. 'See how the rain kicks up, when it's this heavy? When I was a kid I used to tell me little brother they were rain fairies dancing.'

'And he believed you?'

'Well he was only eight. Kids believe anything when they're eight. Anyway, he liked it, stopped him being so scared of thunderstorms.'

When it eased off they ran for Lovejoy's car, which was parked closer than his Golf. He got the decision log kicked off, named the victim's father as his initial suspect. One of their first priorities would be to make him a focus of further enquiries or rule him out.

'Can you hear a dog barking?' Lovejoy said when she'd finished writing it up.

'Fuck, I forgot,' Charlie said.

He ran back to his car. The cocker wagged its tail so hard when he opened the door, he thought its bum was going to come off. Charlie couldn't say he was quite so pleased to see the cocker. It had eaten all the biscuits, including the wrapper, and had crapped all over his passenger seat.

'Never took you for a dog person,' Lovejoy said over his shoulder. 'Oh look, he likes you.'

'Get off me, dog,' Charlie said. 'You're getting shit on my jacket.'

Lovejoy picked him up. 'Sorry guv, but are we supposed to bring pets to murder scenes?'

'I found him on the doorstep as I was leaving, what else could I do? Look at him, he's starved and he's wet. He needs some TLC.'

'And leaving him locked up in your car in the dark is your idea of tender loving care, is it? What kind of dog is he?'

'He's a cocker spaniel.'

'He looks like a bloodhound.'

'Trust me, he's a cocker. I grew up with one.'

'We only ever had short-haired dogs. What are you going to do with him?' The cocker was trying to lick Lovejoy's face while she made baby talk at it. A different Lovejoy, this; not the same one that had a black belt in judo.

'Can't do sod-all with him, Lovejoy. I live alone in a flat and I work all hours.'

'My dad will have him. His old Lab died a couple of months ago, I've been telling him he needs another one to keep him company. It can be just temporary, if you like.'

'Is he going to leave it banged up in a yard all day on its own?'

11

'No, he's on a pension. Like I said, he needs the company. It'll be a good home for him till you get it sorted.'

'All right. But if he's on a pension, I hope he can afford plenty of Rich Tea biscuits. The little bugger eats for England. Come on, we'd better get back to the nick. We have work to do.'

CHAPTER THREE

An absolutely filthy dawn, grey as gunmetal and rain spattering on the windscreen, like someone was throwing gravel at it. Not even the camera crews could be bothered, and neighbours were reduced to peering out through net curtains, so the street was almost deserted except for two miserable uniforms standing outside the front gates in their ponchos. Oh well, that had been him once, it was good motivation to pass your detective exams first time.

The Okpotus lived in a large semi with Gothic windows and bargeboards. He could make out the hilly heights of Mount View to the north.

'Simon Pegg lives round here somewhere,' Charlie said. 'You know, *Shaun of the Dead*.'

'He'd be over in *Crouch End*, wouldn't he?' She pronounced it, *crouchon*, as if it were French. He laughed.

He told Lovejoy to stay in the car and look after the spaniel. They'd had to come in hers, the Golf would need detailing before he could use it again. He waited for the rain to ease then made a dash for it.

Charlie seemed to remember that he and his brother Ben had got beaten up round here somewhere, by a bunch of pikeys, after they gatecrashed a party. Those were the days. And the last time he was here it was on his first and last Tinder date, some girl from Crouch End who wanted him to pull her hair and smack her with a hairbrush while they were having sex. Not his thing really, but dinner had been the business: nettle soup, and chicory and wild garlic gnocchi.

There was a child's plastic ride-on tractor lying on its side in the driveway. Malik was waiting for him in the car port, some polycarb roofing giving protection from the rain.

'Morning, guv.'

'Malik. All right, then?'

Malik puffed out his cheeks, lit up, offered him one. Charlie shook his head. Hadn't had one for a while now, he'd felt quite virtuous putting 'non-smoker' on the admittance forms in A&E, wondered if he could keep it up this time.

'Who's in there, then?'

'Mr Okpotu is just wandering around like he's in a trance. Mrs Okpotu is upstairs. Doctor's been round, had to sedate her, she was a right bloody mess.'

'Kids?'

'Three, she was the oldest. They're in the kitchen with aunts, uncles, you name it. The mullah is there, too. Watch him, he's got a lot of opinions, know what I mean?'

'What's the story, then?'

'She came home from school, around quarter to four, went up to her room. Must have sneaked out again. When her mother went to call her for dinner, about seven, she wasn't there. They rang round all her friends. When none of them said they'd seen her, they rang the local nick.'

'Which friends?'

Malik pulled out his notebook, tore off a sheet. 'Here, I made a list.'

'What happened then?'

'The local Bill took it serious because of her age, and started a low-level search, but they told them there wasn't much they could do until the morning. Anyway, about eleven, Mr Okpotu said he couldn't stand the waiting and went off on his own with a torch.'

'And found her pretty much straight away. Lucky, that.'

'According to him, he was searching for an hour, knew the places the local kids like to go.'

'Anything on him on the PNC?'

'No, nothing.'

'Look, we've got to establish a timeline for all this. You'll have to speak to everyone in the family on their own, find out when each of them reckons they last saw Mariatu alive. But softly, softly, all right?'

'Sure.'

'Ty reckons there's something funny about him.'

'Maybe he's on the spectrum or something. He's in IT,' Malik said, like that meant something.

'I hate this,' Charlie said. 'Kids.'

'Me too, guv,' Malik said, and Charlie remembered how Malik had told him once how his little brother had died when he was ten. Full marks for being sensitive, Charlie.

He went in. There was a lot of shouting coming from the kitchen, sounded like they had the old Arsenal North Bank in there.

There was a framed photograph on a rough-hewn wooden table, a family portrait, carefully posed, the Okpotus with Mariatu and two younger girls. So that's what she looked like, pretty and a little chubby. He doubted that he would recognise her the next time they met.

The door to the living room was open, wooden masks and bright-coloured rugs on the walls, wooden sculptures on the bookcase, some polished bark with words he didn't recognise carved into it.

Suddenly the door to the kitchen burst open and a short, bearded man in a turban and a grey *thobe* rushed out. 'Are you the chief inspector?' Without waiting for a response, he said, 'What are you doing about this? Why are you here? Why aren't you out catching the monster who did this to one of our children?'

'And you are?'

Another man came out, lanky, clear-eyed, almost serene. 'Please, Imam Ahmad, let me talk to them. It is all right, they are doing their job.'

The cleric looked like a balloon about to burst, but he allowed himself to be pacified. The tall man put a hand on his shoulder and guided him back to the kitchen, but as he was going through the door the imam turned around and gave Charlie and Malik a look of venom. 'This is what we get for letting our little ones play with white children.'

'It's not their fault,' the tall man said.

The cleric pointed a forefinger at Charlie, but he was looking at Malik. 'You should go; go and take your Malteser with you!' The door shut behind him.

Malik just shrugged and gave Charlie a grim smile.

'Mr Okpotu?' Charlie said.

'My apologies,' he said and held out his right hand, put his left on Charlie's shoulder. 'And you are?'

'DI Charlie George. I'm deeply sorry for your loss.'

'Please,' Okpotu said and led the way into the front room. Glass crunched under Charlie's feet.

'I am sorry about the mess. My wife, when she heard, she threw things.'

'I understand.'

'Sit. Please.'

'Mr Okpotu, I can't imagine what you're going through right now, and I'm sorry to have to do this. I know you've already spoken to DC Malik here, but I need you to go through this for me one last time.'

Okpotu rubbed his face with his hands. 'Go ahead,' he said. Charlie understood what Gale had been trying to tell him: the man seemed strangely serene for someone who had just found his daughter beaten to death. He was one of those fortunate men who age slowly; his skin was smooth, almost polished. When he smiled he looked as if he was about twenty.

What was the geezer doing with a grin on his face when his daughter was in the morgue?

Charlie asked him if he minded him recording the conversation, then led him through it again. No, there was nothing troubling her, as far as they knew, no, she was too young for boys. She had been truanting from school a couple of times recently, and she could be a little headstrong, but she wasn't a bad girl, not really.

He delivered the account without faltering; it was like he was discussing an interesting book he'd just read. It gave Charlie the shivers. And there was the mother upstairs, drugged up, helpless with grief; now that was more like it.

'So when was the last time you saw your daughter alive, Mr Okpotu?'

'Yesterday morning, when I went to work. She was in the kitchen, having her breakfast.'

'She wasn't here when you got home?'

'My wife said that when she got home from school, she went straight to her room. She thought she was still there, she said she had a lot of homework. When I came home, she called Mariatu down for dinner. When she didn't answer, we went into her room. That was the first any of us knew she had gone.'

'Where do you work, Mr Okpotu?'

He faltered, for the first time. 'I work for Westminster City Council.'

'And you got home from work at what time?'

'Just after seven.'

'That's quite late.'

'We are quite busy at work.'

'And how do you get to and from work?'

'I take the tube.'

'How long does that take you? From when you leave work?'

'Why all these questions, Inspector, am I under suspicion?'

'We're just trying to establish a timeline for events, that's all, Mr Okpotu. So, what time would you say you left work?'

Now, that's a simple enough question, Charlie thought. Why do I have the feeling that he's working out sums in his head?

'Around six.'

'You made a missing persons report at the police station in Crouch End at seven forty.'

'I don't know when it was. As your detective here will have told you, we rang around all her friends' parents first.'

'Mariatu. That's a pretty name.'

He gave a short, barking laugh. 'It's a traditional name in Sierra Leone for Muslim girls. It means innocence.'

'Innocence,' Charlie said.

'Her mother brought her here to get away from all the violence in her own country. It's ironic, don't you think?'

'Well, doing what I do for a living, yes it does seem particularly ironic to me that anyone should ever come to London to try and get away from violence. Is that where you're from too? Sierra Leone?'

'No Inspector, I'm from Nigeria. Mariatu is not mine. Her biological father is dead.'

'I see.'

'My wife, she has had tragedy enough in her short life for ten people.'

'Life, in my experience, can be very unfair.'

'An understatement. As you saw just now, the community here will be very angry. Do you think it was a white person who did this?'

'It is too early to speculate on that. All I know is that your little girl is dead, and I will move heaven and earth to find out who did it.'

'It won't bring her back though, will it?' His voice cracked but instead of tears there was another smile.

'What time did you decide to go looking for Mariatu?'

'What?'

'How long did you wait, after you reported her missing, before you went looking for her yourself?'

'I can't remember what time it was. About eleven o'clock, I think. I just remember that it was getting later and later, and I

18

knew I couldn't just sit here and do nothing. So I got my torch and I went out looking on my own.'

'In the rain.'

'I didn't notice the rain. I didn't really care about it.'

'How did you know where to look?'

'Instinct. A sixth sense, if you like. Somehow, it seemed the most likely place.'

'When you found her, can you describe what you saw? This is important. I know this is difficult, but every slightest detail will help us.'

'I went up the embankment, I was going to go left, something made me go to the right. I shone the torch in an arc, you know, left to right. I didn't see her the first time. I walked perhaps for five minutes, then I turned around and came back, I was almost back at the bridge when I saw something in the bushes. She was lying face down, her arms by her side like this, straight down, and when I reached for her, her head, it was, sticky, there was blood matted right through her hair.'

'And her clothes?'

'Her underwear was, you know, down, around her ankles.'

'And what did you do?'

'I picked her up, she was stiff, you know, like, I don't know, like one of those things you see in shop windows.'

'A mannequin.'

'Yes, a mannequin. I shook her to try and wake her up. What a person would do in such a situation, I did. Is there anything else, Inspector? I should get back to my family.'

Charlie turned off the recorder on his phone. He could compare the transcript later with Malik's notes and those of the two uniforms from Crouch End. He thanked him and said he would keep him informed of all developments.

As they were getting up to leave, Charlie asked him about the wooden sculptures on the bookshelf. 'They are monkeys, Inspector, Mizaru, Kikazaru and Iwazaru – it means, see no evil, hear no evil, speak no evil.'

19

Evil, Charlie thought. No getting away from it in my line of work.

Mr Okpotu went back into the kitchen and shut the door behind him. Someone was still yelling and crying in there.

Charlie went out and stood under the car port with Malik and watched the rain hit the road. 'What now, guv?' Malik asked.

'I'll leave you to it. Good luck with that lot.'

'He's hiding something. The father.'

'Yeah, I know. We have to find out what. And all the while the rain is washing out our scene of crime. Just getting better and better, innit?'

He ran back to Lovejoy's car. The spaniel looked happy, at least.

By eight that morning the squad were all in the Incident Room, the HOLMES team had been there even earlier, setting up the system. It was a circus already: there were two other teams still working cases; there had been four murders in the last fortnight; you couldn't go anywhere in North London these days without someone waving a samurai sword in your face. Even the gangbangers were wearing stab vests.

Charlie had the first crime scene photographs pinned to the whiteboard, together with a map enlargement of the disused railway and the neighbouring streets. And there were the three photos of Mariatu; a recent school portrait Malik had obtained from Mr Okpotu; and two others, taken by the CS photographer earlier that morning, one of her face, the other a close-up shot of the gross injuries to the back of her skull.

DS Dawson – 'the skipper' as they all called him – came over to take a closer look, chewing a bacon butty. 'This one here, of her face, there's a lot of discoloration.'

'We think she was face down when she died.'

'Got a Time of Death?'

'Not yet. We still don't know if this was the scene of crime or if she was dumped.'

When they were all ready, Charlie led them through it, everything they knew so far. There were, of course, a lot of questions. Wes James wanted to know straight away about the area where her body had been found. He explained that construction of a railway line had begun years ago, as part of a rail link to Alexandra Palace, but plans had been shelved and it had just been left for years, a long finger of wasteland running right through the borough. Locals used it for walking their dogs, jogging, and it was also popular with small-time drug dealers and prostitutes.

'Which is why it is known, locally, as Sesame Street.'

'What's that building in the photograph there?' the skipper wanted to know.

'There's a ventilation shaft for the underground inside.'

'What underground?'

'The Northern Line follows the line of the track. Or it was going to. Then they built this road over here and they found it was quicker to build another tunnel over there. So this bit has never been used.'

'So that's where all our taxes go,' the skipper said.

'Is it open?' Wes asked.

'I checked, there's a metal barred gate, it was locked. The CS team are going to check it out anyway.'

'Her old man,' Rupinder said. 'How did he find her so fast? Doesn't add up.'

'That's what I think, too. He is, of course, our prime suspect, until and unless we can eliminate him from our enquiries. To that end, we will have to interview him formally later today, request access to his phone. He says he was at work until six, then took the tube home. I want you and Wes to verify that, first job.'

'What was a kid that age doing out that late?' McCullough said. David McCullough was the new boy on the team.

'You've led a sheltered life,' Wes told him.

'Why did he pick her up?' Gale said. 'He trampled all over the crime scene. Could have been deliberate.'

21

'Picking her up is natural, it's what any father would do. Could be deliberate, yes, but what would you do, if it was you?'

He turned back to the map behind him. 'Access and egress to the scene is difficult. We cannot rule out the possibility that Mariatu was murdered elsewhere, but I consider it unlikely. The closest entry points are here, up the embankment beside the bridge, and here, down this cul-de-sac, between two blocks of flats. If I was going to dump a body and not be seen, I can think of lots of better places to do it. I believe she was murdered where she was found.'

'Was she interfered with?'

'Cannot be sure. Her father said her underwear had been pulled down. That suggests a sexual motive.'

'And the race aspect?'

'Possibly. Let's hope not, but it can't be discounted.'

'When was the last time she was seen alive?' Gale said.

'That has yet to be established. Sanderson, Machin, I want you out at the school this morning, talk to all her friends, everyone in her class, her teacher; let's get everything we can. Here's a list Malik got from her father, you can start with that. The school has called in a team of counsellors to talk to some of the kids, so it's softly, softly, the whole way, all right?'

They nodded.

'Now CCTV. Access to Sesame Street is, as I have told you, via the embankment or down this cul-de-sac here. Both these access points lead off the high street, which means that Mariatu and her killer will be on tape.'

'Along with half of North London,' Winston said from his perch on the radiator near the window.

'And you will know, Viv, because when Wes and Rupe here have gone in every business premises in the high street that has security cameras and picked up every bit of CCTV from every local government office covering this area here . . .' Charlie slapped his hand on the map, 'Then you will help DC White study them in detail, until you find her.'

The look on his face; he wished he'd kept quiet.

'The local nick has given us plenty of uniforms for the house-to-house, we've got sniffer dogs out there; now it's getting light the SOCOs will be combing the area. We should have a lot more to go on by tonight. Meanwhile, Joe, Parm, get onto MAPPA and the sex offenders' register, anyone in a mile radius we should be looking at, let me know.'

'What about this kid's phone, her computer?' Gale said.

'Malik's organising her iPad. Her phone was at the scene. Jack's got it, said he'll get it over to you as soon as they've checked it for prints.'

'Hello, hello,' Sanderson said. He pointed to the TV that was mounted on the wall above the window. Charlie reached for the remote and turned up the sound.

There were grabs of the embankment and the CS team in their white suits, a quick shot of the inspector – what was his name, Mansell – talking to two of his uniforms. Then they cut to the mosque, a ten-second grab of the imam Charlie had met in Okpotu's kitchen saying something about racists. The item finished with the DCI trotting out the usual clichés and asking for witnesses to come forward, a news crawler on the bottom flashed up the Crimewatch and Incident Room numbers, as well as their Twitter handle.

'Well, that should keep you busy,' Charlie said to the skipper.

Charlie turned to Gale. 'Ty, let's get a POD down there, couple of blokes talking to people, show Mariatu's photograph around. Someone must have seen something. Mayer, you're in charge of evidence.'

Lovejoy walked in. The skipper held up his wristwatch and tapped it. 'What's this then, the afternoon shift?'

'Had to see a man about a dog,' Lovejoy said.

'It's all right, skipper, I had her running errands.' The skipper shrugged and muttered something about the teacher's pet. Charlie closed the meeting, told them there would be another one at six o'clock. 'OK everyone, we've all got our jobs, we have to be all over this like flies on a melon. Gale, what is it? You want to see me?'

Gale nodded towards Charlie's office. Charlie led the way in, closed the door behind him. 'What's up?'

'My daughter's sick, guv. She's had to go into hospital again last night. I've been up all night, not feeling that flash.'

'How's she doing?'

'Oxy sats are still right down – bit worried about her, actually.'

'Well, you'd better go and help out your missus, then. You're no good to me here.'

'I didn't want to let anyone down.'

'The skipper will find someone to come in and cover. You have to look after your own, Ty. Off you go, let me know how it goes.'

'Thanks.'

After he left, Lovejoy came in with two takeaway coffees and two sausage rolls in greasy paper bags. 'Brought you breakfast,' she said.

'How's the cocker?'

'Last time I saw him he was snoring in front of my dad's gas fire with a belly full of prime mince. He's even given him a name already.'

'He shouldn't get too fond.' Charlie took a sip of the coffee. A sausage roll, too! Food of the gods. 'What did he call him?'

'Charlie.'

'Because he looks like me?'

'He's a lot prettier than you are, guv.'

His Nokia rang. He winced when he clocked the screen, saw Lovejoy smirking at him. He picked up. 'Sir,' he said.

'Got anything for me?' the DCI said.

'I just did the briefing, sir.'

'Don't get defensive, makes me think you're not doing your job. Get on with it, then. And no stuff-ups.'

He hung up.

Sometimes Charlie wanted to throw the phone through the

24

window. He bit into the sausage roll. It was too hot, and he burned his lip.

They brought the decision log up to date, then Charlie checked his watch. The pathologist had rung him earlier and told him he'd scheduled the PM for ten, moved Mariatu right up the list. That's the good thing about the dead, Charlie thought, they finally have plenty of time to wait.

'Thoughts, guv?'

'Two things. One, what was an eleven-year-old girl doing on a place like Sesame Street at that time of the evening, and two, why was her father lying to us about when he left work?'

'How do you know he was lying?'

'I don't know, Lovejoy, but I think in the fullness of time, evidence will come to light that shows I'm correct.'

'It's just a hunch, then?'

'No, it's body language.' He finished the sausage roll and tossed the empty wrapper in the bin, missed by a good foot and a half. 'We're off to the post mortem. Don't worry, we're not staying for the whole thing, but I need a TOD estimate and a cause of death. You don't have to come in if you don't want to.'

'If I'm going to cut it in this place, I'll have to sooner or later.'

'Yeah,' Charlie said, 'sooner or later. Did you take my car to get detailed?'

'It's going to cost.'

'I'll have to figure out a way for Charlie to pay me back. We'll pick it up on the way back.' He opened the door. 'Come on, then. You're driving.'

CHAPTER FOUR

Last night I lay on the floor and listened to them moving downstairs. They have bright eyes, they do, are unblemished by kindness or mercy. I can smell them. Rustling. Twitching. Looking for something helpless to prey upon.

They can see things, they can, without using their eyes. They keep a map in their brain and they remember all the ways in and out of the dark for a long time. This is because they cannot see very well. Humans can see three colours, blue, green and red, at really high saturations, but rats can only perceive ultraviolets, and only see objects that are very close and even then they are blurred.

But they hear and smell much better than humans, which makes them better suited to the dark. They can detect sounds at frequencies as high as ultrasound. And they have long whiskers, so they can feel everything around them. Their world is not shape but texture. They find their way around in the dark by touch.

They will find constellations in tiny specks of debris, whole stories in a swirl of wood grain. They feel every faint stroke of the brush on a painted fence, each tiny lifted edge of paper on a wall. A tiny grain of sand, a flake of skin – it is like braille to them.

That is what it is like to be a rat. Their world is rich and dark and velvet.

I try to imagine what it is like to live down there all the time, not to have to come back up to the world. Just to smell and hear. I like smells. I can smell things on people, like food and sweat and sex. Most people only live in a world they can see. Most people are so stupid.

Not like them down there in the dark. They scuttle, they shuffle, I can hear them. They leave droppings, they do. You can smell the droppings if you concentrate really hard. I'm the only one that knows about them, no one else knows the secret way down there. I like to go down there, feel like I'm one of them.

You can be free in the darkness.

I was lost there once, the first time. I still remember it. I wasn't even a little bit scared, even though I thought I was never going to find my way out. I didn't mind. There was a part of me that would have been happy, even if I'd died. There's comfort in the dark.

Rats are what are called opportunists. They will eat anything, even dead bodies. It's not because they like eating dead people. It is just because they are there. They don't make them be there. I don't make them be there, mostly.

I've only ever murdered one person. It's not many, really, not in a whole lifetime, when you think about how many it might have been. Opportunities everywhere. I'm not going to do it again, though. Not up here in the light.

I don't want to talk about that any more.

So this is what happens when you die: your body starts to eat itself. It's called autolysis. I know, I read about it in a book.

Your body is nothing special, it is just a place where bacteria live. That's all. Even little girls are like that. And when you die all these bacteria escape, trillions of them, because the body stops providing them with their meals. And so they start to eat you.

And as they eat you, they make waste, and because you are dead you can't get rid of what they don't eat, and so that builds up and it turns a greenish-black colour. It starts at the right hip. I read that in a book, also. You can see it there because that is where the large intestine is closest to the skin.

And because there's no blood moving around, your veins and

arteries are empty, so the bacteria use them to travel around, just like you could walk on the motorway if suddenly one day no one could drive their cars on them any more. And that's why they turn that greeny-black colour more than the rest of you. It's called marbling. Like the cake.

And the bacteria also give off this gas and that's why a dead body gets all swollen up. Because of the gas inside. And that's also why the eyes bulge and the tongue sticks out and the skin blisters and starts to come off. Because of all the gas inside.

And after a while everything inside turns liquid. After two or three weeks, unless someone comes to take you away, you're like this black balloon, full of gas and foam, which is why everyone looks really fat when they're dead, even skinny people.

Some people think the hair and fingernails keep growing after you're dead but they're wrong. What happens is, the skin dries out so much it just looks that way. I know. I've looked at lots of pictures. You can find them on the internet, they're everywhere.

The next thing is, you turn into a mummy, like you see when they open up those old tombs in places like Egypt. Everything inside dries out. It happens quicker if you die somewhere that's hot, like in the desert.

Only this is not what always happens. If you die in a swamp, it is like pickling. This is because there is dead plant matter and the water is very acid and if it is cold as well, it stops the bacteria being active. Like when you stay at home when it snows. The bacteria are like that. They do not like the cold.

But if you are dead and not in a swamp, the last thing that happens is that there is nothing left but your skeleton. It can take years and years for you to be just bones. They know this because there are things called body farms, where doctors can study dead bodies for research.

I would like to work on a body farm, but most of them are in America; one is in Knoxville, Tennessee, and there is another one, a cold weather one, in Marquette, Michigan. That is all they do there, watch what happens to dead people.

And some people say that a person is just a body, and other people think that there is a part of you that no one can see, a part of you that keeps living even though you do not have a body. There are people who have died, but who have been saved and come back to life; they say they saw a white light when they were dying, like they were going through a long tunnel and could see a way out at the end of it. Just like that.

I do not know if I believe this. I have read about murderers, who have killed a lot of people, and they say that when they murder someone, the victim gets this faraway look in their eyes, like they are looking at you but they are seeing something else. The end of the tunnel.

Cats and even birds get this look. I know because I have tried it for myself. It is really interesting.

But no one knows what cats and birds think, if they can see a light, too. Perhaps it is just a trick that your brain plays on you when you are dying. Other people say there is only the dark.

I would not care if it is just the dark. I like the dark.

In the dark you can smell mould and water and dust and dead things, and wet food and electrical wire and old food and wet paper and dust. And there is so much more to hear, like cables humming and traffic rumbling in the street and water dripping and bats chirping.

So I will just lie here and listen. I have to go back down there soon, when the others have gone, when it is safe. I do not like it here, there are so many things not to see, in the light. But once you are in the dark, you can see whatever you want.

I like the rustling, the shuffling, the clawed feet. The orange eyes that can see everything. The black.

I like the black.

CHAPTER FIVE

Lovejoy drove into the underground car park, Charlie in the front, Mayer in the back. Charlie had made Mayer his evidence officer on this one, not his sort of bloke really, always looked as if his dog had just died. His dress sense had expired about the same time as Kurt Cobain, he wore hush puppies and bomber jackets.

'This is pretty grim,' Lovejoy said as they got out of the car.

'Should have seen it in the old days. This is state of the art.'

They could have watched through the observation window but Charlie wanted Lovejoy to get mud on her boots, in a way. When they got upstairs, they put on gloves, booties, and sleeveless aprons. Lovejoy brought out a little jar of Vicks, offered it around.

'You won't be needing that,' Charlie said. 'For one thing, she won't smell, she's only been dead a few hours. And for a second thing, even for the ripe ones, it doesn't help. After a few minutes in there, your body will adjust. All that stuff does is keep stimulating your smelling system, stop you getting acclimatised.'

Lovejoy looked disappointed, as if she'd handed in her homework early and teacher said there'd be no extra marks.

'Biggest problem,' Mayer said, 'when we get back to the nick everyone will smell us. Hope you brought a spare set of clothes.'

They went in. Charlie could still remember back in the day, painted brick and God-awful Victorian tiles and grim lighting. There were still a few places around like that but Haringey was state of the art, like stepping on to a spaceship, stark strip lighting and everything gleaming stainless steel.

The pathologist, Ferguson, had already started. The body bag was unzipped and Mariatu lay on the stainless-steel trolley, still in her muddied school clothes. Ferguson was studying the X-rays on the light board. He glanced around as they came in and nodded at Charlie.

'Thanks for bringing this forward,' Charlie said.

Ferguson grunted, leaned closer to the light board.

'That the cause of death?'

'It certainly did the lassie nae much good. All right, let's start.' He looked at Mayer and Lovejoy. 'Brought a gang with ye?'

'DC Mayer, my evidence officer. This is DC Lovejoy, she's my assistant on this one.'

'Well DC Mayer, let's have your evidence bags, you can remove the personal effects for the family.'

Ferguson started a scalp-to-toe examination, looked in Mariatu's hair, under her eyelids, in her mouth. The left side of her face was misshapen and her left eye seemed as if it was about to pop out of its orbit. He marked it on his autopsy chart.

'Contracoup injury,' Charlie said, when he saw Lovejoy frown.

'You've been paying attention over the years, I see,' Ferguson said. 'You'll be wanting my job next.'

'Not for all the tea in China.'

Ferguson and his assistant rolled the body and Ferguson repeated the process. He took his time on the pulpy mess that had been the back of her head. He extracted several small particles from the wound. Charlie peered at them as Ferguson placed them in an evidence bag with his forceps; they looked like pieces of brick. They still had blood-matted hair attached.

'Massive blunt trauma to the orbital skull. It would have caused gross insult to the brain.'

'She wasn't struck just once.'

Ferguson nodded. 'Repeatedly.' Ferguson unbagged the hands, took fingernail scrapings for forensic testing. 'No marks on the palms.'

31

Charlie nodded.

'What does that mean?' Lovejoy said.

'It means she didn't suffer.' Another quizzical look. 'If you're in pain, you clench your fists, natural reaction, see? Your finger-nails leave marks in the palms of your hands.'

Lovejoy nodded. She looked pale. He'd already warned Mayer to watch her, catch her if she fell. He had a fiver with him that she wouldn't, he was still hoping he'd collect.

Ferguson cut off her clothes with medical scissors; her school blazer, with its achingly poignant motto, *Semper vigilans*, the polo shirt she wore for school stiff and brown with blood. Mayer held out the evidence bags and he dropped them in, one at a time. There were no other injuries, nothing else remarkable.

Finally, she lay there, naked, ready for the final indignities. Her skin was a dusty grey colour, the veins already starting to blue up. Charlie felt the bile in the back of his throat. God help me if I ever stop feeling like this around dead children, he thought.

'You know what I'm going to ask you,' Charlie said.

Ferguson pulled down the face mask. His glasses flashed in the strip light. 'When I arrived at the crime scene, rigor was advanced but not fully present. Body temperature . . . it was a cold night, Charlie, you know I cannot give you anything to be relied upon.'

'You got there when?'

'I arrived at the scene around two in the morning.'

'More than eight hours?'

'She had been deceased for several hours.'

'Had she been moved?'

'She was prone when she died, someone rolled her onto her back some time later. As you can see.'

He started the head to toe. When he came to examine the girl's genitals, Charlie stared at his boots, out of decency. He only needed to know one thing, and Ferguson could tell him that, he didn't need front-row seats to know how the plot went.

32

'There is no evidence of penetration, detective. No vaginal or anal tearing. I'll swab for semen, of course.'

Charlie shook his head, nonplussed.

'Someone must have come along after he grabbed her,' Mayer said.

Charlie nodded. What else could it be?

Ferguson's assistant positioned Mariatu face up with a rubber block beneath her shoulder blades. 'We don't need to stay for this bit,' Charlie said to Lovejoy.

'Thanks Tom,' Charlie said. Ferguson nodded.

Charlie heard a sound, like a dentist's drill, as they were leaving, and shuddered. He needed a cup of coffee, thought about a cigarette, but promised himself only his caffeine addiction would win today.

No one said anything until they got back to the car.

'So did she die where we found her?' Lovejoy said.

'I still believe so, but it has yet to be determined.'

'She looked as though she had sunburn.'

'That's the lividity, Lovejoy; gravity makes all the blood pool at the lowest point. It suggests that she was lying in the prone position for several hours, but there's also some lividity on her back, because her father came along and moved her, and stuffed up the process. But we cannot be certain that she wasn't moved before he came along as well. You all right?'

'I'm all right.'

'Good. It's gut-wrenching, I know. But you don't do anyone any good thinking about anything but finding the fucker responsible, pardon my French.'

He reached out a hand to Mayer in the back. Mayer sighed and took out his wallet, pulled out a five-pound note and gave it to him.

'What's that for?' Lovejoy said.

'Never you mind,' Charlie said. 'I need a coffee. Where are you going?'

'There's a place there.'

'No, not Starbucks, I'd rather drink bleach. There's a place around the corner, run by a couple of Italians. Lesson in life, Lovejoy. You want a decent cup of coffee, never buy from anyone not called Gino or Tony.'

He felt his Nokia buzzing in his jacket pocket. It was the skipper; the phones had been running hot since the piece on breakfast television, he said. He gave him an address and Charlie logged it into his Google maps.

He hung up. 'Things are looking up. We've got an eyewitness. Some kid who was down the railway line, claims he saw something. His mother just rang in. But first I need that coffee.'

Charlie was scrolling through his phone. Lovejoy watched him while she drove. Charlie clicked his fingers in front of her eyes and pointed to the road. 'I have a strong preference for not driving into a lamp-post, especially when I'm in the seventy per cent seat.'

'What you doing, guv?'

'I'm on Tinder.'

'Joking, right?'

'Checking my emails, Lovejoy. And I just got another message from the skipper; there's a jogger called in, reckons they saw something. He's sent Wes and Rupinder to chase it up. 'What's this, then?' They were driving back past the crime scene, the CS van was still there. 'Stop here,' Charlie said.

'Nowhere to park.'

'Drive round the block then,' Charlie said, and got out, signed in with one of the uniforms by the bridge and made his way up the embankment. There had been SOCOs up and down all morning, it was tough going. He was breathing hard by the time he got to the top. Thank God he'd given the cancer sticks away.

It looked different in the daylight, if 'daylight' was the right word for an overcast day in London. So many houses and flats overlooking this stretch of wasteland, right in the middle of London. Gale had said the locals used it for a jogging track and for walking their dogs; the perfect place, if you were a fan of dog shit and empty crisp packets.

Jack had his white coveralls peeled down around his waist and was smoking a cigarette; it had been a long shift for him. He nodded at Charlie. 'Think we found something that might cheer you up.'

'Well, that would be lovely.'

He nodded at the brick shed that the skipper had been so curious about. 'Thought something about that ventilation shaft weren't right.'

'It's a cardboard mock-up?'

'The boys were all finished up, I said no, we're not done till we've had a good look down there.'

'Thought it was locked.'

Jack nodded and led the way over. The steel mesh gate was open; it smelled foul inside. There was a manhole, with a steel fixed access ladder and safety cage.

'We found your murder weapon. It was down the bottom.'

'How did it get down there if the gate was locked?'

Jack motioned for him to come back outside, pulled the gate shut behind him. It was smeared with the metallic residue from the fingerprint powder. Jack nodded at an old milk crate lying in the weeds. 'They stood on that, tossed it through the gap at the top and down the hole.'

'Tossed what?'

'A house brick. Either they brought it with them or they found it lying around here in the grass.'

'You found it?'

'What was left of it. It was in bits. Bloody murder of a job finding all the pieces.'

'How do you know it was the murder weapon?'

'Found traces of blood and hair on a piece of it. My team grumbled to Christ when I told them they had to get down there and look, now they're all patting themselves on the back like it was their idea.'

35

Charlie went back inside. Jack shone his torch down the hole. 'Want to take a look?'

'No thanks.'

'It only takes a minute or two to get down there.'

'I get claustrophobia.'

'Big ugly fucker like you, scared of the dark?'

'I didn't say I was scared of the dark, I said I had claustrophobia. Had it since I was a kid. So, what's down there?'

'Spiders. Big, fat hairy ones with sharp teeth.'

'Very funny. Serious.'

'Goes down about twenty metres. There's a tunnel either side, tracks are long gone, else they never got laid in the first place. Go far enough along you reach another gate, and that leads right to the Northern Line. Don't even need your Oyster card.'

'This gate, the lock's been tampered with.'

'Yeah, I know. We've lifted some prints off it, don't know if it'll do you any good.'

'You never know, we can run them up the flagpole, see if anyone salutes. Who moved the safety grille?' Charlie said, nodding at the steel mesh plate propped against the wall.

'Same bloke what picked the lock.'

'Who would want to go down there?'

'One of those urbex types, I reckon.'

'One of those what?'

'Urban explorers, they call themselves. It's like a sport, like rock climbing, or surfing, except you find places in the city that have been abandoned and locked up, like old underground stations, and they find a way to get in and take photographs.'

'How do you know about that, then?'

'Got a mate who's proper into it. It's like the new skateboarding, for people with dodgy knees. He goes looking for old underground stations, that sort of thing, takes photographs, goes creeping about in tunnels.'

'Sounds loony to me, don't mind me saying. I'd rather be at home watching a good comedy like *CSI*.'

Charlie stepped outside, bent down and looked at the milk crate. Jack said it had been photographed, now he'd seen it they were going to take it back to Lambeth for testing, not that they were likely to get much off it.

'So what have we got?' Charlie said, thinking aloud. 'Little girl wanders up here on her jacksie, he grabs her, tries to interfere with her, she screams and so he hits her with the nearest available, gets rid of the evidence and runs.'

'Unless he did for her somewhere else and dumped her here.'

'Doesn't make sense. He didn't rape her, that tells me he was interrupted. And her injuries indicate a frenzied attack. Dumpers are cold-blooded, my experience. No, it happened right here. It was opportunistic.' They walked back to where Mr Okpotu said he had found the body. 'Someone must have seen something.'

'Hard to see much from here, Charlie. Those trees there, they block the view from the flats. And the houses down there, they can't see much past the edge of the embankment.'

'You're probably right. Anyway, thanks Jack. Let me know what you get off that brick. You're a legend.'

'Come home and tell me missus that,' Jack said.

'Well, this is a bit of all right, innit?' Charlie said as Lovejoy pulled into a quiet street of Victorian villas and flat-fronted artisan houses. Another world from Finsbury Park, but still just a walk to the tube. Nice work if you could get it.

The Williamses lived in a Queen Anne-style house built of red brick, with views over London in the distance. Charlie imagined himself sitting in the bay window with an espresso and a croissant from the local bakery, saying oh look dear, the Gherkin looks well this morning.

He knocked on the door, blood-red enamel paint and a brass knocker from a Jane Austen film set. The woman who answered the door was dressed in Mulberry, no dressing gown with a Burberry cap around here.

'Mrs Williams?' He took out his ID. 'DI Charlie George, this is DC Lovejoy and DC Mayer. I believe you called our information hotline this morning?'

'Yes, my husband called actually. My son thinks he saw something yesterday evening that might help. Come in, come in.'

Nice. She led them down the hallway to the living room. There were high ceilings, moulded cornices, an antique fireplace, Queen Anne mirrors. Bookshelves filled one wall, some Salman Rushdie, Zadie Smith, Iain Banks. Living round here, they have to fill a wall with Booker prize-winners before they can have anyone over for dinner, he supposed.

A Maltese terrier stood on one of the armchairs and barked at him. Charlie held out his hand for it to sniff, and she regarded it suspiciously before accepting the invitation. Satisfied with whatever she found, she licked his fingers then jumped down and tried to dry hump his leg.

'She doesn't normally like strangers,' Mrs Williams said. 'You must have a way with dogs. Molly, get down!'

The dog ignored her. Charlie stroked Molly behind her ears and she settled down.

'She just wanted a little bit of attention,' he said.

'Doesn't every woman,' Mrs Williams said, and Charlie was suddenly glad he had Lovejoy and Mayer with him.

She made coffee with an espresso machine, bright red, which used pods. That was a hundred and fifty to five hundred years to break down in landfill, Charlie thought, and resisted the urge to lecture her on the looming global environmental disaster. That wasn't what he was here for.

'Nice garden,' he said.

There was a mossy ragstone wall, a trough of irises not yet flowering, a child's tricycle, a red and yellow plastic swing. A Weber barbecue with a red lid sat on a hardy square patch of lawn. The wrought-iron bench looked more like a torture implement than garden furniture; there were some prickly stumps of rose bushes if the prisoner was difficult.

A teenager in a hoodie and a try-hard hat was out there pushing a perfect blue-eyed girl on the swing. She was concentrating intently on the enterprise and had not a curl out of place.

Mrs Williams put some biscuits on the table, Fortnum and Mason, pistachio and clotted cream. Get in.

Mr Williams came in. He looked like the sort of man he would trust to do his tax return: neat fair hair and a cardigan, a rugby club tie. They didn't wear ties round where Charlie lived, and he appreciated a good tie. He had the impression Williams had showered and dressed for the interview. That made a refreshing change. Most of his customers didn't even stop taking drugs for a routine statement.

They shook hands. 'I'll fetch the children, shall I?' he said.

The Williams family arrayed themselves on a brown Chesterfield in the living room, Mrs Williams at one end with a teenage girl, maybe fifteen, sixteen, sitting beside her. Her name was Brooklyn and she had been prised with a crowbar out of her upstairs bedroom by her mother. She concentrated on her phone and looked bored and victimised.

At the other end was the kid in the hoodie, his face held together with acne; thirteen, Charlie would have guessed, and trying to look proper hard, not easy when you haven't cracked puberty. His hat was a brown Brixton with a banderole; who was he kidding, even some cheap silver bling to go with it. This was Reuben.

A pretty girl, five or six years old, sat beside him. Her name was Lucee, with two 'e's. She had white hair, pale blue eyes and such pale skin she might have been a ghost. She was wearing a school uniform, the same one that he had seen less than an hour ago, being cut off Mariatu's lifeless body with surgical scissors.

'We weren't here when it happened,' Mr Williams said, 'we both work late during the week. I'm in the City and my wife works in High Wycombe. We're never home before six.'

'Who looks after the little one?'

'Brooklyn is supposed to,' Mrs Williams said, and the teenager rolled her eyes.

Mrs Williams gave Charlie an apologetic smile. 'She was on Facebook, trolling her friends.'

'No one uses Facebook any more, Mum.'

'You were supposed to look after your little sister,' Mr Williams said.

'I can't watch Psycho Girl and Mr Weirdness every minute of the day. I've got better things to do.'

Charlie looked at Reuben. 'So, what happened last night, then?'

'Went out, innit? Got bored.' Not long out of primary school, living in a posh house and trying to sound as though he'd just stepped off a housing estate in Peckham. God give me strength.

'What time did you leave the house?'

'When Manz gets home from school. She were playing boy bands. Hurt me ears, innit?'

'Where did you go?'

'Just walked.'

'On your own?'

'No, took me younger with me. And Molly. The dog, she goes everywhere with us, innit?'

'You took your sister and the dog for a walk?'

'You're proper bright. Just said that.'

'Reuben!'

'It's all right, Mr Williams. You're just bare jokes, aren't you, Reuben? Now, how about you tell me everything you can remember about what happened after you got home from school, and we'll go from there.'

Reuben told them he and Lucee had wandered pretty much aimlessly until they got to the high street, then went down to Sesame Street, as the locals called it. She liked it down there, he said, because she could see in people's windows in the overlooking flats.

Brooklyn made another face. 'You are the *king* of weird.'

Mr Williams made a choking sound. 'How often do you do this?'

'You're not here.'

'That wasn't my question.'

'Perhaps if we could just let Reuben finish his story,' Charlie said. He turned back to the boy. 'Did you see Mariatu Okpotu while you were on your walk?'

'I saw her. She was signifying on me like always. I just give her air. But then I clock this other old boy. Proper clapped. His teeth is all proper rank and he dresses like a gutter-nutter.'

'What made you notice him?'

'He was following her, innit?'

'Following her. What time was this, Reuben?'

'Don't know what time it was, it was getting dark. I was bricking it, real talk. Best believe, I just wanted to get home to my yard. He's a proper scary man, that one.'

'You know him?'

'He's from ends, innit? Manz sees him around, in the street and that.' He leaned in. 'That's a well shabby suit.'

'Thanks.'

'You're tonk man, you work out?'

'Don't have time to work out, Reuben. Too busy chasing bad people.' He turned to Lovejoy, who was still tapping away on her laptop. 'Did you get all that?'

'There's a few words you'll have to translate for me, guv.'

Charlie turned to Mr Williams and gave him his card. 'Do you think you could drop by the station some time tomorrow morning, we'll get that printed up, just need your son to sign it.' He turned back to Reuben. 'Do you think you could describe the man you saw to one of our police artists?'

'You want a picture you can put on the telly?'

'That's right. You've seen them before?'

He nodded.

'Anything else you remember, that might help us, just get your mum or dad to call me.'

41

'That poor little girl,' Mrs Williams said.

'Did you know her?'

'We met her parents once, I think. At a school play. I can't imagine how she must be feeling. All the things that have happened to that woman. Now this.'

'What things?'

Mrs Williams glanced at her husband, gave him a look that said, have I spoken out of turn? 'Just the war and everything, in Africa. I heard they came here looking for a better life.'

Charlie thanked the Williamses for their assistance and reminded Reuben that if there was anything else he could remember about the man with the bad teeth, he was to ask his mum and dad to ring. They would be in touch, he said. He was sure they would soon be bringing the investigation to a satisfactory conclusion.

'We're always telling our children, don't talk to strangers,' Mrs Williams said. 'Poor little girl. That could have been Reuben, or our little Lucee.'

'Rest assured, we will not be letting them out of the house again until the killer is found,' Mr Williams said, with a hard stare at Brooklyn.

They went back to the car. Lovejoy took her time starting the engine.

'That's my ambition, that is,' Lovejoy said.

Charlie raised his eyebrows. 'What is, marrying an engineer and having autistic kids?'

'A nice bit of lawn and a Weber.'

'Don't aim too high, Lovejoy. You'll only get disappointed.'

'A mulberry tree as well. I didn't even see a tree until I was six, and that was in a zoo.'

'What did you make of the little girl?' Mayer said.

'Like I said. They all looked a bit odd to me.'

'And the boy, talking like a roadman.'

'Well, he probably gets bullied at school. The important thing, we have an eyewitness and a murder weapon. Get a bit of DNA from Lambeth, match it to a known offender, all sorted.'

'We all go home, have an early night, I can watch a bit of *Broadchurch* with Charlie's big wet nose in my lap.'

Mayer caught Charlie's eye in the driving mirror. 'She's referring to her dog,' Charlie said.

'Didn't know she had a dog, guv. You got a dog, Lovejoy?'

'He's recent.'

'Lucky you. Those big wet noses.'

There was a long silence. That Lovejoy. If he didn't know better, he would have sworn she did that deliberately. His Nokia rang, it was the skipper. Winston had found something on CCTV.

CHAPTER SIX

DC Viv Winston was leaning back in his chair with his hands in his pockets, staring at the laptop on the desk in front of him. He looked up when Charlie walked in, gave him a sour look. What's his problem, no one said detective work was red lighting all over London and shooting guns out of the window.

'What have you got?' Charlie said.

Winston sat forward, pulled up a file. Charlie watched the grainy images on the screen; the counter on the top right-hand corner said 17.23.

Winston tapped a finger on the screen. 'There,' he said. 'That's her, isn't it?'

Charlie peered closer. Mariatu Okpotu appeared briefly outside the Domino's, was in the frame for just a few seconds, walking towards the cameras, then she was gone.

The skipper came to join them. 'That's her, right?'

Charlie nodded.

Winston pulled up another file, this one in colour. 'This is from outside McDonald's, five minutes earlier.'

'Good work,' Charlie said. He turned back to the map on the wall. 'So she left her house, went to the high street, turned south. Last vision we have is . . . here. Here's the cul-de-sac, leads down to these flats and the disused railway line at the bottom.'

'Which is where Reuben said he saw her.'

'And he said someone was following her.' He turned to Winston. 'In those two CCTV grabs we have, is anyone behind her?'

Winston pulled up the two CCTV files on the screen in task view. They watched over his shoulder, Mariatu wasn't being stalked. Whoever Reuben had seen had already been down on Sesame Street, either waiting for her or by chance.

'How much more CCTV is there?'

'A bit.'

'Well keep going then,' Charlie said. 'I need coffee. Come on skipper, you can bring me up to speed.'

They went down to the canteen in the lift. It was quiet, a few uniforms on their break, radios on the table, nursing mugs of tea. The plasma TV was on but the sound had been muted so the crews could hear the dispatches coming in on their radios. As they walked in, a call came in for back-up for a stabbing on one of the estates. Chairs screeched as two of the crews pushed back their chairs and pulled on their Met vests.

Charlie got Lovejoy and the skipper coffees from the machine and brought them back to a table in the corner, by the window.

'Wes just called,' the skipper said. 'Him and Rupe are just on their way back from interviewing that jogger.'

'What's the story?'

'She was running down by where the girl was found last night. Thought she heard something.'

'What time was this?'

'About six. It was after dark.'

'Who goes jogging at night down there? Some people have a death wish.'

Charlie brought the skipper up to speed on the post mortem, and the fact they now possibly had a murder weapon, and perhaps even fingerprints, from the lock on the steel mesh door on the ventilation building.

Rupinder and Wes walked in. Wes was eating a packet of bacon crisps.

'Thought you were one of those vegan types,' the skipper said.

'Vegetarian, skip.'

'What you doing eating bacon crisps?'

'There's no bacon in bacon crisps. It's all chemicals and flavourings.'

'If you don't like bacon, why do you like bacon flavour?'

'I didn't say I didn't like bacon flavour, man. I just don't agree with killing animals for flavour.'

'Don't make no sense, that.'

'I don't care about being healthy, I'm vegetarian because I love animals, man.'

'For Christ's sake, you two,' Charlie said. 'Rupe, tell me about the jogger.'

He checked his notebook. 'Sarah Dutton. She rang the Crimestoppers line, said she'd heard something last night. The skipper sent us out there to interview her.'

'What was she doing down there at that time of night?'

'She had her Alsatian with her. And a torch.'

'Go on, then.'

'We went back there with her, to see where she heard these noises.'

'And?'

Wes and Rupe grinned.

'Well, here's the thing, we heard screaming, too.'

'It was coming from the flats,' Wes said, 'nowhere near where they found that poor girl. Anyway, we knocked on their door. It was just this white fella with his girlfriend, they was having a little bit of Netflix and chill.'

Rupe grinned. 'And Wes says to him, are you going to come quietly?'

The skipper shook his head. 'Should be doing stand-up, you.'

By six o'clock, the team were gathered in the IR. They all looked tired, it had been a long day. They sat at their desks or slouched against filing cabinets, their jackets off. Charlie told them what they had so far; they believed they now had a murder weapon, he told them the crime unit had found the remains of

46

a brick with traces of human tissue, described how it had been disposed of.

'The pathologist found no evidence of sexual penetration, though her father said that when he found her, her underclothes had been partly removed. This suggests that her attacker had been disturbed in the process of molesting her.'

'Or that he's trying to throw us off the scent,' the skipper said.

'That can't be discounted.'

'Do we think she was murdered where she was found?'

'At this stage, yes.' He referred to his notes. 'We also have a possible eyewitness: a Reuben Williams, he's thirteen years old and goes to the same school as the deceased. He saw her yesterday evening, near where her body was later found. He said she was being followed by a much older man. It was probably the last sighting of her, so I am taking this piece of information very seriously indeed. We now have an artist's impression of the man we are looking for, which we are going to distribute to the media.'

He held it up for them to see.

'Jesus,' Sanderson said. 'He looks like a bashed crab.'

'What's our timeline?' the skipper asked him.

'From the CCTV captures we have so far, it looks as if Mariatu was at the high street here, about five thirty last night.' He traced her movements on the map on the whiteboard with his finger. 'She went down to the disused railway line, where she was last seen alive by Reuben Williams and his sister. Soon after this, she was assaulted and murdered by persons as yet unknown. All the indications from the post mortem support this theory.'

'There were no other injuries?' Wes said. 'She had not been restrained?'

Charlie shook his head. 'No abrasions on her wrists, no other injuries.'

'So she was killed by one blow to the back of her head with a brick?'

'Not one blow, Wes. What the pathologist described to me was a frenzied attack.'

'Sounds personal,' Joe said.

'Perhaps.'

He looked at Sanderson. 'Any luck at the school?'

Sanderson shook his head. 'I spoke to a couple of her mates. They say she used to sneak out of the house and meet them behind the pizza place, smoke, do the usual things teenagers do.'

'Wasn't she Muslim?' DC Lubanski said.

'It's called rebelling,' Rupe said.

'Anyway, they said they didn't see her Thursday night. Said she was going to meet them, and never showed.'

'Well, now we know why our good little schoolgirl sneaked out of the house,' Charlie said.

'What have we got from forensics?'

'Early days. But Jack is hoping to get lifts from the brick, perhaps, but more likely from the gate to the ventilation shaft or the milk crate.'

'Is the father still a suspect, guv?' Lovejoy asked him.

Charlie turned to Malik. 'Did you ask him for his phone?'

'Not really.'

'What does that mean?'

'He left it lying on the table. I borrowed it for a moment. I had the Cellebrite in the car.'

There was a moment. Under the Police and Criminal Evidence Act, officers could search, seize and retain data from a mobile phone belonging to anyone who had been arrested for committing an offence. Mr Okpotu had not been arrested, nor had he voluntarily handed over his phone.

'Should we be doing that, guv?' Lovejoy said.

'If he's in the clear, there's no harm,' Malik said.

'You're his FLO,' Lovejoy said.

Charlie looked at Parm. 'Aside from all that, did you get anything?'

'On the day she was murdered, it had been switched off from 3.07 in the afternoon until 6.32 in the evening.'

'Interesting.'

'We can't use that as evidence,' Lovejoy said.

'No, but we can ask him about it. Let him think we've got superpowers. Let's bring him in in the morning. We need to know why his phone was off. What else do we have?'

'Joe and I checked the MAPPA and the sex offenders' register. We have four offenders who live within a mile radius of our crime scene, two of them have been released from prison in the last twelve months.'

'And?'

'I sent Lube and Mac to interview them,' the skipper said.

Charlie looked at Lube, Lubanski. Her streaked blonde hair looked dirty in the strip lights and she looked washed out. Not even thirty yet. She'd pulled her share of night duties and sixteen-hour shifts to get this far this fast. Hope it's all going to be worth it for her, he thought.

I wonder what people think I look like.

'How did that go, Anna?'

'Only found one of them so far, boss.' She took out her note-book. 'Howard Briggs. Used to be a scoutmaster.'

'What's his form?'

'Four years for indecent dealing. Sounds like boys are more his thing. He has a rock-solid alibi for Thursday night, he works as a cleaner, we called his employer, it all checks out. There's also a Geoffrey Mayfield, he served five years for sodomising an underage boy; one of his pupils, he was a Classics teacher at a grammar school. There's a Darren Hunt, but he's in the Whittington at the moment, so that rules him out. The last one is Timothy Norton, he's got form, not long out, he assaulted an eight-year-old girl.'

'Why haven't you interviewed Mayfield and Norton?'

'Mayfield's landlady said he's gone away, visiting his family up north somewhere, said he's due back tomorrow.'

'And Norton?'

'We can't find him. He rents a workshop in Barndon Street, he's a car mechanic, sleeps there as well, according to the landlord. We tried there three times, but nothing.'

'OK, make sure you talk to Mayfield tomorrow. If he really was up north, we can exclude him from the investigation.' He looked at his watch. 'Lovejoy and I will go and wait for Mr Norton to get home.'

Charlie identified the lines of enquiry; first they had to exclude Raymond Okpotu and Norton from their investigation or make one of them their prime suspect. In the meantime, there was more CCTV footage to watch, more phone leads to follow up, witness statements to log in to HOLMES. They would reconvene in the morning, eight sharp.

Charlie was dog tired, had been on his feet since two, and no knowing when he would see his bed. He went into his office with Lovejoy, dictating entries for the decision log, got it up to date. His Nokia rang. He glanced at the screen and ignored it. Lovejoy gave him a quizzical look.

'Telemarketing,' he said.

Lovejoy closed the log with a snap. 'Now what, guv?'

As they were leaving, the skipper came over and put a hand on his shoulder, lowered his voice. 'The DCI keeps ringing down for you, says you're not answering your phone.'

'I'll talk to him in the car,' Charlie said. 'Come on Lovejoy, you're driving. If our Mr Norton has bad teeth, like young Reuben said, you could even be watching *Broadchurch* tonight.'

'With a big wet nose in my lap.'

'Guv!' the skipper said. He was staring at his desk monitor and a small crowd of detectives had gathered behind him. Charlie went over. He had put up the file photograph of Timothy Norton, split screen with the artist's impression they had got from Reuben Williams.

Could have been twins.

*

I live in two places. There is my world and then there is the other world. In the other world I talk to people and do boring stuff; then there is my world, the real world, where it is always dark and where no one can see you because it's secret. The only rule is that the two worlds have to be separate and apart for ever. If I could, I would stay in my world for ever, but I can't because I have to go to the other world to get things, like food and material for my experiments.

Some people like food. I don't. Food is something you have to have, like petrol for a car and oil for the engine. Otherwise it will break down. I like making shapes with food to make it more interesting, like making a body out of fish fingers and tomato sauce. You have one for the body, and four for the arms and legs. If you have a fried egg, then that is the head, when you tap it really hard all the yolk spurts out everywhere, like it does with a person.

If you don't have an egg, you can use a mashed potato ball and lots of tomato sauce. Even though I am not going to kill anyone else, I like to think about that time I did.

I have a collection of bones, all sorts of bones, that I keep. Birds have a humerus bone in their wing and an ulna and a radius just like humans. Cats are the same. I know this, because I have looked for myself

I never throw away bones. I wanted to keep a bone from the little girl I killed but that would have been stupid and I am not stupid. I wonder what she would have tasted like. I have read on the internet how cannibals say humans taste like pork. Cats taste like a mixture of frog and chicken.

I kill cats by holding their heads in a bucket, but this is not the best way to kill a human, because they are harder to hold still. So I looked it up, I googled where is the weakest part of the human body, and it said the best place to kill someone is hitting them on the back of the head. This is really good because it fractures the front of the skull as well. If you hit the right side of the occipital bone, then the part of the skull diagonally across from it, just above the eyes, will break apart.

The weakest part is called the pterion, it is where the frontal, parietal, temporal and sphenoid bones all join, and it is on the side of the skull, just behind the temple. The anterior division of the meningeal artery runs underneath it. So if you hit someone there really hard, you will rupture the middle meningeal artery causing an epidural haematoma. But it is not easy to do that, especially if they are shaking their head from side to side shouting no, no, like she did.

She shouted, you're hurting me, you're hurting me, and I laughed so much it made me miss with the brick. It took a lot of tries until she stopped moving. It was fun. When you make people die you realise how powerful you are. People laugh at you, but if they know you have killed someone they will not laugh any more, they will be afraid. But I cannot tell anyone, even though I really want to.

So, I have this brick and all this blood on my hands, I have to use this old rag to wipe it off, and then I climb on the crate and throw the brick and I think: what will I do if it doesn't go down the hole? But it does go down the hole. I hear it clanging on the steel ladder and a big crack when it hits the bottom.

And this is what you do when people ask you questions about things you don't want to talk about; you make them think you are stupid. If they think you are stupid, you can do whatever you want. And if you are caught doing something bad, you must look guilty, and sorry; this is not hard, you can practise looking sorry in the mirror.

Sometimes people try and understand why I do stuff and make explanations. These are the people I like best. But if they're like me, I can tell, I can tell straight away, and we stay away from each other.

If you have a soft heart you are daft. I like people who feel sorry when they do something bad, it is easy to make them do

52

things. You just have to learn what it is they are sorry for or what they feel bad about.

The Bible says things like, 'Cursed be he who does the Lord's work remissly, cursed he who holds back his sword from blood.' I do not hold back my sword from blood, but people say this is godless, so I do not understand people. People are mad. I am not.

And anyway, I do not believe there is a God, and if there is no God what is the point in modifying our behaviour? I watch people, and I think most of the time they are good only because other people are watching, and if they are not watching, then because they think God is watching.

That's why I like the dark. I'm not afraid of God but I am afraid of closed circuit television.

CHAPTER SEVEN

They pulled out through the gates, the drizzle on the wind-screen had pixelated the nighttime streets into a blur of reds and greens. Charlie checked his phone; two more missed calls from the DCI, he'd have to ring him back.

'It's Charlie, sir.'

'Did I or did I not say I wanted twice-daily updates?'

'Been busy, sir. Time just got away from me.'

'Where are you with the Okpotu murder?'

'We have a probable TOD and what we believe is the murder weapon is with forensics. Two possible suspects.'

'Is one of them her father?'

'Yes, sir.'

'And the other one?'

'Known sex offender. We're about to interview him now.'

'And you were going to tell me all this, when? On the way back from the Old Bailey after sentencing?'

'Sorry, sir.'

'Twice daily means twice a day, Charlie. Got that?' He hung up.

Lovejoy gave him a look.

'What?'

'Well, he is the SIO, guv.'

'Technically. In practice, he wants the medals but doesn't want to dodge any bullets. FONC is the sort of bloke who doesn't actually lead any charges, just goes around after the battle and bayonets the wounded.'

'Not wise to keep winding him up.'

'How does he expect me to close off the investigation if I'm in his office every five minutes reading him witness statements?' Charlie wiped the condensation off the passenger window and peered out at the Essex Road. 'Things have changed since I grew up here, Lovejoy. Everywhere you look there's CCTV cameras now. You'd think it wasn't possible to commit any sort of crime and get away with it in this day and age.'

'But they do.'

A bloke on a bike was looking over his shoulder and shouting at a pedestrian who had nearly walked in front of him. A homeless man in a dressing gown and deerstalker went the other way, pushing a Tesco trolley piled with plastic bags.

'When a man tires of London, he tires of life,' Lovejoy said. 'Who said that?'

'Samuel Johnson.'

'He was a writer, wasn't he?'

'He produced the first ever dictionary of the English language, which was ironic, because he had Tourette's. I suppose his editor censored out all the expletives.'

'So, did he ever get tired of London?'

'He did, when he was dying. He said he wanted to go to Islington; it wasn't part of London then. Maybe he went to see the Arsenal. That makes a lot of people lose the will to live. What about you, Lovejoy, do you like London?'

'I used to like the idea of it, when I was living with my mum. We lived in Southend. I thought London would be glamorous.'

'Everywhere is glamorous after Southend-on-Sea. So, is that why you moved? For the glamour?'

'My mum died, and then my dad got ill, so I moved in with him.'

'Like a good daughter.'

'Something like that.'

'Do you still think it's glamorous? London?'

'When I first got here I tried ketamine and I saw Liam Gallagher outside a pub in Primrose Hill. That was it for glamour and rock 'n' roll. After that it was just brown drizzle and Wetherspoon's. These days I earn enough money to live here but not enough to enjoy it. Outside of work, the only people that ever talk to me are Polish waiters. What about you?'

'I hate the place. But that goes without saying, I was born here. Wouldn't live anywhere else though.'

'What do you hate? Name six things.'

'Stan Kroenke.'

'Who's Stan Kroenke?'

'American businessman who owns the Arsenal. He runs it from an office in Delaware and has screwed us up royally.'

'That's one thing.'

'Pigeons because they crap everywhere. Foxes. Boris Johnson. Fat blokes who take their shirts off in parks on hot days. And my pet hate, top of the list—'

She never got to hear it. His phone rang; he thought it was the DCI again, but then he realised it wasn't the Nokia ringtone, it was the Arsenal club song. He pulled out his iPhone.

'Ben. What do you want? I'm working.'

'Love you too, big brother.'

'Better be important. And no, I cannot help you with your parking fines.'

'It's Will.'

'What's he done now?'

'No idea. Someone found him collapsed in a lane.'

'Shit.'

'Some bloke rang me. Think it's his boyfriend. Apparently, he's been dropping all kinds of tablets last few months.'

'Reckon we should go and see him?'

'You mean me, don't you?'

'You have the money and the time, I don't.'

'What's the point? Remember the last time? All that way, and all that money, and as soon as he was off the ventilator he told me to sod off. That was a very expensive lesson in human nature.'

'Have you told Mum?'

'What good would that do?

'Where is he?'

'The hospital's called Saint Vincent's, it's in Darlinghurst. I called them, they said they'd ring me if there's any change. Look, you're working, I'm sorry. Just thought I should let you know.'

'All right, keep me posted.'

'Yeah, later.'

He put the iPhone back in his jacket pocket.

'Everything all right?' Lovejoy said.

'My kid brother's in a bit of strife.'

'What kind of strife?'

'He was playing around with drugs for a while, now the drugs are playing around with him. He's in hospital. It was only a matter of time, I suppose.'

'How old is he?'

'Old enough to know better. You ever been one for substance abuse, Lovejoy?'

'I did a bit of stuff when I was younger, but never saw the attraction really.'

'They say for some it's like a painkiller, only for the emotions.'

'Is that how it is for him?'

'Maybe. Some people have it tough. I mean a lot of people have it tough, a shit childhood wasn't invented yesterday. Some just get on with it, others don't. Will was a lovely little kid, I remember, a bit sensitive, but he's grown into a right proper prat.'

'Is he going to be all right?'

'Don't know. This is not the first time, but one day it will be the last time. Know what I mean?'

'You going to see him?'

'He lives in Sydney.'

'Australia? Why did he move there?'

'Well,' Charlie said, 'I suppose he got tired of life.'

It was an attractive, late Victorian, mid-terraced two-bedroom house in what the locals called the ladder north of Finsbury Park. It wasn't the sort of place he had been expecting. There was a late model Beemer parked on the forecourt.

The man who answered the door wore a pink shirt open at the second button to reveal a thick rope of gold chain. He looked as if he'd just stepped out of the high-rollers room in a Beirut casino.

Charlie showed him his warrant badge. 'Detective Inspector George, Major Incident Team. I was looking for Mr Timothy Norton.'

'He's not here. How many more times? You people have been coming round here all day.'

'And you are?'

'My name is Bahremi. I am his landlord.'

'His landlord?'

'He rents the workshop from me. It is all quite legal. I've been through it all with the council.'

'I'm sure you have.'

A dark, plump woman, absolutely dripping with gold, appeared in the hallway behind him. There was a short exchange between her and the man in rapid-fire Farsi.

'The police? Again?' she said to Charlie in English. 'Why are you here? What has Mr Norton done?'

'We're hoping he can help us with our enquiries is all, madam.'

'Is it about that poor little girl who was murdered?'

'Yes. Do you know anything about it?'

'Only what we saw on the television. Do you think Mr Norton is mixed up in it?'

'As I said, he's just helping us with our enquiries at this stage.'

'I told you there was something not right about that man,' she said to her husband.

'Has he been renting long?'

'Two months.' He looked at his wife for confirmation.

'A good tenant?'

'He pays his rent on time, otherwise, well, we hardly see him.'

'Do you know where he is?'

He shrugged and shook his head.

'Well, Mr Bahremi, here's my card. If you see him, tell him we'd like to speak with him.'

Lovejoy was waiting in the car. Charlie leaned in the passenger window. 'Anything?'

'No, guv.'

There was a wooden gate. Charlie could make out a crudely handwritten sign, complete with misspellings, under the sodium street light:

Mechanical Repairs. Work Garanteed.

'Are we going to wait?'

'Nothing better to do,' Charlie said, and got back into the passenger side.

Charlie took out his iPhone, started scrolling through the news on the Arsenal website. He wondered aloud if, as a police officer, it would be considered bad form to organise a hit on Stan Kroenke.

'I don't know how you can spend so much time thinking about football,' Lovejoy said.

'Better than thinking about that little girl lying in the morgue. Sometimes I need to tune out for a bit, Lovejoy, so I can do my job. This is the thing about football, see. It's a distraction, and everyone needs a distraction, whether you're a murder detective or you've been on the dole for two years and your big day out is going to the Westfield in Stratford.'

'Didn't think anything got to you, actually.'

'Oh, things get to me; they get to everyone sooner or later. My last job, that doctor bloke nearly took my arm off with a scalpel, then he jumped fifty feet on to a concrete car park while I was talking to him. I was cleared by the DPS, but you think I slept easy that night or the next one? Things get to you. Not human if they don't.'

'There's times I've wondered if I'm cut out for this,' Lovejoy said. 'Like back there, in the morgue. You remember, when I said I wanted to go to the ladies to pee. I threw up.'

'Yeah, I know.'

'You did?'

'As long as it doesn't stop you doing your job,' Charlie said.

'When was the last time you threw up, guv?'

'When Stan Kroenke said he was going to take over Arsenal. Hello, here we go. Here comes our likely lad.'

They jumped out of the car and approached him. Charlie watched him fumble with the padlock on the wooden gate. He looked as though he had got his clothes at random from an Amnesty clothes bin, and he was so ripe that Charlie actually took a step back. 'Mr Norton?'

'Cops,' Norton said.

'DI George and this is DC Lovejoy. Mind if we have a word?'

'I knew you lot would be around.'

'How did you know that, Mr Norton?' Lovejoy said, on the front foot straight away. 'Are you psychic?'

'I heard about that little girl. It was on the news.'

'Mind if we come in?'

Norton finished unlocking the gate. They followed him inside. There was a wooden shed with a car on bricks, the engine leaking oil on a tarpaulin that had been spread on the concrete under it. There were ancient wooden shelves around the walls, crammed with rags, tools, boxes of spare automotive parts, old newspapers, oil cans.

'Brilliant,' Charlie said, 'looks like the Ferrari factory, this does. How do you keep it this spotless?'

'Can't work with cars without there being a bit of mess.'

'How's this one looking?' Charlie asked, kicking the coach-work of the piece of crap he had on blocks. 'What is this, an Astra?'

'It's a Corsa, 1999. I'm rebuilding the motor, so I can sell it.'

'Good for you, should be a handsome quid in that. Get a lot of work, do you?'

'Enough.'

'Let's get this straight. You work here, and you sleep here?'

'Saves money on rent.'

'That your heating?' Charlie nodded towards the single-bar heater on the floor next to a spare wheel.

'It's all right when the doors are closed. Dark. Cosy.'

Norton pushed aside some oily rags and a torn cardboard box and pointed to a stained red plastic kettle and two stained enamel mugs on a greasy workbench.

'Want a cup of tea?'

'Got any Orange Pekoe?'

'Any what?'

'Don't worry then.' Charlie looked around for somewhere to sit. The dining suite was a milk crate and a wooden cable spool. Charlie wandered around with his hands in his pockets, as if he was thinking of buying the place. There was a little area at the back that had been separated off with a bit of curtain; Charlie clocked a stained mattress and some rumpled bedclothes, sur-rounded by fast-food containers, chicken bones standing up in the boxes like little soldiers. There were used Kleenex tissues balled up everywhere. It stank.

He stopped in front of the television. My microwave is bigger than that, he thought. 'See this TV, Lovejoy, my gran had one of these. It was black and white. You had to bang it on the side with your fist when you turned it on to get a decent picture. Is that black and white, Mr Norton?'

'Course not.'

'Just interested. How long have you been here?'

'I had a place in Upper Tollington, but I had to leave.'

'Because they found out you were a sex offender. You were living with your brother before you went to prison.'

'Don't have a brother, don't have any family. They're all dead.'

'I'm sorry for your loss.' Charlie leaned in. 'Don't tell me, you had fish fingers and tomato sauce for lunch.'

'How do you know that, then?'

'I'm a detective. Also, there's a fish-finger packet lying on the floor over there, and ketchup all over this plate. See the one I mean? It's on the floor here next to the Bible. Don't mind me saying, you don't look like a God-fearing man.'

'I thought I'd give it a bit of a read. When I was inside, there was a priest, he told me it was never too late for anyone.'

'That was nice of him. By "never too late for anyone", was he referring to the fact that you were doing three and a half years for abducting and indecently assaulting an eight-year-old girl?'

'I done my time for that.'

'Yes, but not very much time, was it, Mr Norton? The maximum term for that is actually life. If I'd been the judge, I would have been tempted to have a right proper look at the rule book.'

'Lucky you weren't the judge then.'

'Yes, it was lucky. According to the files, you were out in two for good behaviour.'

'I'm sorry for what I did.'

'Well, that makes everything all right then. Is that the bathroom?' There was a brick outside toilet. You didn't see those much any more, Charlie thought; the garden around it was overgrown with weeds.

'Like I said, this place is only temporary.'

'Where do you shower?'

'Where do I what?'

'Where were you yesterday evening from five o'clock?' Lovejoy asked him.

Norton turned around. He seemed startled, almost as if he'd

forgotten that she was there. 'I was feeding the ducks in the park.'

'Was anyone with you who could verify that?'

'Just the ducks,' Norton said, 'but they aren't talking.'

'Oh, I get it,' Charlie said. 'That was a joke.'

'We have a witness,' Lovejoy said. 'He says he saw a short, scruffy-looking bloke with yellow teeth down by that bit of disused railway line last night, right where they found the little girl.'

'I'm not short.'

'But you were down there?'

'I told you, I was feeding the ducks.'

'The person he saw was scruffy and he had dodgy teeth,' Charlie said. 'That remind you of anyone?'

'Expensive that is. Dentistry.'

'Can we have a look at your phone?'

'Don't have a phone.'

'You don't have a mobile phone?'

'Don't need one.'

'How do you post your selfies on Instagram?' Lovejoy asked him.

'What was it, Mr Norton?' Charlie said. 'How did it happen? Not your fault, really, I suppose. You didn't mean to do it, did you? You were just out for a walk, you saw her down there, it was getting on dark, just too hard to resist. It wasn't like you planned it.'

'I don't know what you're talking about.'

Lovejoy leaned in, which was brave of her, Charlie thought. 'What have you been doing today, Mr Norton? Our officers have been trying to speak to you all day, and you haven't been here.'

'No law says I have to be.'

'So where were you?'

If he says 'feeding the ducks', Charlie thought, I am going to stick a ratchet extender where the sun don't shine.

63

'Just walking. I like to walk.'

'Trying to forget what you did to that little girl?'

For the first time Norton looked animated. 'I didn't do nothing to the girl! I told you, I don't do those things any more.'

'I wish I could believe you,' Charlie said.

'You've still got the urge though, haven't you?' Lovejoy said to him.

'Maybe. You want the truth, it never goes away. I wish it would. But I didn't do it. Swear to God I didn't.'

'No good swearing on something you don't believe in. Well, thanks for your time, Mr Norton. We'll leave you to it.' Charlie stopped, took a last look around. If there was any evidence hidden in here, he wondered how they would find it. It would take Jack and his team at least a month just to sort through it. 'You should put up some pictures. Make it look nice. For when you bring girls home.'

'Proper comedian, aren't you?'

'I can be. Can't I, Lovejoy?'

'Oh yeah. Right funny, him.'

'Goodnight Mr Norton. We'll talk again soon.'

When they got back to the car, Lovejoy was seething. 'It was him. Dirty bastard. Why didn't we just drag him in?'

'Lovejoy, once we arrest him we're on a clock. I want all my ducks in a row before we do that. So far, all we've got is an eyewitness who said he saw him near where the little girl was murdered. If it was him.'

'It was him, written all over him.'

'Don't get too far ahead of yourself. One thing that bothers me is the MO. The little girl he assaulted in Colchester, he abducted her in a van. This crime is completely different.'

'He's learned from last time, guv, if he'd offed the girl in Colchester, chances are he wouldn't have been caught. Besides, like you said, this wasn't planned, it was opportunistic.'

'All the more reason to get everything sorted before we charge him.'

'He'll do a runner, for sure.'

Charlie took out his Nokia. 'I'll ring the DCI, ask him for a surveillance team to keep an eye on him until I can put enough together for an arrest warrant. Don't worry, Lovejoy, he's not getting away.'

CHAPTER EIGHT

Charlie checked his watch when he got back to the nick, tried to work out how many hours he had been on his feet. He sat down at the laptop, went through the day's witness statements, and before he knew it, it was midnight. He stared at the camp bed folded away in the alcove in the corner of his office and he just couldn't face it. Be nice, he thought, just to be at home in my own bed for a few hours. I never sleep right on that bloody thing and I'll have to have my wits about me tomorrow.

He got his keys, went down in the lift, jumped in his car. He sniffed. It smelled like pine and leather. He remembered now, Lovejoy had taken it down the road to get it cleaned. He should do it more often, though he supposed he'd probably change his mind when he saw the charge on his credit card bill.

There was typically nowhere to park in the street. He finally found a spot down the end near the high road; might as well have walked. He turned off the engine, sat listening to the clicking of the motor as it cooled. The moon raced across dark scudding clouds, a fox ran across the street, like it owned the place. He saw a light flickering in the top-floor window of the flat over the road, that psycho watching porn or playing Minecraft, he supposed. Only cops and misfits still up at this hour.

He couldn't stop thinking about Norton. Had to be him, didn't it? As soon as Jack got back with the forensics, there had to be something he could nail him with. So far all they had was the girl on the CCTV, and the kid who said he saw him following her, down the disused line. He couldn't get an arrest warrant on that. Tomorrow, he told himself. Tomorrow everything would fall into place.

That bloody horrible little shed he lived in. There had to be something in there that they could use to finger him, as long as he didn't dispose of it before they had a chance to get a search and seizure.

It was sort of nice sitting here with no one talking to him, but it was getting cold already. He got out and walked fast back up the hill, only thinking of his bed now. You only realised how stuffed you were when you finally gave in to it.

He fumbled with his house key, took him three tries, he was that tired. Funny, he didn't remember leaving the light on. For a moment he thought about flopping down, on to the couch, just for a minute. No, screw it, he'd come home to get away from dossing down just anywhere and waking up with his neck twisted around like a glove puppet. He let his jacket drop on the carpet, threw his briefcase on the stairs and stepped over it. He made sure he had the Nokia in his pocket, couldn't even go to the khazi without that. The top of the stairs looked like the ascent to Everest base camp. Come on, Charlie, just get up there and into your bed, man. Set the alarm. Six a.m. A good, solid five hours. That's the business.

As he walked into the bedroom, a hand went across his mouth and an arm circled his chest from behind. 'Don't move,' a voice said. 'I've got a gun and I'll blow a hole in you the size of the Blackwall Tunnel.' The hand travelled down his chest to his groin. 'Now what have you got for me?'

'Please,' he said. 'Not now.'

'You say no, no but he says yes, yes. Now which one am I going to believe?'

She pushed him forward and he lay face down on the bed. He felt her weight on his back.

'The Blackwall Tunnel? You realise real criminals never talk that way?'

'I'm not a real criminal,' she said, rolled him over and put both his hands on her breasts. She was wearing one of his t-shirts and not very much else. 'Do I feel like a real criminal?'

'What are you doing here, Pip? I'm rostered on, I told you.'

'I thought you'd be pleased. By the way, someone pooped in your kitchen.'

'Oh God, that must have been Charlie.'

'Who's Charlie?'

'He's a cocker spaniel.'

'You've got a dog?'

'Course not. He wandered in, he must be from round here somewhere. I gave him to a friend to look after. Did you clean it up?'

'I'm your girlfriend, not your housemaid.'

'You mean it's still there?' He got off the bed and went down to the kitchen. Look at the time. He got the Ajax and the paper towels. He could hear Pippa in the bedroom; she'd put music on: 'Marvins Room'. Well, he couldn't disappoint. He remembered what Ben had told him. Never ever say no, bro, two reasons: one, with a face like yours, you never know if there'll be a next time, and two, you're a bloke, it's the principle of the thing.

So much for sleeping.

When he came back to the bedroom she was kneeling on the bed, facing away from him, holding the brass rails of the bedstead. She was moving her butt in time to Drake, who was singing about being in the club too long.

'Do that butterfly thing with your tongue, Charlie,' she said.

He took off his clothes; all he wanted was a shower, but felt the time was inopportune. He knelt on the bed behind her and she started to grind herself against him. Like the lady said, his lips said no, no, his body kept saying yes, yes. He was going to pay for this tomorrow but now was now.

He put his fingers down the front of her pants. She was already wet. He kissed the back of her neck and she squirmed around and held his face in her hands and put her tongue in his mouth. I could be dreaming this, he thought, I'm that tired. God help me if I'm dreaming this in my office or in the DCI's office.

He had been hoping for a quickie, but he should have known better. If he wanted to sleep with blonde Amazons, he would have to do the right thing. 'Keep it down, you'll wake the whole borough,' he said, but she wasn't listening.

But you can't rush these things; he didn't want her going away disappointed and finding some other bloke. So he took his time, built up to it, finally she grabbed his hair and almost suffocated him, he felt her thigh trembling, it was a sign she was close, to hell with the neighbours.

When she'd finished she rolled over and curled up with her knees to her chest and lay there, trying to get her breath. She wasn't the kind of girl who needed more, only one show a night thanks, so that was something, considering his present condition. As a rule he would gently part her legs and find his own way to ease the tension, but not tonight.

At last, Charlie thought. Sleep.

He spooned behind her and was out as soon as he closed his eyes. He woke with a start, his heart hammering against his ribs. He fumbled for his watch: shit, half past six, he'd forgotten to set the alarm.

How could it be half six? Jesus. That felt like five minutes.

He jumped out of bed, fumbled for his clothes lying across the bedroom carpet. Where was his briefcase? Where was his jacket? He found it lying in the hallway – it needed a good dry clean – raced upstairs and threw on one of his good suits. He thought about coffee and cornflakes, decided he didn't have time. Took him five minutes to find his car keys. He was about to run for the car, remembered Pippa upstairs, better get her up, or she'd be late for work too.

But she was already awake, she was in the bathroom, standing in front of the mirror, stark naked.

'Not your usual sartorial elegance,' she said, watching him in the glass as she brushed out her hair.

'Haven't even got time to comb my hair,' he said.

She ran a hand across the close-shaved bristles. 'There, it's fixed. You've got semen on your tie.'

'Not mine, I didn't even come.'

'Not from one of your suspects, I hope.'

'What? You got a potty mouth. It's mayonnaise from the chicken sarnie I had for lunch.'

'That's a relief.' He had to get going, but he couldn't take his eyes off her. She smiled, reached a hand behind her, and squeezed his crotch. 'I think he wants a day off.'

'He can't have one.'

'Poor him.' She squeezed past. 'You had your chance. Anyway, I can't be late for work.' She got in the shower, turned on the hot water. 'You had another dream last night.'

'What dream?'

'You shouted out that the angel of death was after you.'

'You're making that up.'

She put her head around the shower screen. 'Who's Lucifer?'

Charlie thought about him, perched up the top of that tower, with the scalpel in his fist and that look on his face. Could have stopped him jumping, if I'd wanted to. 'No idea.'

'When am I going to see you?'

'I don't know. I told you, I'm on call all week.'

'That poor little girl who was found. Are you in charge of that?'

'That's why I don't know when I'm going to be free next.'

'I'm going to my dad's birthday lunch Sunday week. Are you still on call then?'

'Depends where we are with the case. You want me to meet your parents?'

'You don't have to. Unless you just want to keep sleeping with me, you know, no complications. At least I'll know where I stand.'

'Where is it?'

'I'll text you the address, if you like.'

'Do that.'

'I'll understand if you can't come.'

'I'll try, all right?'

She opened the shower door and put her head round. 'And if my mum tries to chirpse you, tell her to fuck off.' She grinned and shut the door again.

'Yeah, I can see me doing that,' he said. He went into the kitchen and turned on the hot tap. As he went out of the door he heard her screaming as the water upstairs ran cold. He grinned and ran for his car.

These are the things I don't like: bright lights; loud noises; people asking me questions and wanting to know stuff about me; people shouting at me; people treating me like I am nothing.

Other things I don't like: jigaboos; and my father.

These are the things I like: little girl's knickers, as long as they are white; school playgrounds. I like to watch. You can learn a lot.

I also like watching flies try to get away from ants, if you take their wings off; using a magnifying glass to burn moths on the curtain; taking birds out of a nest and watching to see what the mother bird will do.

Most of all I like smells. You can tell everything about someone by the way they smell, you can tell what they think and how they think. I have read about it online and in books, smell can affect a person's emotions, or even their memory. No one knows I notice smell but I do, smell is the most important thing.

Like the smell of soil when it has just been turned over by a spade. The smell is not always the same, it is different depending on where you dig. If it smells like ammonia or it has a rotten egg smell, it means the water cannot run away, or there is no air getting into the ground. The smell comes from bacteria, not the ground. It is the smell of what we are when we die.

Most people only notice really big smells like cheap perfume or vomit. But everything has a smell, and smells have a name. Like petrichor. Petrichor is the name for the smell when rain falls on dry earth. Petra is Latin for rock. The ancient Greeks thought that *ichor* was the blood that flowed through the veins of a god. So it is a really good word.

What happens is that when it is dry, plants give off an oil, and the clays and rocks around it absorb the oil. When it rains, the raindrop lands on a porous surface and, as it seeps down, it forms small bubbles, and these float back to the surface with the oil and something called geosmin, which is made by the bacteria that live in the soil. So what we can smell is the plants and the bacteria, not the rain. The rain just makes it happen.

Petrichor.

Hundreds of thousands of years ago, when humans prayed for rain when there was a drought, petrichor was like a prayer they had made that had been answered. And our little primeval brains still like that smell.

Humans can tell over ten thousand different smells. That is nothing compared to rats. Everything a rat touches, every time it sniffs the air, it learns different things. A rat cannot only register scents, it can tell changes in atmosphere or emotion by the chemicals in the air.

Sometimes I wonder what it would be like. I get down on all fours and try it for myself, and sniff the floor, the bits of food, the grease, the smell of rubber and shoes and electrical wire, and metal. Everything has a different smell.

Rats also have a second scent receptor, called the vomeronasal organ, to pick up scent marks left by other rats. A rat can tell by even the tiniest drop of urine who produced it, what sex they were, whether they are in heat, whether they are pregnant or available for sex, their social status, even if they are stressed. Humans think urine is bad and dirty but it isn't.

Because people do not like urine smells, they have to borrow smells to confuse other humans. Like aftershave and perfume.

That policeman wears aftershave. People call them fragrances, but fragrance is not always nice, fragrance is just something people use to hide themselves and their real smells. A long time ago, when people started wearing leather, they used oils, musk, ambergris and civet to hide the dead animal smell of the leather.

The policeman's aftershave has juniper and cade oil, cistus labdanum, two chemicals called quinolines and Safraleine, as well as petit grain, and guaiac wood from Paraguay.

I do not like these smells.

The policeman acts like he is in control, all buff and bristles. He likes the sound of his voice, he thinks he says clever things, but he isn't clever at all. He likes to dress and smell so people will notice him, but he is stupid, he doesn't know it is better if people do not like to look at you, then you can hide away, in your own dark.

I bet people are scared, wary, when he walks in the room, because he is so hard, so certain, so sharp; even like his clothes will cut you, with such sharp creases.

He doesn't really know anything, because he does not like the dark, no one really likes the dark. The dark behind my eyes, they can't go there, they cannot ever find their way without the light and that is why I am cleverer. Policemen like saying things on the television like 'something has come to light' and 'let me be clear'. But things aren't ever clear, not really.

I like to watch people, study what they do. I practise in the mirror, because people, they cannot smell, so they have to rely on what they see to try and understand, and the eyes are not like smell, they cannot tell you the important things.

The more you practise the different faces, the better you get at it. It is like acting, like on the television, everyone you meet, they are just actors, like I am; none of it is real but everyone is so good at it, you think it is. You can show them one thing and they will look at that and while they are looking at that, you can do something else.

Most people want to believe in the good, that is what is wrong with them. I never believe in the good. That is why I am clever.

That is what you do, you make people think you are one thing then they never guess you are something else.

74

CHAPTER NINE

'Ben.'

'Do you know what time it is?'

'Early bird catches the worm.'

'I'm a futures broker not a starling. Christ, it's Saturday.'
Charlie heard him talking to someone in the background, one
of his ski bunnies probably.

'How's Will?'

'Still in ICU, last I heard.'

'Which was when?'

'What? I don't know. Yesterday. Do I need an alibi?'

'Let me know if you hear anything more.'

'No, I'm going to wait till three in the morning and tell you
then.'

The grumpy bastard hung up. Charlie checked his watch.
A quarter to seven. If he'd woken him up, he'd woken his girlfriend as well. Time for a morning glory, he should be thanking
him.

The Incident Room was buzzing when he got in. He
stopped by the whiteboard on the way to his office, stared at
Mariatu's face smiling back at him. Have to close this one. It
won't bring her back, but it might stop it happening to someone
else.

I promise you, I'll find out who did this to you.

There were three arrows leading away from her picture: one
led to Norton, one to Mayfield, the last to Raymond Okpotu.

He was eager to take down that last picture. For God's sake, he thought, don't let it be him.

Raymond Okpotu eyed them warily. He still looked fresh, as if he had come back from a week at a spa retreat. He even looked relaxed; in Charlie's experience, geezers with something on their conscience sat a little hunched up, as though they were hiding something in their lap. He had on a quilted ski jacket, a white shirt, freshly ironed. He kept his hands in the jacket pockets.

'Thanks for coming in, Mr Okpotu.'

'Have you any news about my daughter's murder, Inspector?'

'We're following a number of leads. In the absence of an eye-witness, these things can take time. But we are doing everything we can.'

'How can I help?'

'We just want to fill in a few gaps in your statement.'

'My statement? Am I . . . am I under suspicion here?' He looked at Lovejoy, then back at Charlie. 'Should I have a solicitor?'

'You are of course entitled to legal representation, if you feel it's necessary. But at this stage, we just want to clarify what you told us about your movements on the day your daughter was murdered.'

He took his hands out of his pockets and folded them neatly on the desk in front of him, one on top of the other like a pair of gloves. 'What is it you are unsure about?'

'You said you left work at around six o'clock. Is there anyone in your office who can corroborate that?'

'Why are you doing this, Inspector? We are the victims here.'

'Is there anyone who can corroborate your statement?'

He looked like a rabbit caught in the headlights. 'I don't know.'

'How many people work in your office?'

'Around twenty.'

'One of them must have seen you leave.'

'I was working in my office, I had the door shut.'

'That's not quite true, is it?'

His Adam's apple bobbed in his throat. He leaned in. 'How do you know this?'

'Are you saying our information is incorrect?'

He blinked slowly.

'If you have an innocent explanation,' Charlie said, 'just tell me now, and let's get this out of the way.'

'My daughter is dead. Am I the one on trial here?'

'We're just doing our job, Mr Okpotu,' Lovejoy said. 'I'm afraid in many of the cases we have to deal with, the murderer is known to the victim.'

'You really think I would hurt . . . my little Mariatu?' His face, so composed for so long, suddenly crumpled. A fat tear rolled down his cheek.

'Please, Mr Okpotu,' Lovejoy said, softly, 'just tell us where you were that afternoon.'

'Does my wife have to know?'

'If it doesn't affect the case, then she won't hear it from us.' He pushed the box of tissues across the desk.

'I have a girlfriend.'

'What time did you leave work?'

'It was around three. I went to see . . . do you need her name?'

'We'll have to speak to her, yes. We'll need her to corroborate your story.'

He rubbed his face with his hands. 'Her name's Lilian Garner, 22 Inglewood Lane in Richmond.'

Charlie checked his notes. 'How long were you there?'

Raymond Okpotu studied his shoes. 'I don't know. Till about six.' He reached into his jacket pocket and pulled out his mobile phone. 'Here, you can check for yourself. You can do that, right?'

Charlie was relieved. In a way it got them off the hook. He took it.

77

'Is there anything else?'

'That's all,' Charlie said. 'Thanks for coming in.'

'I know the way out,' he said. Then he was gone, leaving the door yawning open behind him.

Charlie tapped the phone on the edge of the desk. He felt shabby.

'We had to exclude him,' Lovejoy said. 'He wasn't going to come out and tell us himself.'

'He still has an hour he can't account for.'

The Nokia rang in his pocket. It was the DCI. He took a deep breath and held the phone to his ear.

'Charlie. My office. Now.'

'Shut the door.'

The DCI reminded Charlie of his accountant. His desk was neat, terrifyingly empty. There was a blotter, a pen, and a photograph of the DCI's family in a square silver frame. The wife and children seemed almost geometric in their positioning. At the DCI's elbow was the document he had been reading when Charlie entered. He put it out of view underneath the blotter.

Charlie appreciated this level of anal retention, in an accountant.

'Where the hell have you been?'

'Working, sir.'

'My other three DIs manage to report to me twice a day, without fail. I wonder why it is you can't?'

There was a long silence. Charlie blinked. 'Is that a rhetorical question?'

'Don't be a smartarse.'

'I can't keep running back to the office, it's not where work's done.'

'You do have a phone, don't you? How hard is it to pick up the phone and call in? It's what the others do.'

'I shall endeavour to be more conscientious in the future, sir.'

They looked at each other. The DCI couldn't decide if

Charlie was having a go, but he let it slide. 'Last time we spoke, you said you had a murder weapon and two suspects.'

'Jack and his team recovered a house brick, on which they detected blood, hair and brain matter. It was found, or bits of it were found, at the bottom of a ventilation shaft, located inside the brick building near the murder scene.'

'And the two suspects?'

'One is her father, of course; the other is one Timothy Keith Norton. He was on the sex offenders' list, lives only half a mile from where Mariatu's body was found. I also have three others on our TIE list, also convicted sex offenders; one was at work from four until midnight, and this was verified by his employer. The second one is in hospital.'

'Something serious, I hope.'

'He has cancer of the right testicle.'

'And they say there is no God. What about the other one?'

'The skipper sent McCullough and Lubanski to interview him. So far, no luck. There was no answer at his flat and the neighbours say they haven't seen him. Intel are trying to find him now. We should have him by the end of the day.'

'Tell me about the father.'

'He was the one that found the body.'

'You think he killed her then went back later and recovered the body to confuse the forensics?'

'Possibly.'

'That would be smart. Did he have a motive?'

'Not really, no.'

'Why kill her at the railway line?'

'Better than killing her at home.'

'It indicates prior planning. Domestic crimes are usually done on impulse.'

'We still need to exclude him from the investigation, especially as he lied to us in his original statement. He said he was at work until six, but he just revised his story, said he was with a girlfriend in Richmond.'

'You've dragged him in here for another interview without checking with me? You realise the local mullah is kicking up a shitstorm in the media? He's telling everyone the murder was racially motivated.'

'We have to exclude him from the investigation as soon as possible.'

'How did you know he was lying?'

'Well, the GPS on his phone.'

'He gave you his phone.'

'Well, yes.'

'Before you had this information or afterwards?'

'Does it matter now?'

The DCI lowered his voice, as if his wife and the vicar were listening. 'Jesus fucking Christ!'

He didn't use profanities very often, so Charlie surmised he wasn't best pleased.

'This is why I need you to check in with me regularly, Charlie. I'm not always in favour of your unorthodox methods.'

'Actually, it was one of my team using their initiative. But I take full responsibility.'

'I'll hold you to that.'

Charlie let him fume.

'We'll talk to the girlfriend.'

'Tell me about this Norton character.'

'Released from Bullingdon Prison seven months ago, got three and a half years for the abduction and indecent assault of an eight-year-old girl, Samantha Parkes, taken from a funfair in Wilton Dene. Currently renting a workshop half a mile from where Mariatu Okpotu's body was found.'

'A workshop?'

'There's a sign on the gate that says he's a car mechanic.'

'Where does he live?'

'In the workshop. Before this, he was renting a flat in Upper Tollington Park for five months, but then his neighbours found out about his prison record and made it uncomfortable for him to remain.' Charlie looked up from his notes. 'One of them beat him up.'

The DCI shrugged. That was rotten luck for him. 'Mobile phone?'

'Says he doesn't have one.'

'How does he keep in touch with all his Facebook friends?'

'Intel are on to it.'

'Must be the only bloke in London who doesn't have a mobile phone. How does he get work?'

'Honest guv, if you saw this geezer, you wouldn't trust him with your motor. He's got one car in his shed, some wreck he says he's going to do up to sell.'

'Does he have an alibi?'

'He said he was at the park feeding the ducks. Thing is, we have an eyewitness, a thirteen-year-old boy, who puts him at the old railway line, following the deceased, the afternoon she disappeared. That was the last time she was seen alive.'

'Confirmed?'

'Came in with his father, last night. We showed him Norton's photograph from the file, and he says he's positive that was the man he saw.'

'So why haven't you arrested him?'

'I was hoping for something from Lambeth. We haven't got enough to charge him. I don't want to start the clock running until I've got solid evidence.'

'He could be destroying that "solid evidence" as we speak, now he knows we're on to him. I'll get you the warrant. Bring him in.'

'But, sir—'

'But me no buts, Charlie. Collar him. Now.'

Charlie went to the whiteboard, stared at Raymond Okpotu's photograph. He drew a red circle around Norton's mugshot and a question mark next to Mayfield's.

'OK people, listen up, the DCI is getting a warrant for

Timothy Norton. Soon as I have it in my hot little hand, we're going to pick him up and charge him.'

'Have we got enough?' Wes said.

Charlie shrugged. 'Word from on high.'

'Guv,' White said. 'Look at this.'

Charlie went over. White's desk was basically a tuck shop: there was a Crunchie bar, a packet of cheese and onion crisps, half-eaten, and two empty cans of Coke. It amazed Charlie that the laptop worked; the keyboard was covered with bits of biscuit.

'This is the CCTV from the betting shop,' White said.

Wes and Rupinder peered over Charlie's shoulder at the grainy black-and-white vision.

White tapped his finger on the screen. 'This is him, isn't it?'

Norton was somehow distinctive in his nondescript way. He was wearing a Batman t-shirt, a stained Harrington, jeans a size too big. Charlie checked the clock on the right-hand corner of the screen: 17.23.13. So at five twenty-five on the Thursday evening, they could prove that Timothy Norton had not been feeding ducks in the park, he had been down at the disused railway line, just as Reuben said he was.

His Nokia buzzed to life in his pocket. That was quick work with the search warrant. But it wasn't the DCI, it was Morton from surveillance. 'Our boy's on the move,' he said. 'Just got in a car parked in the street outside. What do you want us to do?'

'Keep him in sight,' Charlie said. 'The DCI's organising a warrant. If he tries to get any further than the local offie, grab him.'

'Right,' Bruin said and hung up.

'He's on the move,' Charlie said.

Five minutes later, Bruin rang back. 'He must have seen us,' he said. 'He started driving all over the road. Just missed a bus and an old lady with a walking frame and drove right into a lamp-post, the daft sod. He's slumped over the wheel, there's blood everywhere. We've called an ambulance. Got that warrant yet?'

CHAPTER TEN

The Emergency Department at the Whittington was rammed, as usual. It was a Saturday, the most popular day of the week to get injured, especially if you were a kid playing football or netball. There were three trolleys in the corridor, paramedics in a hurry to get away; all the plastic seats in the waiting room were taken, a bloody bandage here, a shrieking kid there, the NHS on overload.

There had been two major motor-vehicle accidents in the last hour, a car versus pedestrian in Tottenham and a T-bone between a taxi and a lorry at some lights in Islington. Charlie saw the taxi driver lying on a trolley with an oxygen mask over his face just before a nurse whipped a curtain shut around him. Didn't like the colour of him. Looked like one for Ferguson at Haringey.

They found Timothy Norton in one of the cubicles at the end. He had been handcuffed to the trolley and Bruin was sitting in a plastic chair fiddling with his phone. They were a scruffy lot, surveillance, Charlie thought; Bruin looked as if he'd just got out of bed.

He jumped to his feet when he saw Charlie and Lovejoy, eager to be away. 'When was the last time that bleeder had a bath?' he said.

'Did he give you any trouble?'

'Only when he breathed out. My grandmother smells better than he does.'

'Did you take a look in the van?'

'Yeah, it was piled with stuff. I called Jack, he said he'd send a team down there. As soon as you get them the paperwork, they'll take it back to Lambeth for a right going-over.'

'Good job. Is he all right?'

'Staging, I reckon. But he's not going anywhere in that van of his any time soon.'

'What happened?'

'He must have seen us watching him. Took off like a bat out of hell, didn't get any further than the high street, overcorrected on a bend, went straight into a lamp-post.'

Timothy Norton lay on the trolley in the same Batman t-shirt he had been wearing in the CCTV capture two nights before. Charlie was glad he wasn't a nurse, having to clean him up, you'd need a fire hose and some industrial-strength bleach to get this bloke clean. The coppery taint of the blood from his head wound overlaid his rank odour of sweat and rotted teeth and motor oil.

Charlie took a closer look at the gash in his scalp. 'Does it hurt?'

'No,' Norton said.

'Pity. Well, a couple of stitches and you'll be good as new. If it were me, I'd take a couple of Panadol, you're going to have a proper headache later.'

'Why am I handcuffed?'

Charlie showed him the arrest warrant. 'Timothy Norton, I am arresting you on suspicion of the murder of Mariatu Okpotu. You do not have to say anything. But, it may harm your defence if you do not mention when questioned something which you later rely on in court. Anything you do say may be given in evidence.'

'I didn't do it.'

'Is that why you tried to do a runner in your van?'

'I wasn't trying to do a runner.'

'What were you doing, then?'

'I know what you lot are like. You're going to try and fit me up for something I never did.'

'I don't have to fit you up, Timothy, I reckon I have you bang to rights.'

'I'm going to be sick,' Norton said, and he leaned over the edge of the bed and Charlie jumped back out of the way, but not far enough and not in time. First the spaniel craps in his car, now a kiddy-fiddler throws up on his Corneliani. What had made him wear it, today of all days? No point in getting it dry-cleaned, he supposed, it would be back to the charity shop for the suit. What a crying shame.

That's it for you, Mr Norton. I'll bloody nail you now.

Jack stood in the street, suited up, his mask down around his chin. He was making notes on a clipboard. He gave Charlie a look when he saw him. 'You get some right muckers, you.'

'Find anything?'

'Jimmy Hoffa. Amelia Earhart. MH-370. All in there, I reckon.'

'Bit of a mess, isn't it?'

'Looks like my son's bedroom. How long has he been living there?'

'Two months, the landlord reckons.'

'I've known hoarders that don't have this much stuff. Going to take us all day, this.'

'Anything that looks promising?'

'Lots of used tissues everywhere, and that outside toilet, Jesus Christ, didn't ever flush, the dirty bastard.'

'What about the bedroom?'

'Is that what you call it? Nothing incriminating exactly, old clothes, takeaway boxes, dead cockroaches. The mattress has got stains all over it, of course, we'll take it back to Lambeth and see what we've got.'

'What about his van?'

'It's been towed. If there's so much as a molecule from that girl, we'll find it.'

Charlie suited up, and Jack led the way inside. The warrant and premises search books lay on the bonnet of the disused car. Jack's team worked silently, intent. They had plenty to keep them busy. Two men in knee-length rubber boots and head-to-toe waterproofs were carrying a toilet cistern out of the outside toilet. Charlie gagged and turned away.

'You know that 130-ton fat-berg they found in the sewers?' Jack said. 'I think we found its twin sister.'

'I don't know how you blokes do this job.' Charlie pointed to the old motor, still on bricks in the middle of the shed. 'Where did that come from?'

'I've checked the VIN number, it's definitely registered to him. Looks like it's been on those blocks for months.'

'Guv, take a look at this.'

One of the SOCOs called them over. He'd found a cheap plastic ring-bind folder behind a box of spark plugs on one of the shelves. Inside there were yellowed newspaper cuttings dating back to 2010, about the disappearance of a girl called Tiffany Strong.

'Do you know who she is?'

'Not yet,' Charlie said. 'Bag it for me. I'll take it with.' He called Parm on his phone, told her to put Tiffany's name into the PNC, get him the details.

'Some of the pages are stuck together,' the SCO said.

Jack shook his head and made a note in his clip folder.

'There's something else.' The SCO led them over to the shelves. 'These were tucked in behind it.' He held open a plastic shopping bag.

'Underwear,' Charlie said.

'They won't fit him, by the looks,' Jack said.

'They appear to have been washed. I used the wood's lamp and some of the items are positive for semen.'

Charlie followed Jack back outside. Jack lit up, coughed.

'What got him the last time?' Jack said.

'Forensics found blood in the tyre well in the boot of his car. Even though it had been detailed.'

'Well, his van hadn't been cleaned in a good long while. So if she was there, or anything of hers is in there, we're going to find it.'

'How soon?'

'Everyone wants something yesterday.'

'Come on, Jack.'

'No, you come on, Charlie. We've got no money, they've cut our budget to ribbons. You want your evidence faster, lobby your MP, don't give me a hard time.'

Charlie took the point and turned away; let Jack enjoy his close encounter with cancer in peace.

'Inspector!'

Mr Bahremi marched towards him, sharp suit, bits of gold everywhere, the proper business. 'Inspector, what is happening here?'

'Your tenant is at the station, helping us with our enquiries, Mr Bahremi. Meanwhile we have been authorised to conduct a thorough search of these premises.'

'Is it true, then, that he killed the little girl?'

'He has not been charged at this stage.'

'What is this going to do to my business?'

'Excuse me?'

'I will have to get rid of him. I won't have people thinking that I am the sort of landlord who harbours filthy people in his own house. You ought to cut his nuts off.'

'You lot are going to need help down here,' Jack said over his shoulder.

'That's for the local uniform to sort,' Charlie said. 'As long as the locals don't tamper with my evidence, Mr Norton's Jacobs are not my concern.' He extracted himself from Mr Bahremi and past the police cordon. His iPhone rang. Please don't be the nursing home, he thought.

'Ben.'

'Busy?'

'What do you reckon? How's Will?'

'He's out of ICU.'

'How's he doing?'

'Discharged himself.'

'You are kidding me. Where's he staying? Has he got mates?'

'You know as much as I do, Charlie.'

Charlie got in his car. A crowd had gathered outside the police tape. Some of them shouted things at him, someone was banging on his window. He flicked on the central locking.

'I still think you should go over and see him.'

'Mate, he's a big boy, he's not our responsibility any more. What am I going to do, tell him Mum's cross and he's got to come home?'

'What if he does for himself?'

'It's his life. You can't save everyone, Charlie.'

Got a point there, Charlie thought. He headed back to the nick. He thought about the folder in the sealed evidence bag on the seat beside him. Tiffany Strong. What the hell was that all about?

CHAPTER ELEVEN

Wes and Rupe were leaning on Wes's desk, staring at the laptop screen.

'I cannot listen to this bloodclaat a second time,' Wes said. 'I'm going downstairs to get coffee.'

'What's the story, morning glory?' Charlie said.

'We found Mayfield,' the skipper said. 'Wes and Rupe have just finished the interview.'

Rupe fiddled with the mouse and went back a couple of minutes on the file. He pressed play. Charlie leaned in. Wes and Rupinder sitting in the interview room, a man in a tweed jacket and Hugh Grant hair sitting on the other side of the desk. Any other situation, Charlie thought, he would have taken him for a university professor.

'I first realised I might be a paedophile when I was about fourteen,' Mayfield was saying. 'Of course, I didn't know there was such a thing when I was that age. But while my friends were talking about the girls in our class, I mean just *all* the time, all I could think about was . . . the boys in the primary school across the road. I knew, without anyone ever telling me, that I would get into trouble if I ever said anything about it. My childhood was a nightmare. I thought I would grow out of these feelings, but of course I didn't. I got older but my attraction to boys of that age remained the same. I realised the only way to deal with the situation was to compartmentalise these feelings. It's not hard. People do it all the time, keep all the parts of their lives separate. It's how people have affairs, isn't it? But with me, the stakes were much, much higher.'

He saw Wes sit back, throw his pen on the desk. He would have stopped the interview right there, but Rupe leaned in, encouraged him to keep talking.

'I was very strict with myself. Like an anorexic, I suppose, I was only allowed a limited diet of my own fantasies. That way I could live what appeared to everyone else to be a normal life. I kept myself apart. I wanted to be like others. I even tried sex with a man once, a man my own age.'

'What happened?' Rupinder asked him.

He flicked at the comma of hair hanging over his eye. 'I didn't like it. It was boring for me. I'm attracted to young boys, and *only* very young boys. It's what I am and what I have to live with every day. But I'm not like those slavering child molesters that are depicted in films and television. You can see that for yourself. I am a civilised man. I have self-control.'

'Is that what you are?' Wes said. 'Civilised?'

Mayfield bristled. He crossed his arms and looked at Wes down the length of his nose. 'I was born this way, detective, it was not a choice. It's no different to being gay, or transgender. That's even *trendy* these days.'

'Yah, I don't think a kiddy-fiddling Mardi Gras will ever catch on, man.'

'I know what you think of me,' Mayfield said to Wes. 'But remember this, I did not choose to abandon my humanity and decide to prey on young boys, even though there have been times when a lifetime of self-sacrifice brought me to the edge of despair. I have considered suicide more times than I care to admit. It would have been easier, of course, to have become a priest. Some do. But there are many of us, more than you would imagine, who hide their secret longings and every day go about their business, harming no one. I don't look at child porn, I respect society's position on this. I understand it and agree with it. But the fact remains, I have been a paedophile my entire life.

It was *not* my choice, that was God's. *My* choice was not to act on it.'

'But you did act on it, didn't you?' Rupinder said to him. 'That's why you're here.' He took a photograph out of the file in front of him, a photograph of a small boy. 'Do you remember Thomas Daniels?'

Mayfield stared at the photograph for a long time. 'It wasn't planned. I was at a friend's birthday party. Thomas kept coming up to me, wanting me to play with him. He wouldn't leave me alone.'

'So it was his fault?' Wes said.

'I didn't say that! It was just . . . the temptation was just too, just too much. If only he had played with the other children and not . . .'

'Not – what?' Rupinder asked him.

'He had the face of an angel. Such blue eyes. I was enchanted. Mesmerised.'

'And so you abducted him?'

'I did no such thing! He came willingly with me. I said I would take him to the park, to . . . feed the ducks.'

Charlie looked up at Lovejoy, who raised an eyebrow. 'Perhaps it's a private code,' she said.

He returned his attention to the screen. 'And did you?' Rupinder asked. 'Feed the ducks?'

Mayfield swallowed hard, remembering. 'No.'

Rupinder glanced at his notes. 'The doctor who examined him afterwards said he had a dislocated elbow and a half-inch tear in his anus.'

'I got carried away. I didn't mean to hurt him.' He tapped the edge of the desk with his finger, making his point. 'I would never, ever, hurt a child.'

Wes had been leaning back on his chair. There was a loud noise on the tape as he suddenly leaned forward again. 'So ripping some poor little kid's arse apart doesn't hurt the boy?'

'I was inexperienced. I accept that.'

'You know what happened to that little boy?'

'I'm sure you're going to enlighten me.'

'When he was ten years old, he tried to drown himself in the bath.'

'Why are we talking about this? I have paid my debt to society for what I did. It will never happen again.'

'We are investigating the death of an eleven-year-old girl on Thursday night on the disused line near Clannis Court.'

'You seriously think I had anything to do with that?'

'Did you?' Wes asked him.

'I told you, I have no interest in girls of any age. And I certainly wouldn't hurt anyone, not intentionally.'

'Where were you between four p.m. and midnight on Thursday?'

'I told you, I was in Manchester, I was visiting a friend.'

'Your friend can verify this?'

'Of course.' He reached into his jacket pocket, threw his mobile phone and his wallet on the desk. 'Check my phone, my credit-card accounts.' He reached across the desk, pulled Rupinder's notebook and pen towards him. 'Here, this is my friend's name and number. Call him.'

'We will,' Wes said. He picked up the mobile and started scrolling through it.

'I am not going back in there,' Mayfield said.

'In where?'

'Prison. Do you know what it's like for a man like me? They called me KFC. It stands for 'Kiddy-Fucking Cunt'. I was assaulted in the showers, almost every day, and if it was too bad and I had to go to the doctor, when I came back I found my cell had been trashed and my things had been stolen. They looked down on me for one moment of weakness, when most of them had lived a lifetime of cruelty and depravity. No, I will never go back in there again.'

'I'll get this thing downloaded,' Wes said and walked out of the room.

Rupinder wrote the credit-card numbers on his pad. Mayfield crossed his legs and sat back.

'This is the bit that gets to me,' the skipper said.

Mayfield put his elbows on the desk. 'You seem like a decent fellow,' Mayfield said.

'I try to always put myself in someone else's shoes,' Rupe said. 'As you can imagine, I've had a fair bit of discrimination myself.'

'What people don't understand, it's not the sex that messes children up. It's the fuss afterwards. That's the problem.'

'The fuss?'

'What happened to Thomas – it was what people said to him afterwards that damaged him. Do people ever think about that?'

'I suppose not,' Rupe said.

'There are no absolutes. What is wrong, what is right, it depends on the times we live in. Having physical relations with little boys, it wasn't a crime in ancient Greece. The great men of classical history, Pythagoras and Socrates and Plato, they all acknowledged the beauty of a romantic attachment between an adult male and a younger one. In fact, they thought it was perfectly *normal*. Socrates got most of his students from a boy brothel. Plato would have thought it was quite – logical.' He waited for Rupe to laugh. He didn't. 'Such relations were *enshrined* in the constitution of Sparta.'

'Don't know how you could sit there and listen to that shite,' McCullough said, over his shoulder. 'I would have been across the desk and nutted the dirty bastard.'

'Which is why Rupe is brilliant in interviews,' Charlie said, 'and you're not.'

Rupinder paused the file.

'Did he check out?' Charlie said.

Rupinder nodded. 'Alibi is solid. Not even any kiddy porn on his phone.'

'That just leaves our Mr Norton, then.'

93

The DCI emerged from the lifts. The skipper looked at Charlie and gave him a look. 'And lo, a Greek God descended from the heavens to speak to the people.'

'Keep your voice down, crissake.'

The DCI clapped his hands together. 'How are we doing, Charlie? Have we got this Norton bloke banged up?'

'He's still at the hospital, sir. He tried to abscond and drove into a lamp-post.'

'I told you that would happen. Is he all right?'

'Few stitches. I should be able to interview him this evening.'

'Good.'

'Not that good, sir. The clock's ticking and I still haven't got anything back from Lambeth.'

'Did they find anything?'

'Jack rang me, just now. They've found a t-shirt. With blood on it.'

'There you are, then.'

'It might not be her blood.'

'Bound to be. This is a tap-in, Charlie. No excuses on this one.' And he walked out again.

Timothy Norton sat in the white tracksuit and black pumps that the custody sergeant had given him when his own clothes had been seized for forensic examination. He looked dazed. There was a bandage on his head; the doctors at the Whittington had put eleven sutures in a head wound, checked him for concussion, and pronounced him fit for purpose.

He gave off a pungent odour of antiseptic, urine and fear sweat.

The court-appointed solicitor sat next to him, a snappy dresser this one, the West Ham commemorative shirt from the 2015 season with PAYET written on the back, Primark jeans and a pair of scuffed Converse. Already trying to provoke me, Charlie thought.

He thought of the old joke: what always looks good on a West Ham supporter? The answer, of course, was an Alsatian.

'When was the last time you had a bath?' Charlie said to Norton.

'Is this relevant?' his brief said.

'It is to me.'

'Can we just get on?'

Charlie opened the cellophane on the DVD pack with his thumbnail and slotted one into the double deck, pressed the record button, and yawned, for Norton's benefit. His brief frowned in disapproval. That was more like it.

'We are in Interview Room One, Essex Road Police Station. My name is DI Charles George, also present is . . .'

'DC Lesley Lovejoy.'

'Paul Mason-Gilles.'

They all stared at Norton, who stared back. His brief whispered in his ear.

'Timothy Norton,' he said.

This was going to be a long evening. 'Timothy Norton, you have been arrested on suspicion of the murder of Mariatu Okpotu on the first of March 2018. Do you understand the offence?'

Norton nodded.

'Aloud. For the tape, please.'

'Yes!'

'You don't have to say anything, but it may harm your defence if you do not mention when questioned something which you later rely on in court. Anything you do say may be given in evidence. Do you understand the caution?'

'YES!'

'You don't have to shout, Mr Norton. The microphone is right here.'

The smell was debilitating. Norton's brief moved his chair another fraction of an inch further away from his client. Pity they couldn't open a window. How did a bloke allow himself to get in such a state? His teeth were rotting in his head, there was some sort of white scum on his lower lip, and he could have trapped a moth with the hair in his ears. His fingernails were chipped and jagged, and were rimmed with grease and dirt. Charlie wondered what a psychologist would make of him.

'So. You've been at it again, Timbo?' Lovejoy said, and Norton, who had been staring at Charlie, was taken off guard.

'What?'

'Done it again, have you? Another little girl? Got a bit carried away this time.'

'Hold on,' the brief said to Charlie. 'What is she doing? Do you have a question for my client?'

'We have lots.'

'Then please ask them.'

Charlie shuffled the papers in front of him, as if he were looking through the notes on the case for the first time. The silence stretched. The solicitor fidgeted. Norton looked at the acoustic tiles on the ceiling.

'Mr Norton, do you remember when we spoke to you yesterday evening? We asked you where you were between four p.m. and six p.m. on the night Mariatu Okpotu was murdered. You said you were feeding the ducks in the park.'

He blinked slowly and nodded.

'Would you pass me the CCTV images, please?'

Lovejoy unclipped a plastic folder and took out some full-colour images and slid them across the desk. Charlie turned them around so that Norton and his brief could see them clearly.

'These are exhibits MVO/5, MVO/6 and MVO/7, they were taken from a CCTV camera outside the betting shop on the high street. You'll notice the time: 17.23. How do you explain that?'

Norton shook his head.

'We have a witness who said he saw a scruffy middle-aged man in a Batman t-shirt under his coat following Mariatu along the disused railway line around five thirty. When you were feeding the ducks.'

'A scruffy middle-aged man? That wasn't me.'

'Are you denying that you were there or denying that you're scruffy?'

'I wasn't there.'

'He has made a positive identification from a photograph.'

'Well, he's wrong.'

Charlie tapped the photograph with his finger. 'Is he? Would you like to tell me what you were doing in the high street at 5.23 p.m., seeing as you clearly weren't providing unnecessary carbohydrates to amphibious birds?'

'I don't remember.'

'You don't remember?'

'It's a long time ago.'

'It's forty-eight hours ago. My mother can remember what she was doing two days ago and she's got Alzheimer's.'

He had a quick, whispered conversation with his solicitor. He saw him wince, when Norton breathed on him.

'Mr Norton wishes to revise his statement.'

'I thought he might.'

'He was confused about which night it was. On the night in question he was on a Tinder date.'

'A what?'

'Tinder. It's an online dating app.'

'I know what Tinder is. Mr Norton, you don't have a mobile phone. You can't be on Tinder if you don't have a phone.'

'I lost it.'

'That was convenient.'

'Well really, I threw it away.'

'Did you lose it or did you throw it away?'

'I threw it away.'

'Why?'

'I got tired of it. I was angry.'

'What were you angry about?'

'Women. Tinder. She didn't look a bit like she did in her profile. That wasn't the first time. So I thought, hell with it, and I threw it in the bin. It was better when we didn't all have mobile phones.'

'Where did you dispose of your phone?'

'In a bin. Don't ask me where.'

'Where?'

'I don't know. I don't remember.'

'But you have an account, with a telecom provider.'

'It was one of those pre-paid things. I hadn't had it long.'

'Where did you get the phone?'

'In London somewhere. Wish I'd never bothered now.'

Charlie made a note on his pad.

'So you are now testifying that on Thursday the first of March, at around 5.20 p.m., you were on a Tinder date?'

He nodded.

'Where?'

'In that café there. What's its name? The Fine Grind.'

'And your Tinder date, she can verify this for us?'

He nodded.

'What was her name?'

'I don't know. She never told me.'

'How long were you there?'

'I don't know. Half an hour.'

'You were speaking to a woman for half an hour and you never learned her name.'

'She was a proper cow. She wasn't a bit good-looking, like. Looked nothing like her picture.'

'Yes, you've mentioned that. What was her Tinder name?'

'Don't remember.'

'You're not doing yourself any favours here.'

'You said you wanted to know where I was. I'm telling you.'

Charlie nodded at Lovejoy. She opened the file in front of her, took out a photograph of a smiling eight-year-old girl in a school blazer. Then she took out another, placed it beside it, turned them towards Norton. In the second photograph, the girl was not smiling, and had a front tooth missing and her left eye was swollen closed.

'Remember her, Mr Norton? Samantha Parkes, abducted from a funfair in Wilton Dene. Judge only gave you three and a half years because of the early plea. You served an extra five months for refusing to take part in a rehabilitation programme for sexual offenders. Any reason for that?'

'Psychologists. All wankers.'

'Well, I suppose you would say that. He told your parole board you were a high risk to reoffend. They ignored him.' Charlie touched the girl's photograph with his fingertips, to draw Norton's attention back to it. 'Such a pretty girl before all this happened.'

Norton glanced at the photograph, then looked away again.

'I didn't hurt her. I loved her.'

'Like you loved little Mariatu?'

'Little who?'

'Mariatu Okpotu. The girl whose head you bashed in with a brick.'

'Harassment,' the brief said and whispered something to Norton.

'Did quite a bit of damage, didn't you?' Charlie said, tapping his finger on the girl's photograph. 'Do you like hearing them scream? Did Mariatu scream much?'

'Inspector, my client has already attested that he has no knowledge of this crime.'

Charlie nodded to Lovejoy, who brought out two more photographs from the folder and placed them on the desk.

'Do you recognise her?'

Norton shook his head.

'Her name is Tiffany Strong. She went missing from Duddington in Oxfordshire eight years ago. She was on her way home from school. The parents blame themselves for letting her ride home on her bike. Me, I blame whoever abducted her.'

'People should be more careful with their kids.'

'You were questioned with regard to her disappearance. You were living half a mile away, you were seen in the area at the time she went missing.'

'I told them then, I'm telling you now. I know nothing about it.'

Lovejoy reached into her briefcase and took out the evidence bag with the black folder they had found in Norton's shed.

'For the tape, I am showing Mr Norton the black plastic folder that was recovered from his possessions at his place of residence at the rear of 29 Barndon Street.'

'What about it?'

'You said you didn't recognise the photograph of Tiffany Strong, but this folder has numerous photographs of her, as well as cuttings taken from the newspapers, detailing her disappearance in August 2010.'

'I did that years ago. Forgot all about it.'

'Why did you keep newspaper cuttings about a little girl you say you don't remember?'

'You lot tried to pin that on me. I were going to write a book about it. Police brutality and all that. That's what the folder were for.'

'They never found her. Technically, she could still be alive. I think it's not having any sense of closure that destroys the people left behind. Do you know what happened to her father?'

Norton shrugged. Couldn't care less.

'Developed a drinking problem. Lost his job, broke up with his wife. He committed suicide two years ago. Hung himself from a beam in the garage. Shame.'

'Like I said, nothing to do with me.'

'Are these anything to do with you?'

Lovejoy placed several more photographs on the table; Jack had sent them the file from Lambeth.

'For the tape, I am showing Mr Norton photographs of evidence exhibits, MVO/29 through to 50, items of girls' clothing found in a Sainsbury's shopping bag in his place of residence.

Can you tell me how you came to be in possession of these items?'

'Found them.'

'Where did you find them?'

'In the laundry in the high street. So I took them home.'

'Why did you do that?'

'It was a whim. Reckless, me.'

'Some of these items have your DNA on them.'

'No law against DNA is there?'

'Did you know the local police station had received a number of complaints about items going missing from washing lines? Do you know anything about that?'

'Should I?'

Charlie checked his notes. 'You were living in Upper Tollington Park until just before Christmas. What was the reason for the move?'

'I wanted to be closer to the art galleries.'

'Amusing. They ran you out of the estate, didn't they, when they found out what you'd been inside for?'

'People like to talk.'

'What people like to do, is raise their kids without some twisted pervert trying to assault them.' He glanced at the brief. 'Speaking in general terms, of course.' Another glance at his notes. 'When we interviewed you, yesterday, you said you had no family living.'

'I don't.'

'But that's not quite true, is it? Your father is currently living in Suffolk, and you have three brothers, also living, two in the Home Counties and one in Oxfordshire. Do you make a habit of lying?'

'They're all dead to me.'

'Ah, so you were being metaphorical. There was my mistake. I thought you meant it literally. Just to be clear, when we ask you questions, like, for instance, did you kill Mariatu Okpotu, we mean it absolutely literally. You do understand that?'

Norton leaned forward in his seat, showing interest in the interview for the first time. 'My father used to abuse me.'

'Physically or sexually? Or metaphorically?'

'I'm the victim here. He's the one that made me like I am. Him.'

'What do you mean, made you like you are? What are you, Mr Norton?'

'Introverted.'

Charlie leaned back, tapped his biro on the edge of the desk. The silence dragged. He reached into his pocket. 'For the tape, I am offering Mr Norton a Skittle.'

'No thanks, I don't like Skittles.'

'I like the Tropical Skittles best, but they were all out.' He put one in his mouth, chewed on it for a bit. 'Look, Timothy. Tim. Which is it you prefer?'

'Mr Norton to you.'

'Think of this as your opportunity to explain your side of things. Full disclosure. We've found the murder weapon and we know it's going to have your fingerprints all over it, as well as the gate on the ventilation shaft. Your DNA will be all over her clothes. Did you take anything of hers? Did you? Because we're going through your shed, your car. If you took it, we're going to find it. It's just a matter of time before we charge you. This is your chance, your window of opportunity if you like, to explain your side of things. I know you didn't mean to do it. It just got out of hand, right?'

The solicitor sighed and leaned forward. 'My client has—'

'I don't know what you're talking about,' Norton said.

'If you don't know what we're talking about, *Mister* Norton, then why did you try and abscond in your van?'

'Because I don't trust coppers, that's why. You're going to try and fit me up for this, and I'm telling you, I didn't do it.'

His brief leaned in. 'Inspector, is it necessary to point out that, at this stage, you have no solid evidence linking my client to this horrendous crime. You have a thirteen-year-old boy, who says he thought he saw my client, but he was some distance away and it was getting dark. Unless you have something a little more substantial than that, I would suggest that we wait until you do.'

Charlie smiled, to disguise his frustration. He told FONC this would happen. He looked up at the clock. 'Nineteen twenty-five hours. I'm suspending the interview.'

He nodded to Lovejoy and they walked out.

CHAPTER TWELVE

Belting it down, the windscreen wipers were finding it hard to keep up. A crisp packet flew across the street as though it had been shot out of a gun; he saw a young woman wrestling to keep her skirt and her umbrella from flying up around her head, no success on either front. She retreated into a doorway.

'Filthy weather,' Lovejoy said.

'Hadn't noticed.'

They were on the Blackfriars Bridge. London looked like a goldfish bowl that hadn't been cleaned for a week. He stared at the Houses of Parliament, wrapped in scaffolding now, through a grey swathe of rain, Barry's homage to London's Gothic past falling down around their ears. He'd read that there was a danger the hot-water system could have blown the whole lot into the Thames at any moment. A quick way to fix the country's problems.

'Where did you sleep last night?' Lovejoy asked him.

'In the office.'

'Can't be very comfortable.'

'It's not.'

His phone rang. The DCI. He took a deep breath and answered it.

'Sir.'

'Twice a day, Charlie, that's all I ask for. I come in to the office, go down to the IR and I ask the skipper where you are; he says you've been and gone without so much as a word to your SIO. Explain?'

'Forgot, sir.'

There was a silence at the end of the line.

'Sitrep.'

Wanker, Charlie thought. You were a quartermaster in the Terries for a couple of years when you were eighteen, now you talk like you won a VC at Kandahar. 'Waiting on Lambeth, sir. We've had him for twenty-four hours already, we'll need an extension from the super.'

'I'll see to it. Where are you?'

'The skipper got a call from some geezer who said he shared a cell with him at Bullingdon. Said he had information that might help us.'

'My office, as soon as you get back.'

'Sir.'

He hung up.

Charlie sucked his teeth, thought about checking the Arsenal website for a bit of light relief. They passed Doggett's, Lovejoy let herself get stuck behind the number 45 bus to Clapham Park.

'You do it deliberately, don't you?' she said.

'Do what?'

'You know what I mean.'

'No, I don't.'

'Wind him up.'

Charlie didn't answer. He did know what she meant.

'What is it you don't like about him?'

'We don't have time. We're nearly there.'

'It's cos he's posh, isn't it? You don't like his Home Counties accent. And he doesn't like you because you're from Walthamstow.'

'We're professionals. That has nothing to do with anything.'

'The class thing. It's everywhere. Especially the Met.' She fiddled with the radio. 'Nice For What'. Drake again.

'We gonna get a roll on for this Dal-ton?' she said, in her best Drake voice.

'Would you Adam and Eve it? Tells me, to my bleedin' face,

that he's been using a burner phone, then he says he dumped it, and he doesn't know where. You have got to be kidding me. Then he meets a woman on Tinder. Who's going to swipe right on that low-life? He's having a laugh, innit?'

'I don't know.'

'What don't you know?'

'He plays dumb. I worry that it's an act and that he's really, really smart. You're right, I think he's playing us.'

Another South London council estate, look at it, no wonder London had a crime problem. It looked like Alcatraz from the outside, dark stairwells around a square of ryegrass, a few puddles of tungsten under the streetlamps. It was a maze for those who didn't know their way around it, gangland heaven for the dealers and the roadmen in hoodies and jeans.

It was places like this that made him grateful for growing up in a terraced house with just one violent drunk to deal with. He clocked the graffiti on the walls, at least it was a bit of colour. One of the rubbish skips was charred, where someone had set it on fire. There was a teenager sitting on a kid's swing in the middle of the courtyard, dealing in plain sight, he eyeballed Charlie right back. A car alarm was going off somewhere in the car park, and either the owner or the thief hadn't figured out a way to turn it off.

He checked the scrap of paper with the flat number. The lifts were out of order, of course, so they took the stairs. Bob Wetherby lived on the second floor.

He looked as if he could have been a boxer in his prime, but his prime was a long time ago. He was gone to fat now, his hair was thin, and he was at the tracksuit-and-pizza stage of his life. He let them in straight off, didn't ask to see their ID, he knew what a cop looked like, he didn't need to be told.

Inside it smelled of damp and smoke.

There was a bedroom, a living room and a kitchen-diner. It still had the original 1960s kitchen cupboards by the looks;

they would love these over in Finsbury Park, he thought, a renovator would charge a fortune. The effect was spoiled by the plaster peeling off the ceiling and the mould creeping up the walls. The tap was dripping.

Never mind, there were some nice desert plants on the windowsills.

'First time I've ever had a view,' Wetherby said.

There were a number of responses to that, but Charlie just said, 'Good for you,' and stood at the window and admired the dull grey sweep of towers and terraced houses of South London, all the way to the Surrey hills.

'This was classified a hard-to-let flat, because there's smoke damage,' Wetherby said. 'Doesn't bother me.'

'May we sit?' Charlie said.

He perched on the edge of the ancient sofa. The arm came loose as he sat down and he settled it back on its screw. Wetherby seemed not to mind.

'Most of the estate is Bengalis,' he said. 'They're more welcome than I am in most places these days, so I count myself lucky to be here.'

'Keeping out of trouble?'

'I am,' Wetherby said, with the fervour of a true believer. 'I really am.'

'That's good then.'

'People think it's crap, but it's not. It's like a real community round here. Them next door, I help them fix their tap, just a washer needed replacing is all, they bring me rice and dhal, even a box of mangoes. They're proper nice people. They even asked me if I wanted to babysit their kids.'

'To which you said no, right?'

'Course.'

Lovejoy was clearly impatient to get on. As soon as Wetherby drew breath, she said: 'You called the hotline, said you had information for us regarding Timothy Norton.'

'I heard on the news that you'd arrested him.'

'He has not been charged. He's helping us with our enquiries at this stage.'

'You have to watch that bloke. He's cunning.'

'How is he cunning, Mr Wetherby?' Charlie asked him.

'I've seen how he does it. Used to do it to the screws inside. He were always smiling and ingratiating hisself. But he's dark, proper dark.'

'You shared a cell, I believe?'

'For three months, until I asked to get moved.'

'Why did you do that?'

'Couldn't stand it. Messing with my head, it was. Things he said. Stopped me getting better.'

'What sort of things did he say?' Lovejoy asked him.

'Well, when they turned off the lights, we'd be lying there in the dark, and I thought he was asleep, and he started talking aloud, about these fantasies he had.'

'What sort of fantasies?'

'About little girls. He had one all worked out, getting her on her own like, and having sex with her. Then killing her. He went on and on about it.'

'It was a fantasy, was it?'

'Do you want a cup of tea?'

'No thanks, Mr Wetherby.'

'I got some Extra Strong.'

'Just tell us about these fantasies. Did he indicate to you that he intended to carry them out?'

Wetherby stared at his hands, interlocking his fingers around and around, as if he was trying to work out a difficult knot in a piece of old rope.

Finally: 'No intended about it. What I reckon is, he'd already done it.'

'You think he had killed someone?' Lovejoy said.

'Sure of it.'

'Do you have any evidence of this?'

Wetherby shook his head. 'Just the way he talked, you know.

Something about him. After a while it wasn't like a fantasy. It was like he was remembering.'

'Did he say anything, anything at all, about who the victim might have been?'

'No, I told you, he's not daft, that one.'

Charlie waited, Lovejoy was about to open her mouth but he silenced her with a look. The oldest trick in the book; if you want to interrogate someone, just shut up and let them talk. The silence dragged. Finally, Wetherby shrugged. 'That's all I can tell you really.'

All the way out here, Charlie thought, to hear some bloke talk about curry and daydreams. He knew Norton was a killer. What he needed was evidence. He declined another offer of a cup of tea and left.

'What was he in for?' Lovejoy asked him when they got back to the car.

'He was a teacher. He penetrated a five-year-old boy, one of his pupils.'

'Why didn't you tell me before we went in?'

'Because it would have prejudiced you against him, and I needed to hear what he had to say without you giving him attitude.'

'You think I would do that?'

'Wouldn't you?'

She started the engine. 'I'm not sure,' she said, as they pulled back on to the Blackfriars Road. 'Did he really say the people next door wanted him to babysit their kids?'

'He did.'

'Shouldn't someone tell them?'

'Not allowed. Besides, he says he's cleaned up his act.'

'That's not good enough for me.'

'Then I'll leave you with that moral quandary, something to occupy your sleepless nights. I have enough to keep me awake. Watch that cyclist. You don't want to end up sharing a cell with someone who has bad dreams.'

CHAPTER THIRTEEN

The skipper was standing by the kettle making a cup of tea when they got back to the IR. 'Do you want one?' he said to Charlie.

Five years he'd been working with the skipper, five years he'd been asking him the same question and getting the same answer. It was almost like a litany, a religious ritual they went through every day.

'I don't like tea,' Charlie said. 'I only ever drink coffee.'

'We got instant.'

'No thanks.' There, they'd got that out of the way. 'Skip, have you heard from Lube and Mac about his Tinder date?'

'They should be back soon.'

The phone rang on the skipper's desk. He picked it up, muttered something in reply and looked up at Charlie. 'Reception. Mrs Okpotu's down there asking for you.'

'Mariatu's mother?'

Well, that was one out of the box. He called Malik on his Nokia.

'Guv.'

'Where are you?'

'I'm with Mr Okpotu. He wanted to know what was happening with our suspect.'

'I've got his wife here.'

'What?'

'Doesn't he know?'

'He told me she was upstairs. Hang on a minute.'

110

Charlie waited on the end of the line.

Malik came back on. 'We'll come and get her.'

'Take your time. I'll go downstairs and see what she wants.'

Mrs Okpotu was sitting in the reception with an anorak over her pyjamas; she had the thousand-yard stare that Charlie had seen countless times on the faces of the bereaved. The fact that she was in her nightclothes and was staring vacantly at the wall didn't make her in any way remarkable to the zombie who was screaming insults at the station sergeant on the other side of the reinforced glass or the rest of the human wreckage littering the plastic chairs.

'Mrs Okpotu? DI George. You were asking for me.'

She nodded without speaking. She reminded him of one of the people he'd seen get dragged up on to the stage at a Strictly Come Trancing show a couple of months ago near the Elephant and Castle.

He couldn't take her up to the IR, not with her daughter's pictures all over the whiteboard; he found an interview room downstairs and sat her down. 'Can I get you anything?' he said.

She shook her head. She looked like she'd just walked out of a car crash.

'How did you get here, Mrs Okpotu?'

'I walked.'

'You walked? All the way from Finsbury Park?'

'It's not far.'

'In your dressing gown? It's raining. You're soaking wet.'

'I've walked further than that, wetter than that. You have no idea.'

He remembered her husband had told him that she'd come to London twenty years ago to escape the civil war in her country. No, he probably didn't have any idea.

He said to her, 'I'll only be a moment,' and went outside, asked one of the uniforms for a dry towel and got a cup of tea.

When he came back in she was sitting with her head on her arms; for a moment he thought she was asleep.

He didn't want to think unkindly of her, but the thought hit him that he had seen better-looking corpses. Her skin had that same dusty blue pallor to it and her cheeks were sunken into her skull. Her breath was rank. He thought about the family portrait he had seen in the hallway of her home, couldn't believe this was the same woman.

It was only when he handed her the cup of tea and she reached for it that he realised she had no hands. He stared at the stumps, and then back at her. She caught him looking and wriggled her sleeves down over them. Or perhaps it was just to protect them from the hot cup.

His Nokia buzzed. It was Malik again. 'Sorry about that, guv. We're on our way in. I don't know how she got out, she was supposed to be sedated. Her husband thought she was asleep in the bedroom.'

'Not your fault, my son. Come and find me when you get here, we'll be waiting for you downstairs. Hope Mr Okpotu brought her some nice warm slippers, her feet must be freezing.'

He hung up. 'That was my detective, Mrs Okpotu. He says your husband is very worried about you. You didn't tell him you were going out.'

'Have you found my daughter yet?' she said.

'Found her?'

'You have to find my little girl. She was the only good thing to come out of my country, the only good thing.'

'Mrs Okpotu. You do know, your husband has told you everything? DC Khan has told you?'

'Told me what?'

Charlie experienced a sense of everything shifting under his feet. Had he missed something? 'I'm sorry, Mrs Okpotu, but your daughter is dead. There is no question about this. Your husband found her, and he's made a positive identification.'

'No, that's no possible,' she said, quite reasonably. 'You are mistaken.'

She shook her head, they stared at each other. Her eyes horrified him. He looked away first.

As soon as he did she started to wail. The teacup dropped out of her stumps and the milky brown tea dribbled off the edge of the desk and on to the floor. It wasn't just crying, he was well used to that: this was a banshee scream that came from the pit of her. She filled her lungs and did it again, bending at the waist, then crumpled on to the floor. Charlie went to the door. There were uniforms gathered outside, just staring at him. He motioned to two of the women PCs, thought that would be the right thing.

He thought about Norton sitting in his cell downstairs, calling the custody sergeant, I asked for two sugars in my tea, this has only got one. Maybe they had it right back in the old days, he thought, throwing them into a pit in Bridewell. That bastard. Look what he's done.

This was the hard part of his job, the grief. People didn't just weep politely, like they did at funerals when their old mum had passed on in a nursing home; with murder they wailed, they choked, they lost control of their bodies. And the bloke who did it is protected by PACE laws and a brief in a West Ham shirt.

Charlie stood back, feeling responsible, as if he should have done something. He let the WPCs pick her up off the floor, settle her back in the chair, put their arms around her, do what they could. Mariatu means Innocence, he remembered, and Innocence is dead.

Raymond Okpotu stood outside the interview room, looking lost. The composure he had displayed in the first twenty-four hours had quite evaporated. He looked like a man who had just watched his house burn down. A police doctor had been called, his wife was still wailing behind the closed door, it sounded like she was being tortured in there.

113

'Did you tell her that her daughter is dead?'

'I thought she knew, Mr Okpotu. Hasn't anyone told her?'

'Of course she *knows*. But you didn't have to say the words. Nothing you people have done has made this easier for us. At first you even thought it was me.'

'We're only doing our job.'

'What is going to happen to the man who did this?'

'No one has been charged, as yet.'

'But you have arrested someone?'

'We haven't completed our investigation yet.'

The look he gave him, pure contempt. Another shriek from the other side of the door. He winced. 'Most people don't go through half the things that she has. You saw her hands? Rebel soldiers did that, the Revolutionary United Front they called themselves. They came to her village, and killed her father in front of her, and then they raped her and cut off her hands. She said the boy who did it was twelve years old. You have heard of these child soldiers? You wonder, how can a child do such a thing? Then he put her stumps into hot tar to stop the bleeding. She survived this thing, this terrible thing, she had a child because, you know, just because it's rape does not mean a baby will not come from it. It was a girl. She said she grew to love her so much. But she died. Malnutrition. Then there was a man, he helped her. She married him, she said he was a good husband.'

'Mariatu's father?'

A nod.

'What happened to him?'

'What do you think happened? The war.' He gave a shrug. 'So then finally, she got away, came here, looking for a better life. For a while, I was able to give her that. Now this.'

The doctor arrived, went into the interview room. 'I should go in,' Raymond Okpotu said and the door closed behind him.

Charlie's Nokia rang. It was Jack, from Lambeth. Charlie listened, and after he'd hung up he called upstairs, for the skipper.

'Now then,' the skipper said.

'Any news?'

'Nowt that's any good.'

He listened for five minutes as the skipper briefed him on what Lubanski and McCullough had found. When he was done, Charlie sighed and went to the window. At least it had stopped raining. He rang upstairs. 'It's Charlie, sir.'

'Don't tell me you're actually going to brief me on what's going on?'

'On my way up now, sir.'

'I'll hang the bunting out,' the DCI said, and hung up.

Such a nice office, Charlie thought. They breathed a different kind of air up here, he thought, like walking through business class after economy. Nice pine desk, lots of light, no annoying buzzing from the strip lights. I'd like to be a DCI one day. Just need an attitude transplant. Change where I was born on my birth certificate. Used to know blokes who could do that, when I was with CID.

'So, Charlie. Tell me the good news.'

Charlie was hoping for the offer of refreshments, perhaps one of those bourbon biscuits FONC kept in his drawer. Looked like they were off-limits for blokes who didn't report in twice a day.

'Jack just called me. Nothing so far.'

'What about the t-shirt you found, the one with blood on it?'

'Blood was Norton's.'

'There must be something. You said they found the murder weapon.'

'Positive for the deceased's blood and tissue, they also retrieved one of her hairs. They found a partial fingerprint too, it's going to be hard to get a match. They are positive, however, that it doesn't belong to Norton.'

'How does that work, then? If the brick was the murder weapon, it would have his prints all over it. You said this was

115

a crime of opportunity, so he wouldn't have had time to put gloves on.'

'Yes, sir. It's puzzling.'

The DCI glared at him as if the lack of evidence was somehow his fault. 'What else?'

'They found some fibres on her clothes, but they've confirmed that they came from the woollen jumper her stepfather was wearing when he found her. And results on nail scrapings, semen on her clothes, they'll take days yet.'

'What about his van, this shed where he was living?'

'It will be days before we get the result on that.'

'We haven't got days.'

'That's what I said, sir. At which point, Jack reminded me of the budget restrictions placed on them by Westminster and advised me to take it up with my local MP.'

'Smartarse.'

'Not really, sir. He has a point.'

'What did they find?'

'Girls' clothes and a folder.'

'Girls' clothes?'

'Vests, underpants, skirts, that sort of thing. Some of the items tested positive for semen.'

'Sick bastard. Go on.'

'At first, I hoped the items we found belonged to the deceased, but we showed the images to her father, and he doesn't recognise them. The local police have advised us they have had a number of complaints about items going missing from washing lines in the area around where Mr Norton lives. One of the items we recovered had a name tag inside it. Wes and Rupinder checked on it, there was someone with that name who lived at the other end of Mr Norton's street. They visited her and showed her images of some of these items and she was able to identify several of them.'

'So, he's a snowdropper.'

'Among other things.'

'What else?'

'They also recovered a black plastic folder. It contained newspaper cuttings about a girl who went missing in Oxfordshire eight years ago. Norton lived in the area at the time and was questioned about her disappearance.'

'What did he have to say about that?'

'He said he had collected them at the time in order to write an exposé about how the police had tried to frame him for a crime he didn't commit.'

'He's having a laugh.'

'So far.'

'What about his alibi?'

'He said that at the time in question he had a Tinder date in the local café.'

'A Tinder date. What kind of bloody woman would go on a date with him?'

'Parm looked into that for me.' Charlie opened his file and pushed a printout across the desk. It was a Tinder profile, *Tim, 46, business proprietor.*

'That's a photo of Ricky Gervais.'

'Unusual angle. Still, you would have thought he was still easily recognisable.'

The DCI held a hand to his forehead. 'This fella is seriously disturbed. Did you track down his date?'

'Parm is still working on it. But Wes and Rupe interviewed the café proprietors and they say they remember him being there some time between five and six on Thursday evening; they seem to remember his personal fragrance more than they remember him. He sat in the corner with a woman for a few minutes, but the owners can't remember what time they left. So it's not really an alibi at all, at this stage, because the Fine Grind is only five hundred yards from where the girl was found.'

'The Fine what?'

'Grind, sir.'

'It's got to be him. Got to be. There must be something. You told me he didn't have a mobile phone. How does he get on Tinder unless he's got a phone?'

'It was a burner phone. Parm is looking into that as well. But if it's true what he says, and he ditched it before he did for the girl, then we're still back at square one.'

'He used the phone for Tinder. Let's get the records for it and track it. He's our killer, I know it, I can feel it in my water.'

Charlie didn't want to think about the DCI's water, so he changed the subject. 'The warrant was executed yesterday morning, sir. We'll have to let him go this evening. We have nothing we can take to the CPS.'

'You have to find me something, Charlie.'

'Can't give it to you if it's not there.'

'All right. But we'll keep him under surveillance. I don't want him trying to skip off again. Keep me informed.'

By the time Charlie got back to his office, most of the crew had gone home, they'd been hard at it the last seventy-two hours, and he didn't begrudge them getting some kip. He slumped into his chair, Lovejoy came in and they brought the log up to date. She asked him if he wanted anything else, and he said, no, go home. I'll see you in the morning.

He checked his iPhone; he'd had it switched off all day. There were two missed calls from Pippa and a text: HOW R U? She was a teacher, for God's sake. What kind of example was that? There was another, longer, message from half an hour ago, reminding him about her old man's birthday. He'd forgotten about that.

There were three missed calls from Arlington Mansions and two more from Ben, just to say that he hadn't heard any more from Will and was he going to the Southampton game next Saturday?

Charlie thought about going through the witness statements again, perhaps he'd missed something, but then the frustration and fatigue overwhelmed him. He grabbed his Stone Island from the back of the chair, locked the office behind him and

118

headed for the lifts. DC White was still at work, he was so bloody young, the glow from his computer screen made him look like a teenager doing his homework.

He thought about calling past the custody suite on his way out but, hell with it, he'd let the DCI tell Norton's brief the good news. He didn't think he could stand the smug look on the bastard's face.

CHAPTER FOURTEEN

Charlie got home, took a Punk IPA from the fridge, and slumped on to the sofa. He considered watching a DVD of the Invincibles, reliving the glory days of Vieira and Bergkamp to cheer himself up, it was that or go to bed, but his head was running away with itself. His Nokia rang. Oh, for God's sake.

It was Reuben's mother.

'I'm sorry to be ringing you so late. But you said we could, any time.'

'Has Reuben remembered anything that might be of help, do you think?'

'Actually, it's more about what I just heard on the news. Is it true, you've let him go?'

'Our enquiries are continuing, Mrs Williams.'

'But he's dangerous. I read in the newspapers, he's on that offenders' list. He hurt some poor little girl near Oxford somewhere.'

'I can't comment on what the papers say, Mrs Williams.'

'It's just I'm worried about my kids. Men like that out there, on the prowl.'

'I'm not at liberty to discuss the case with you, Mrs Williams. All I can say is that we have been working around the clock to bring this case to a successful resolution. But we do not have the evidence to charge anyone at present.'

'But my Reuben saw him following that poor little girl!'

'That, on its own, is not enough to bring to a court of law, I'm afraid.'

'What will it take before you people do something? Some other poor girl getting killed? If the police won't protect our kids, who will?'

She hung up on him. Well, Charlie thought, that's a nice end to the day. There was a dull pain behind his eyes. He closed them, just for a second, the next thing he knew there was someone hammering on the front door.

Charlie opened the door and leaned against the jamb with his bottle of IPA and thought, but didn't say, well who the fuck are you? A raised eyebrow would do it, at this time of night.

The geezer had Frank Begbie eyes and a horseshoe moustache; he also had a mullet, and you didn't see a lot of those these days. He was the sort of bloke his old man used to go to the football with: they were all called Knuckles or Psycho or Dog.

Ironically, the first thing out of the geezer's mouth was: 'Have you seen my dog?'

'What sort of dog is that then?' Charlie said, and put his IPA on the hall table. It was good beer and he didn't want it getting spilled in the very likely possibility of a bit of a barney.

'He's a fucking spaniel, innit?'

'Is that a cocker fucking spaniel or a cavalier fucking spaniel? Or a water fucking spaniel. Cos a water fucking spaniel, they're bigger.'

'Are you having a laugh?'

Charlie noticed Dog's eye tooth was a little out of whack. Maybe someone had smacked him. He seemed like the sort of bloke that would get smacked a lot.

'No, it's a serious question,' Charlie said. 'When you're looking for someone – or for someone who also happens to be a dog – you have to give a precise description or how do you know who you're looking for? Height, eye colour, breed, it's all very important.'

'Have you seen it, or not?'

'This is my point, see. A dog is a sentient creature, so by

121

rights it is a "who" not an "it". Have you ever studied much philosophy?'

'You're a fucking loony, you are.' He turned to go.

'How long have you had the dog?'

'What's it to you?'

'Just curious, mate. Fond of it, are you?'

'Fond of it? It's my girlfriend's fucking dog, I'd as soon drown the fucking thing. When I find it, I'm going to give it a fucking good hiding. It's always running off. Open the fucking door for a minute and it's fucking gone.'

'Why do you reckon that is, then?' Charlie said.

'Because he's a fucking shit of a dog.'

Charlie took another swallow of IPA to calm himself down, and thought about hitting Dog with the bottle. Come on, son, be civilised, talk to him normally, like you would any other serial killer. 'I don't suppose you've ever considered treating him with some kindness and respect?'

'Have you seen the fucking dog or not, shit for brains?'

Charlie put down his beer, tried to stay calm. Then again, no PACE laws to get in his way when it came to dealing justice for a spaniel, not as far as he knew. 'Christ, you're ugly. I've seen Dobermans better looking than you.'

Dog took his hands out of his jeans. His fists were full of nugget rings, and he had tattoos on his knuckles. 'Do you know who I am?'

'Yeah, I know who you are. You're the bloke in the flat over the road that always plays his music too loud and is always shouting and carrying on. Don't ask me how I know this but you also have a criminal record, two common assaults and an ABH.'

'How the fuck do you know that?'

'I just said, don't ask me how I know, and there you go, asking me. You don't spend too much time visiting the kingdom of intelligence, do you?'

Dog poked Charlie in the chest with his index finger. 'You ought to mind your fucking self.'

'In what way?' Charlie said.

'Because if you don't, you'll end up eating your breakfast through a tube.'

Charlie was going to point out that all he ever had for breakfast was coffee, so that was doable with or without Dog's help, but instead he said: 'Jesus, you've got bad breath. I think you might have gingivitis.'

Dog grabbed Charlie by the shirt and pushed him against the door. Big mistake. 'No need to be like that mate,' Charlie said, and reached over and grabbed his right hand, locked it in place. His left hand came up fast, almost snapping Dog's right elbow at the joint. Charlie brought his right leg across and around in a sweep for greater effect and down he went.

Suddenly Dog found himself lying face down on the doorstep, right about the spot where Charlie had found his spaniel that Thursday night. He gasped, dribbling blood from his nose where he had cracked it on the concrete. Could have chipped a tooth as well, Charlie reckoned, by the way he was howling. He could have that checked, when he got the gingivitis sorted.

Charlie now had one knee on his right elbow, and a hand on his right wrist, it gave him a nice bit of leverage. Dog's wing wasn't quite as tough as the leg joint on his old ma's Christmas turkey but nearly. This would definitely count as police brutality if he was at work, he supposed, but he was off duty so in his mind it didn't count.

'The fuck,' Dog said. 'You're breaking my arm!'

'Not yet,' Charlie said, and told him to keep his voice down, he was disturbing the neighbours. 'We have enough of that sort of thing around here. People making too much noise, playing their music too loud, gunning the engine on their motors, know what I mean?' He applied a little upward pressure and what came out of Dog was a high-pitched whining sound, like a badly tuned radio. 'Now look,' Charlie said, 'I haven't seen your dog, but if I had seen him, I think he would like me to send you a message.'

Dog wriggled a bit, so Charlie pulled a bit harder, and said, do you want to make a wish before we break it? Finally, he stopped moving about.

Charlie put his mouth close to Dog's ear. 'Now listen here, you low-life scrote, the RSPCA have restricted powers, they probably couldn't even fine you for what you did to that dog. Me, however, I am unfettered by legal process in such matters, and if I ever see you mistreating one of God's own creatures ever again, I will smash you like a plate at a Greek wedding. Am I making myself crystal, old son?'

He heard a bit more static, but he supposed that was a yes. He eased off the pressure a little.

'Now repeat after me: I will endeavour to be kind to all animals from now on. Say it, go on.' Dog was panting, must be hurting quite a bit, he supposed.

'I will be kind to animals . . .'

'No, "kind to *all* animals . . ."'

'I will be . . . kind to . . . fuck, you're breaking my fucking arm, you cunt.'

It wasn't the epithet Charlie had been hoping to hear and he twisted a little harder until Dog was better able to express himself.

'Repeat: "I will be kind to all animals, or someone from the RSPCA will come and cut my jacobs off," say it!'

' . . . or someone from the RPSA will come and, oh fuck me, my arm . . .'

'You don't even know what the RSPCA is, do you?'

At last they got through it, and Dog promised to be good. Charlie didn't believe a word of it, but at least he had made his point, on behalf of cocker spaniels everywhere.

'I am going to let you up now,' Charlie said. 'I would advise you to go directly home, because if you think this is terrible, you don't know me very well.' He gave Dog a final little tug on the arm, just for fun really, and then he got up, levering himself with a knee placed somewhere between the seventh and eight vertebrae of Dog's thoracic spine.

Dog scrambled to his feet, clutching his arm, shouted some idle threats and ran off. Charlie went back inside and shut the door.

Result.

Cocker spaniels 1, Total Wet-wipes 0.

CHAPTER FIFTEEN

Back in the day, the Whitechapel Road was all Jack-the-Ripper tours and Bollywood video shops; it was proper Middle East London now, second or third generation, men in skullcaps and women in hijabs, Islamic bookshops and halal shops, street stalls selling papayas and scarves and rainbow dust mops. A car pulled up at the pumps, radio full blast, playing what sounded like Somali tunes.

They were parked in the service station across the road from the funeral home. Charlie sipped his coffee and scrolled through his phone, left the surveillance to Lovejoy, who seemed keen about that sort of thing.

'Are you on another football site?' she said, after a while.

'It relaxes me.'

'No, it doesn't, it just winds you up, guv.'

'Better than getting wound up about not being able to nail the bloke who did for the little girl.'

'We're getting a lot of stares.'

'We're two white people sitting in a car across the street from the city's largest mosque. Wasn't that long ago that that nutter Osborne drove a van into people outside the mosque in Finsbury Park. Don't blame them for being nervous. Vehicle ramming goes both ways these days.'

'Why have they come here for the funeral? We're a bit of a way from where they live.'

'Still not that many funeral homes for Muslims in London,' Charlie said. 'This is about the oldest one. Christmas, New

Year's Eve, it's always open. Funerals arc dead quick if you're a Muslim. No hanging about like us.'

'Won't have been easy for the Okpotus, then.'

'No, there's been a bit of strife about that. But because of our inquiry, the coroner wouldn't release the body.'

'It's got to be Norton.'

'Here we go,' Charlie said, as the funeral cortege pulled out of the gates into the street. A pink hearse; that was a poignant touch, he thought. Lovejoy was about to start the car but Charlie put up his hand to stop her. 'We don't need to follow them, we know where they're going. Just see if anyone else does, someone who doesn't look like they belong.'

'We're clutching at straws here, guv.'

'Straws, Lovejoy, are all we have. So, let's clutch.'

It was a long drive out to the wilds of Ilford, in Charlie's book. They got there before the cortege and waited in the car park, at a discreet distance. There were three funeral cars for the mourners, even a coach had been laid on. Others arrived in private vehicles.

Lovejoy turned off the engine. Charlie tapped impatiently on the dash with his fingers.

'Do you reckon it's true, that killers go to their victim's funeral?'

'It's the perceived wisdom, Lovejoy.'

'You don't believe it?'

'I've never caught anyone this way.'

'So why are we here?'

'What the DCI wants, the DCI gets. I am a humble public servant, as are you. We are here, serving the public, as directed by our superiors.'

Lovejoy found the binoculars in the console, Charlie went back to his iPhone. Never mind what he'd said to Lovejoy, he couldn't concentrate on the football. He kept going through it in his mind, over and over; there had to be something he'd missed.

'The Williamses are here.'

'All of them?'

'I suppose they feel invested. Seeing it was Reuben who was the last one to see her alive.'

She handed him the glasses. He fiddled with them, re-focused. 'Always him, holding the little girl's hand.'

'They're an odd family. Ever heard the little one speak?'

'Not now you come to mention it.'

'Her big sister's not much better. Just a text bump away from a serious deficit. She'll be Snapchatting over the grave, that one.'

He handed her back the glasses.

'They don't have a casket,' Lovejoy said.

'I know.'

'What, they just put her in, like that?'

'She's in a shroud. It's the way they do it. They have to be buried facing Mecca. Me, I'm going to be buried facing away from the Emirates, so I can finally rest in peace.'

'Never thought about it before, where Muslims go to get buried.'

'Well, we're all different. Trouble is, they can't be cremated, it's against their religion, so it creates a bit of a problem on a little island. A few years ago there was this plan to dig up everyone in this old cemetery in Tower Hamlets and bury all the Muslims there. There were three hundred thousand people in it, that's a lot of dead bodies, more than a Tarantino film. It didn't get passed. Are we done?'

She put down the glasses and shrugged. 'So now what?'

'We keep the file open. We go through all the witness statements again, look for something we missed, all the while trying to keep up with the backlog of other cases. Pray for a breakthrough.'

'On the TV we haul Norton in, conduct a brilliant interrogation, trap him in a lie and he breaks down and confesses.'

'That would be nice, but that's not going to happen. What's going to happen is the team are going off roster, we arrest those two gangbangers who did for that other scrote in Tottenham, we catch up on our paperwork and our sleep, and I am going to see my girlfriend, who has probably forgotten all about me by now.'

'Not that one who works for the CPS?'

'No, we broke up. This one's a teacher. Pippa. Short for Philippa.'

'Nice name,' she said, but her voice had an edge to it. He decided to leave that one alone.

They drove back to the nick. Charlie stared moodily out of the window the whole way, thinking about the Okpotus, saying the *janaza* prayer over their little girl before following her shrouded body to the cemetery; they'd just lost more than he'd ever had. He had to get over this feeling that he'd let them down.

Or maybe I've missed something.

But what?

CHAPTER SIXTEEN

The school was two storeys, made out of London stock brick, reminded him of his own alma mater, depressed the life out of him on this cold, wet, grey morning. Sent a proper shiver up him, it did; his memories of school were the fights behind the bicycle sheds, getting his brothers out of scrapes, getting whacked by the headmaster. Not that long ago, either, corporal punishment was supposed to have been banned, he only found out about that after he left.

Being bright didn't help any, so he spent half his time trying to pass enough exams so that he could have a life afterwards, the other half trying to be as stupid as the blokes he called his mates. As it turned out, trying not to appear too clever was good training for his current profession. Just ask his DCI.

He stopped off on the way to the main building to watch some of the kids playing a scratch match in the playground, blazers chucked on the wet asphalt for goalposts. Those were the days, before you were old enough to realise that you were crap and you were never going to play in front of the North Bank at Highbury, as it was then.

'What are you doing?'

There was a kid watching him, couldn't be more than seven or eight, already on the lookout for dodgy adults.

'I'm a scout for Arsenal.'

'Arsenal? They're crap,' the kid said.

'Who told you that?'

'My old man. Spurs are the best, man.'

Charlie saw the headlines now: 'Police Inspector Throttles Child in School Playground'.

Just walk away, Charlie my son.

The school was a two-storey turn-of-the-century building, most famous for having produced a recent *Big Brother* winner. Charlie was pleased to see that Arsenal Community were one of the sponsors on the canvas poster hung on the gates, the red and white badge right there next to the school's cheerful logo.

The school secretary gave him a visitor's pass, directed him to a Portakabin at the back of the school, near a sad little toilet block. Most of the kids were still in her classroom, even though the bell had gone. They were flocking around her, her all blonde and blue-eyed, looked proper funny among all the hijabs and junior afros.

She was busy and didn't see him straight off, so he waited. He felt some kid tugging on his sleeve. 'High key love those shoes, man,' he said. 'They're just barts.'

'Thom Browne's.'

'What damage?' he said, rubbing his fingers together.

Charlie bent down. 'Saw some geezer down the high street, mugged him for his kicks, know what I mean?'

'No, you dint, you're bacon, man. I can smell it. You here to chirpse our teacher?'

Bacon. To his face. What was it with kids these days?

'Don't blame you, she is buff.'

'Is she a good teacher?'

'She is all right, I guess. So what sort of cop are you, then?'

'Murder squad.'

'No way. How do you do that, then?'

'I studied hard at school.'

'I don't believe you, man. Everyone knows cops are just stupid, man.'

'Jaxon, what are you saying?' Pippa came over, gave him her special smile. 'What's he been saying to you, Charlie?'

131

'We were discussing his future career path. He wants to join the Metropolitan Police Force.'

'You've got to pass your maths test on Monday first.' She clapped her hands. 'Come on, everyone, go home. I've got to get the room ready for tomorrow.'

Charlie was impressed at how reluctant the kids were to leave. When he was a kid, the bell went, he was out of there faster than Usain Bolt.

'Didn't expect to see you,' she said, after Jaxon had finally been shunted out of the room.

'You said you wanted to show me where you worked. Told you I'd drop in some time.'

'I didn't know you meant it.'

'I never say anything I don't mean.'

'That's scary. Not used to that.'

'Christ, it's freezing in here.'

'They keep promising to get me a heater. Most of the kids keep their coats on all day. Do you like the classroom?'

'Nice. Did you decorate it all yourself?'

She laughed. 'Had a bit of help. Some of the drawings the kids do are quite good.'

'Is this you?'

He pointed to a crayon drawing of a tall, straw-coloured stick figure surrounded by lots of smaller stick figures with brown faces. Everyone in the drawing was smiling. In the background someone seemed to be stealing a car, but he couldn't be sure.

'How can you tell?'

'Lucky guess.'

There were cut-out mobiles the kids had made hanging from the ceiling, umbrellas and raindrops, which he thought was good preparation for kids for a life in England. On one wall was a hand-drawn poster, WHAT SHALL I DO NOW? Underneath were suggestions: Read a Book, Write a Story, Help Your Friend. There was nothing about Cut Off Ann Jenkins's

Pigtail with the Craft Scissors, which had been his answer to the same question, a decision he still regretted.

'Nice,' he said, looking around. There were alphabet letters stuck around the powder-blue walls, alongside hand-drawn pictures of fish and cows and sheep, cut out of coloured cardboard and hung on string with clothes pegs. It was what he remembered best about primary school when he was a kid, a lot of cutting out and Patricia Riley wetting the chair every other week.

There was an entire wall covered with crayon and felt-tip pen pictures of flowers, which was – he supposed – last week's project. There were matchstick people and red suns and dogs bigger than people. 'Not bad,' he said. 'I never got my stuff put up on the wall when I was at school.'

'I'm sure I can find a space if you'd like to have another go,' she said.

'Competition's still too good for me,' he said. 'Maybe after I've had a bit more practice.'

'I don't put up all the drawings they do. Some of them are a bit disturbing.'

'Well, it's the area, innit? Get a lot of problems, do you?'

'When you get a five-year-old suspended for violence, you know you're pushing it uphill.'

'You do know a good percentage of your class will end up as future clients of mine, one way or another? As night follows day.'

'I suppose my job is to try and take business away from you.'

'Well, good luck with that.'

'It's a bit depressing. Had a kid earlier in the year, brought a marker pen to school, or I thought it was a marker pen, but when you took the top off, it had a blade instead of a marker. I took it off him and the parents were straight up here, demanding it back, said I was stealing; father said he'd carve me up himself if I didn't hand it over. That's the mentality.'

'Children live what they learn.'

'What about you, Charlie. What did you learn?'

'At school? I learned to think like a criminal.'

'But you turned out all right.'

'Maybe. Not everyone agrees with you.'

'I think you're all right. So what happened?'

'Maybe I had a good teacher. None of them were like you, mind. Mrs Bowers had a bumfront and a moustache.' He put his arm around her waist, tried to pull her close. She wriggled away.

'I'm at work, Charlie George! You can't do that. You want to get me the sack!'

'What's the problem, I'm not one of your pupils.'

'So having sex in the classroom with a murder squad detective is all right, is it?'

'I wasn't thinking about sex, but as you've brought it up . . .'

She gave him a don't argue, and went behind her desk, for safety's sake.

'So, what are you doing tonight?'

'Why?'

'I was going to ask you out. Dinner, or something.'

'I can't. I've got an urbex.'

'A what?'

'It's my new thing. Haven't you heard of it?'

'Yeah, I've heard of it. Sounds proper mad. Can't you call it off?'

'Come with us. My girlfriend Sar will be there as well. Luca, the guy who's guiding us, he's like an urbex legend.'

Charlie tried to hide his disappointment. Crawling around old train tunnels hadn't figured in his plans, but he supposed he should go with it, be the modern man. Perhaps there would be an opportunity for some urbex and chill if they could get rid of the legend.

'Is it legal?'

'I don't suppose so, but who cares? You've got to live a little.'

'I don't know, I'll think about it.'

'Not scared, are you?'

I have claustrophobia, he wanted to say, really bad. But he couldn't tell her that, he didn't want to sound like a proper wally. Yeah, I can bench-press two hundred pounds, but I'm scared of the dark.

'I'll meet you at the Banker in Chancery Lane. Seven o'clock. Don't wear your Italian suit, Charlie. You're going to get down and very dirty.'

That smile again. Loved to tease, this one. 'Great,' he said. 'Look forward to it.'

He dropped his visitor's pass at the reception, walked back across the school yard. A few kids in school uniforms hanging around, a girl in a hijab, looked a bit like Mariatu, she gave him a long stare, for a moment he thought she was her.

'What are you doing here, Inspector George? Why aren't you out looking for the man who murdered me?'

He kept walking. That was the worst thing about open cases, the guilt. You always thought there was something you should be doing, even though you were already doing everything you could.

This was a different Pippa, in her tech-wear hoodie and urbex backpack and black North Face mountain trainers. Her friend had designer stubble with the right amount of grey in it, a baseball cap and a t-shirt that said DO EPIC SHIT. Oh, and a snood.

He was prepared to dislike him but told himself to give the guy a chance.

They were playing snooker upstairs, their beers resting on the mantelpiece.

'This is Luca,' Pippa said.

They shook hands. It was like holding a wet fish. It put Charlie on his guard. Tell a lot about a bloke by his handshake.

'You said there were three,' Charlie said to her.

'She couldn't come. It's all right, Luca's the expert. He knows the way.'

Glad I came then, Charlie thought. Don't think I like the idea of you exploring down under on your own with this bloke.

'Ever done anything like this before?' Luca said, strutting around the table and potting the yellow, the green, and the brown, rapid fire.

'What, played snooker in a pub?'

'Urban exploration.'

'Got lost on the underground once. I was pissed, though. Does that count?'

Charlie tried to quell the sick feeling in his guts. He really wasn't looking forward to this. But he was going to make himself do it; sometimes you just had to face your fear, at least that's what they said. He certainly wasn't going to let this wanker see he was scared.

'I've been an urban explorer for almost fifteen years now,' Luca said. 'I think of London as if it were a person. What you see on the surface is just for show. What makes it what it is lies out of sight, unseen. Hidden even.'

'Luca's a psychologist,' Pippa said, almost apologetically.

'Do you ever think about what lies beneath, Charlie?'

'The pavement, you mean?'

'It's quite crowded down there, there's gas, telecom cables, old post-office train tunnels, the underground, military tunnels. And there's no maps – none available to the public, anyway – for any of it. It's fascinating.'

'And you've found a way down there, have you?'

'There's endless ways into it. The government can only guard the really important ones. They don't want another religious fanatic like Guy Fawkes getting ideas.'

He lined up the black, potted it, with a sound like a gunshot. He asked Charlie if he wanted a game. Charlie said he didn't play, which was only partly true. He didn't play well, and this guy would massacre him.

'So where are we going tonight?'

'Nothing too complicated, as neither of you has much

experience in this. Thought I'd just give you an appetiser. An old underground station that's quite near here. Of course, once you get into it, there's all sorts of things down there. It's the new frontier, more accessible than outer space.'

'You boldly go where no one has gone before.'

'I wouldn't say *anyone*, but very few people. It would amaze you what's down there. There's a Roman baptistry under Oxford Street and a Roman amphitheatre that can seat six thousand people, right under Guildhall. A city's history is always there, just under the surface. You only have to dig a little.' A superior smile. 'Like you do with a person. Shall we go?'

Luca took them down an anonymous back street to show them the curious façade of the Chancery Lane Deep Shelter. There were two black painted doors: one said 'FIRE EXIT DO NOT OBSTRUCT', the other 'NO PARKING 24 HOUR ACCESS.'

'It used to be the London terminal of the hotline between the White House and the Kremlin,' Luca said. 'It was in lockdown during the Cuban missile crisis back in the sixties. It has the deepest bar in London. You should see it now, it looks like the set of an Austin Powers movie.'

'You've been down there?' Charlie asked him.

'It's like the Tower of London for the urban explorer. You have to do it, even if it isn't that interesting any more. Empty now, of course. The world's gone digital. Thought you'd know about this place, in your job.'

'I stay away from the spooks. A couple of times we've been pulled off a murder, the blokes from over the river come in and take over. Suits me. I don't want anything to do with poisoned umbrellas.'

'Bloody rabbit warren under Whitehall. Bunkers everywhere, that's where they're going to put all the senior civil servants if that maniac Trump presses the red button for a joke, screw the rest of us. Apparently, the Queen's got her own private underground station on the Bakerloo line so she can get the hell out when the time comes. Hope she remembers her Oyster card. Here we are.'

They turned down a side street; there was a six-storey building, obscured by scaffolding that stretched out over the pavement, and a blue wooden hoarding. Already Charlie's fingers felt numb with cold. He put his hands in the pockets of his Stone Island. 'Don't worry,' Luca said. 'It will be cosier when we get down there.'

He'd spotted a cab parked at the end of the street. They waited in a doorway until the cabbie finished his rest break. After he'd clicked on its lights and driven away, Luca reached into his backpack and pulled out three hard hats and three high-viz jackets.

'Put these on,' he said. 'If anyone sees us, they'll just assume we're working.'

Charlie was glad of the dark, the other two couldn't see how he was shaking. He was sweating and he felt nauseous, hadn't felt like this since that time years ago he caught a ferry to the Scilly Isles.

They followed Luca to the centre of the road, to the traffic island. There was a grille, he lifted it, pulled it out of the way. In one practised movement he was through the hole and scrambling down the ladder. Charlie saw the light from his torch bobbling as he made his way down. Pippa followed him.

Shouldn't have had that beer, he thought. If I throw up now, I'd rather the ground open up and swallow me.

But then he remembered that that was exactly what it was going to do anyway.

They went down a long set of vertical ladders, what Charlie supposed was a ventilation shaft. Luca was right, it was a comfortable hoodie temperature down here. This would suit some of those poor homeless bastards sleeping in the freezing cold right over their heads. Luca flicked his torch around the walls.

When they were settled, Luca peeled away the high-viz jacket, pulled his snood up round the lower half of his face, double-looped, in case there were any CCTV cameras he didn't know about. Charlie looked around, trying to focus on something, anything, to control his panic. He could smell his own sweat for God's sake.

They followed a narrow tunnel, there were oxblood tiles on the walls, some wire gates and rusted steel pipes, some old fuse boxes and a white sign with red letters: DANGER HIGH VOLTAGE. Luca pointed out an ancient poster on one of the bare brick walls:

METROPOLITAN BOROUGH OF HOLBORN
IMPORTANT NOTICE

PROHIBITION OF SMOKING

Smoking in this shelter is an offence
against the Defence Regulations
Offenders will be prosecuted and their
shelter tickets may be withdrawn.

D.T. Griffiths
ARP Controller.

'Second World War,' Pippa murmured.

Luca nodded. 'People used the underground for shelter in the first war as well to get away from the Zeppelins. But back then, you had to buy a ticket. They say there was one day in 1918 when there were three hundred thousand Londoners going round and round on the Circle Line.'

Luca showed them the old platform, it was like being in a vast cave, just the soft moaning of wind from the empty tunnels, something scuttling in the dark where the train lines used to be. He led the way to a storage room, there were a couple of stainless-steel ticket machines from the seventies, 40p written on them, and then a list of stations. It was hot, sweaty and dank, smelled like a mouldering hospital. Charlie felt like he was drowning in the dark. He leaned against a wall, closed his eyes, Christ, he was losing it. His hands clenched into fists.

'Don't think your friend is looking too good,' Luca said to Pippa.

'Claustrophobia,' Charlie said.

'You should have said.'

'Didn't want to spoil the party.'

'Well, not much else to see here. Let's go back up.'

He didn't need a second invitation.

When they got back to the street, Charlie stood for a long while, his hands on his knees, willing himself not to be sick.

Luca put a hand on his back. 'You all right, man?'

'You're sweating like dough,' Pippa said.

'And that's always attractive,' Charlie said.

Luca offered him a cigarette. Christ, he wanted one right now. Instead he threw up in the gutter.

He heard Luca chuckle. 'Well, at least he didn't do it while we were up the ladder.'

His cheeks were burning but he felt so bloody cold. He felt Pippa's hand patting his shoulder. 'Can't believe this,' Charlie said. 'Five years of doing murders and I've never even felt queasy once.'

'Well, we're all different,' Luca said. 'I cut my thumb a couple of weeks ago and I fainted. Out like a light.'

'Me, I am never going down a bloody hole ever again.'

'How do you survive the tube?'

'At least there's lights. I can keep a grip if there's light.' Charlie took a deep breath, the air sweet and cold. Pippa put her arm around his waist. He really didn't want her sympathy, though.

'Well, we'd all best be getting home,' Luca said, and hitched his backpack on his shoulders. 'I'm on the Piccadilly Line.'

'We'll walk to Chancery Lane,' Pippa said.

'OK. Have a good night.'

He was about to walk off, but Charlie called him back. He decided he didn't mind Luca so much after all. 'What kind of shrink are you?'

'I deal with all sorts of things. I could probably cure your claustrophobia, or put you in touch with someone who can.'

'I'll just stay out of dark tunnels. That wasn't what I had in mind. See, I don't have a budget for profilers, and I've got this case I'm working on, I can't figure it out. I'm looking for some quid pro quo.'

'What's the pro you're offering in exchange?'

'Arsenal tickets.'

'I'm a West Ham supporter.'

That explains the wet-fish handshake then, Charlie thought. 'West Ham are playing at Emirates, last game of the season. I don't know how much you charge by the hour, but minute for minute, Arsenal cost more than a Harley Street surgeon these days.'

Luca grinned. 'Got yourself a real cheeky lad there, Pippa. All right. Come and see me tomorrow morning. I don't start seeing clients till ten so come in any time after nine. Use the stairs, the lift is tiny and keeps breaking down.'

Charlie walked Pippa back to Chancery Lane, decided against taking the tube himself; enough was enough for one night. He could get the number 17.

She seemed distracted on the walk back, he thought perhaps he'd embarrassed her, but finally he got it out of her, her ex had been sending her text messages from prison. He asked her what he'd said to her, but she said she didn't want to talk about it. At the start of the night he'd been hoping she'd come back to his place, but she said she had to get up early for work. He thought he was about to get the 'it's not you, it's me' speech, but instead, she said: 'Are you still all right for Sunday?'

'What's happening Sunday?'

'It's my father's birthday. I told you, we've been invited over for lunch. I said you wanted to come. Don't tell me you forgot.'

'You want me to meet your parents?'

'Is that too serious for you, Charlie?'

'You're proper off the wall, you are. One minute we're breaking into disused Tube stations, next you want to have a Sunday roast with your rents.'

'They've been wanting to meet you.'

'Have you been talking to them about me?'

'I might have mentioned you a couple of times.'

'What do they think about you going out with a cop?'

'They think I could do better for myself.'

'That's forthright. Well, they're probably right.'

'Are you coming or not?'

'Where do they live?'

'Fulham.'

'I thought you were going to say Ilford.'

'Cheeky bastard. You want an Essex girl, go down a Wetherspoon's and drop twenty pence on the floor.'

'Posh though, innit? The only other person I know who lives in Fulham is a police commissioner. What does he do, your old man?'

'He's a professor. But my mother's the one with the money, you sexist bastard. She's in property, she's made a freaking fortune.'

'What do they think of you being a teacher, then?'

'They think it's a very worthy occupation and they can't understand why I'm wasting my life on it. Shall I pick you up twelve-ish?'

'Do I have to wear a bow tie and bring tea cakes?'

'Just don't say fuck, and bring a bottle of wine that's made from grapes.'

'Do they make wine like that then?'

'Be on time for once.'

'If I'm late, I've got a blue light I can stick on the roof.'

142

They stopped outside the station, Pippa gave him a long, slow kiss that she knew would make sleep just about impossible. Then she pushed through the barrier and down the escalator.

There was an *Evening News* placard outside the station: LONDON CRIME WAVE OUT OF CONTROL. The media were having a field day on the latest statistics, sixty-seven murders and forty-two stabbings so far this year. That, and the moped crime: they had a point, he supposed, but he couldn't help but take it personally. All the way home on the bus he thought about what Mrs Williams had said to him on the phone.

'What will it take before you people do something? Some other poor girl getting killed?'

But she's right, isn't she? That's the stakes we're playing for here. Whoever did this, they're going to do it again.

CHAPTER SEVENTEEN

The dark is what lies beneath. It breathes heavy and slow, hiding from the light. I like it down there. It calls us, it does; we don't even know.

All the tunnels and humming cables and mouldering bones and the slurry of our lives, harking back to us, a murmur, a vibration we cannot hear. Up there, they pray to the light, faces turned to heaven. It is down here they should come with their candles and bones.

The ancients, the Greeks and the Romans who knew about all the different gods, they called it the Shades. They had reverence, they did. I read all about it.

There is no darkness like the darkness you find down here. It is the blackness you see after you die. But most people are stupid. They are all so afraid of what lies beneath, they raise their arms up to the sky; but it is what knows them and drives them, the root and dark wellspring, waits to take them, takes all of us in the end.

People don't want to know what's down in the dark, they don't want to look, don't want to know what makes them what they are. Like the sewers and the waste of the world, all the slurry of life we want to forget, it is churning and moving and calling, always. The primitive heart that is the damp, rotting dirt we come from.

It took her back today, it did. Just in a linen cloth, she was; soon she'll melt and fold back into the ground, she'll be a part of it again, all rotted and sweet.

144

She got herself murdered, she did, it wasn't my fault. It was not like I had planned it.

If everyone just leaves me alone, it will be all right.

Just me down here, in the dark.

CHAPTER EIGHTEEN

Charlie stared at the tube map as his carriage pulled out of Oxford Circus and into a tunnel. St Paul's, Victoria, Waterloo, Temple, Blackfriars, Charing Cross. All of England's history right there, all the old things that made the new people that live here what they are. You almost think you've got investment in it; the old church, the kings and colonies and castles. But all they are now is train stations and tourist traps and tube stops for currency brokers.

He tried to pull his mind back to the case, closed his eyes, put himself on that disused railway line that Thursday evening. Norton was there, skulking about after his Tinder date, Reuben and his weird little sister just headed home. Still hadn't found the woman. That could be key.

But it wasn't Norton's fingerprints on the brick, or someone else had picked up the brick after she'd been killed with it and got rid of it. Or else the problem was Lambeth, or the latents themselves, they weren't well enough defined. No matter what they told you on the television, forensics wasn't infallible.

But what if it wasn't Norton? Could there have been someone else down there? That was down to him then, the classic SIO mistake of following the first trail of breadcrumbs in view. He should go back and take another look at Mayfield and the scoutmaster, what if their alibis weren't as cast iron as they seemed?

He got out at Chancery Lane, came up the underground stairs to an ice-blue sky hung with vapour trails, Joe the Juice

146

on one side for the healthy people, a Caffè Nero for the caffeine addicts like him. He got a takeaway flat white with an extra shot and went looking for Luca's office, found it inside an old Tudor building, with a timber frame and a cruck roof. There was a bicycle rack outside and Charlie wondered which one was Luca's: the racing bike or the old trundler with the wire basket on the front.

Racing bike. He'd be wearing Lycra even if he was just cycling a hundred yards from those apartments over there.

He avoided the lift, as advised, and took the stairs to the third floor. There was a nice reception with a view through the windows over High Holborn, a radiator, a couple of ancient tobacco-brown leather armchairs and a mother-in-law's tongue on the desk.

Luca came straight out, must have heard his voice, didn't even wait for the usual I'll tell him you're here. He was transformed by the open-neck shirt and smart trousers, he even had a waistcoat, like he was ready to coach a World Cup semi-final. That was a nice touch, he thought, for a shrink; made him look more like a tactician and a motivator than a head-doctor, a man of the people. The magenta-tinted glasses were a masterstroke.

'Recovered from the other night?' he said.

'I'm all right.'

'It's a challenge, the dark. We all long for the sky. We do not wish to think on that which lies below, in the dark of the ground.'

'Who said that?'

'I did. Just then.'

He led him into his office, all mahogany and framed degrees, with an impressive library on one wall. There were two studded leather chairs. They sat. Luca crossed his legs in a professional manner. 'You have half an hour,' he said. 'The clock is ticking.'

'Have you read about it?' Charlie said. 'In the papers. The little girl who was murdered last week.'

147

'I know about it. That's your case?'

Charlie nodded.

'What do you want to know?'

'I want to know what kind of person I am looking for. I am told, by the government pathologist, that she was the subject of a frenzied attack. Frenzied, that's an unusual word to use in cases like this.'

'Can I ask what she was murdered with?'

'This is not public information so I'd ask you to keep this confidential.'

'Of course.'

'A brick. It was, as they say, to hand.'

Luca thought about it. He steepled his fingers, frowned a bit, channelling Freud, Charlie supposed. Didn't look a bit like a bloke who nipped down manholes to poke about in old underground stations. 'Have you heard of the amygdala?' he said.

'It's a part of the brain,' Charlie said.

Luca seemed surprised that he knew that.

'I got some amygdala on my shoe once. Gangland shooting.'

'Right. Well. You'll know it's not very big, about the size and shape of an almond. It sits right here, above the eyes in the pre-frontal cortex. It plays a critical role in empathy, in how we recognise and react to, say, fear, in the faces of others. Researchers are able to measure activity in the brain these days.'

'I've seen it. They put electrodes on people's heads and wire them up to a machine.'

'In essence, yes. In short, you can show two people the same images; say, of a child in pain, Bambi dying, that sort of thing. One of them will have an extreme reaction to it, another person the needle won't even flicker, so to speak. Nothing. I imagine the people you deal with every day fit into that category.'

'Can't argue there.'

'What you may also have noticed: if someone doesn't recognise fear in others, they often don't feel it themselves. Someone who can't feel fear is both reckless and dangerous. People think

148

they will recognise such a person when they meet them. But it's not that easy, because they become masters of imitation. They know their inner world is different from other people's, so they have to learn the art of camouflage, teach themselves to portray a whole range of emotions, without actually feeling them, so they may manipulate the world around them. A lot of serial killers and a lot of corporate executives fit this description quite closely, which is interesting. It explains much about the world we live in. You should always watch out for the life and soul of the party, the one that everyone is drawn to; chances are they beat their dog and have an outstanding restraining order from their ex.'

'How does that help me?'

'Well if you can't recognise these people by what you see on the outside, then you have to look at their past. That's where you'll find the red flags.'

'That's why we have a sex offenders' register. But we've drawn a blank on that so far.'

'I don't mean their criminal past. Perhaps your murderer is a new offender. The clue will lie in their childhood.'

'Serious?'

'I shouldn't say this, but we have very similar professional lives. For both of us, what we do is largely useless.'

'Not always useless. I do bang people up occasionally. I'm not always giving football tickets to nut jockeys to try and persuade them to do my job for me.'

'What I mean is, Charlie, we're both here to fix problems that can't be fixed. You didn't hear this from me, but to be honest, once a child has been damaged, you can't actually fix them. If someone has suffered violence or sexual abuse as a child, they don't get over it, no matter how many times they come to see me, or you. The abused become abusers, or they become permanent victims. That's the maths.'

'They're screwed up, permanently. Is that what you're telling me?'

'That's not a clinical term I'd use. But you can't fix wiring once someone's pulled it out from the wall. You can't transplant the cortisol receptors that go missing along the way and high cortisol makes bad things happen.'

'So what do you do, then?'

'You do what I do every day. Try to alleviate the damage and stay cheerful.'

'So your profile of my murderer is someone whose old man didn't buy them a football for Christmas.'

'Look for the outwardly healthy subject with the screwed-up past. Two and two never make sixty-eight.'

'At that rate, I'll be banging up myself.'

He sat back, yawned. 'You asked me for my advice. Don't forget to leave your number with my receptionist on the way out, so I can pick up those tickets for the West Ham game.'

Charlie thanked him for his time and got up to leave. He had a thought and stopped at the door. 'What you're saying, you reckon that is always true?'

'There's always exceptions.'

'My question is, you ever had anyone in here who was like, *born* evil? Someone who was just born *bad*, no reason?'

'We don't like outliers in psychology. We prefer to have a reason for everything.'

'I was thinking about that guy, Bundy, in America. They say he had a pretty normal childhood, as childhoods go, and he became a mass murderer. Billy Connolly, he got battered like fish, and he turned it into comedy. Doesn't make sense.'

'Appearances can be deceptive. Sometimes we just don't look deep enough.'

'Get out of it. That Jeffrey Dahmer, they said his mother took drugs when she was pregnant and her and her husband used to argue all the time. If that was a trigger, half the kids in Britain would have body parts next to the fish fingers in their freezer.'

'It's not an exact science.'

'If it's not exact, it's not a science. Not saying I don't agree with you, I reckon you're right, we're both trying to fix things that can't be fixed, that people get damaged and that. But I'm not convinced that it's true for everyone, not any more.'

'So what's your scientific opinion?'

'Nothing scientific about me, as you've noticed. But me, I just think that people don't want to believe in evil, that some people are just born that way.'

Luca shrugged.

'One last thing. A personal question.'

'Personal? I don't know if I can answer one of those.'

'Pip. How do you come to know each other?'

'Really, you should ask her that.'

'I'm asking you.'

'What's on your mind? I'm a married man, Charlie.'

'That never stopped anyone.'

'Well, we met here at this practice, a very long time ago.'

'She used to be a client?'

'She still is.'

'What's she seeing you for, then?'

'I'm afraid I can't discuss that. That would be breaching the rules of patient confidentiality.'

'Any red flags, doctor?'

'Like I said, Charlie, I'm not at liberty to say.'

'Enjoy the game. Way Arsenal are playing, I reckon the Hammers will win.'

Back down in the street, he stopped with his hands in the pockets of his Stone Island, looked at the people around him, going about their business, all of them with baggage locked away inside their heads. A Billy here, a Bundy there. Gave him the creeps.

He headed down the steps to the tube, tried not to think about all that ground over his head, the lights going out, the tunnels collapsing in on him. You silly bastard. Get your mind back on the job. Read witness statements, look for any red

151

flag you missed, go back through Norton's file again. Find this Tinder woman.

He thought about Timothy Norton, wiping his hands on a greasy rag and smiling to himself. Won't be smiling much longer, my son. You are not getting away with this.

His Nokia rang on the way back to the nick. The DCI, what again? He didn't answer. There were three others from the skipper. When he rang him, he said he'd had some calls on the Okpotu case; a couple of time-wasters and a teacher at the school, didn't say what she wanted, it didn't sound urgent; he'd also had a call from Sutton police, Mayfield had been picked up and questioned for loitering around a playground. Oh, and some good news. Lube and Mac had tracked Norton's mystery Tinder date. Some uniforms were bringing her in now.

When he got back to the nick, the skipper was sitting at the end of a long desk, a can of Coke and a packet of cheese and onion in front of him, looking through some printouts.

'Looking a bit flushed this morning, skipper.'

'Aye, I've joined a gym, go for an hour every morning before I come in to this madhouse.'

'Cheese and onion all part of the fitness regime, is it?' Wes said.

'Need some sustenance, don't I? I'm proper jiggered. You try doing ten kilometres on a treadmill before breakfast, see how hungry you get come nine o'clock.'

'Well, you're looking well for it.'

'Why don't you just sod off, you shandy-drinking southerner.'

Wes burst out laughing and, after a moment, so did the skipper. Lubanski patted him on the back as she made her way back to her desk with a mug of instant coffee. 'Take no notice, women like men who are a bit cuddly.'

Charlie turned to her. 'So Lube, the skipper here tells me you've found Norton's red-hot date.'

'It was more him than me,' she said, nodding at McCullough.

'How did you do that?' Charlie said to him.

'I went back to the coffee shop, found the waitress who works Thursdays. She's a lot more observant than that old prick that owns it.'

'What did she remember?'

'She said the woman he was with couldn't get out of the place fast enough. She remembered her because she couldn't understand what she was doing with Norton, called him a smelly creep. Anyway, she gave me a description, so I got out my phone, did a search on Tinder for Finsbury Park, and we got lucky. Waitress ID'd her from her profile.'

'Get in. That's brilliant, that is.'

McCullough nodded. 'Parm found her name, her Facebook page, her A-level results and all distinguishing marks in about five minutes when we got back. Scary.'

'Immigration said she went to Majorca Friday morning,' Lubanski said.

'She's skipped?'

'According to her Facebook it's just a winter break, she's back today.'

'Good how people put all this stuff online,' McCullough said. 'Helps burglars no end.'

'We've got two uniforms picking her up from the airport now,' Lubanski said. 'You want to run the interview, guv?'

'Finders keepers. You talk to her, I've got to go upstairs, brief the DCI on that gangbanger shooting in Brent. I'll check in when I've finished.'

Life goes on; he'd had two other cases during the week they were rostered on. He'd closed them both, but they took time and manpower. They had to brief the CPS, he had to keep the DCI up to speed on all of it.

FONC was in a lugubrious mood, sharing insights about leadership – he must have been reading a book in the garden over the weekend – and about what Charlie needed to do if he ever wanted to get promotion. Charlie kept checking his watch right the way through the meeting, but if FONC noticed he didn't say anything. Charlie didn't mention the possible breakthrough in the Mariatu case. If it went belly-up, he'd only wear another bollocking and get lectured again about his leadership, or lack of it.

When he got back downstairs, the interview with the mystery woman from Tinder had only just started. He went into the observation room with the skipper and Lovejoy to watch on the video link.

Her name was Paula Taylor, the skipper said, she was 41, looked a bit of all right for her age, that is until she opened her mouth. He could hear his old mum in his ear. 'Common as muck,' she would have said, under her breath, never mind that her own husband was bog Irish and she left school at fourteen. They had standards back in her day, even in Walthamstow.

She had shoulder-length blonde hair, she was wearing a fur coat over the top of a sundress, and she was brown, or brownish, something you didn't see a lot of in London in the middle of winter. She had gold hoops everywhere, wrists, ears, around her neck, and rings on every finger. He could just imagine her face when Norton walked in to the Fine Grind.

'Is this about my ex? Because if it is, I didn't fucking touch his car. He can't prove a fucking thing.'

'It has nothing to do with your ex-husband, Mrs Taylor.'

'It's not Mrs it's Ms. I don't want to be associated with that knobhead.'

'For the tape, DC McCullough is adjusting his notes to read Ms and not Mrs,' McCullough said.

Charlie smiled.

'If it's nothing to do with him, what have you dragged me in here for? The two coppers who arrested me wouldn't tell me sod all.'

'You are not under arrest, Ms Taylor. We believe you can assist us in our enquiries.'

'They dragged me out of the airport like I was a crim or something. I could sue you for damage to my fucking reputation.'

'I apologise for any embarrassment you were caused,' Lubanski said. 'We believe you may be a potential witness in a murder inquiry.'

'Murder? The fuck you talking about?'

'You haven't heard the news?' McCullough asked her.

'I been in Spain, love, I didn't get this brown from sitting under a sunlamp.'

'You met someone before you left, who is of interest to us in an ongoing investigation. His name is Timothy Norton. You arranged to meet him at the Fine Grind café on Thursday the first of March, using the Tinder dating app.'

'That gormless munter?'

'Well, that was what we thought,' McCullough said. 'I mean, I wouldn't have thought he was your type.'

'Did you see the photo he put up in his profile? Wasn't even him, I google-imaged it later, it was some actor bloke half his fucking age. If I wanted a smelly fat fifty-year-old, I would have stayed with me husband, wouldn't I?'

'You were disappointed,' Lubanski said.

'Couldn't believe it when he walked in and sat down. Ker-ist, he stank like India on a hot day.'

He saw McCullough wince. His sister had married a Sikh orthodontist from Wembley. They had enough of the old racism from the suspects, without copping it from the witnesses as well.

'His profile said he liked cooking and going out to dinner. Imagine eating anything he'd touched. Looked like he'd been scraping a new tunnel for the Northern Line with his fingernails. I was that mortified. I swear I saw something moving in his hair.'

'What time did he come into the café?'

'We arranged to meet at quarter to five, he didn't get there till five past. I was about to go home. Wish I had now.'

'How long did you stay?'

155

'Too bloody long, quarter of an hour, maybe longer.'

'Why didn't you just get up and walk out?' McCullough said.

'I tried to, but he wouldn't let me. Got real narky about it. He said: "You can't go, we're on a date." He had this funny look in his eyes, scared the shit out of me, it did. I was afraid if I left that he'd follow me.'

'So what did you do?'

'I told you, I was frightened, I let him buy me a coffee, and while he was ordering I messaged a friend of mine, told him to come and get me.'

'So you sat and talked to him?'

'He did all the talking.'

'What did he talk about?'

'All he wanted to talk about was cars. Obsessed, he was. I didn't understand a fucking word. That's right, then he told me I had nice eyes and asked me if I had any kids. I said, yeah, I got a couple, boy and a girl, and he said that's good, I like kids. He said once we got to know each other better he could take them to the park.'

Charlie heard the skipper mutter something under his breath.

Lubanski and McCullough took a moment as well.

'Ms Sutton, what time did you leave the café? This is important.'

'It was just after twenty past.'

'Are you sure?'

'Course I'm bleeding sure, love, every minute with that bloke seemed like an hour. Eventually my friend arrived, he's a bouncer at the World's End, he walked in and said to me, it's time to go, then leaned over the table and told the bloke that if he ever came near me again he'd rip off his arm and beat him to death with the wet end.'

'So then your friend walked you home?'

'Lovely man, he is. One of life's gentlemen. Beat anyone to a pulp for you, if you asked him. I'd go out with him myself, but he's got a girlfriend in Crouch End, twenty-three; girls our age, we can't compete, can we?'

Lubanski didn't rise to the bait. 'Was it dark?'

'Getting on dark, I suppose.'

'Did you see where Mr Norton went?'

She shrugged. 'Didn't give a toss, as long as he wasn't near me. What's he supposed to have done?'

'A little girl was murdered on the disused railway line about a hundred yards from the Fine Grind, about the time you left the café or soon afterwards.'

'You think it was him?'

'As we said, Ms Taylor, our enquiries are ongoing.'

'I knew it, I knew there was something not right about him.'

'Thanks for your help,' Lubanski said. 'Here's my card. If you remember anything else that you think may be relevant, please get in touch.'

Charlie and the skipper left the room, Lovejoy just behind them; they passed Paula Taylor in the corridor. Charlie caught the overpowering blast of her duty-free perfume.

'Well,' the skipper said, 'that don't prove nowt either way. We're right back where we were.'

'Something will turn up,' Charlie said, but he was getting less convinced every day.

CHAPTER NINETEEN

Another Saturday lunchtime, an early kick-off, Southampton in March, the business end of the season; it was looking like another year without Champions League football, unless Wenger could pull a rabbit out of the hat and win the Europa League. Charlie queued up for a pie with Ben, hands in his jacket pockets, staring at the menu board.

'Why is that one called the Bergkamp?' Ben said.

'It's a chicken pie. Chickens can't fly.'

Charlie sometimes forgot how long he'd been going to Arsenal games. Ben was one of the newbies, didn't remember the Bergkamps or the Rocastles, didn't remember bike chains and threepenny bit rings either, and didn't even blink when they told him the price of a season ticket. He wouldn't have come within a mile of Highbury back in the day. At Charlie's first game, he was launched up and down the terrace whenever there was a goal or a fight, and he once saw his old man piss in the back pocket of the bloke in front. What was he thinking, taking a six-year-old boy up the North Bank in those days?

He remembered that one time his old man got in a rumble, they'd gone down the old Boleyn Ground – what a shitty place that was. He must have been all of five foot nothing and he was terrified. They were going down the street one way, and there was a bunch of West Ham supporters coming towards them, and they saw the old man's red and white scarf and that was it, it was on. His old man had shoved him in a doorway and said stand there and don't move.

It scared him it did, the fight; not that he thought his old man might get hurt, but the look on his face. He liked to hurt people, that bastard, and when he came back, knuckles all bruised and torn, with blood on his shirt, he had a big grin on his face, like he'd done something really good. And then the police came on their horses and the old man had grabbed him by the shirt and they ran, he remembered looking over his shoulder and seeing a policewoman, caught her eye through the crowd for a moment, and she saw him too, and he still remembered what he felt in that moment: shame, pure shame.

'I don't get it,' Ben said. 'About the chicken.'

'Bergkamp wouldn't fly. He had a phobia. Used to drive or take the train, even for the European games.'

'They let him do that?'

'It was in his contract.'

'They should have a few more joke pies like that. The Mesut Özil. Expensive, looks good on the outside, but there's nothing in it.'

'The Almunia,' Charlie said. 'Just as they give it to you, it slips through your fingers.'

Ben gave him a blank look.

'He used to be our goalkeeper.'

Ben looked over his shoulder, nudged his arm. 'Mate, look who that is over there.'

'Is that really him?'

'You should go over and say hello.'

'Get out of it. He must get that all the time; must drive him fair round the twist.'

'Go on. Say hello, I'm Charlie George, who are you?'

'Then what, ask him if he wants my autograph?'

'Tell him you're a famous cop. He'd like that. Most of the idiots in here wouldn't know who he is any more.'

'Everyone knows who Charlie George is, and no, I am not going over there and making a complete wet wipe of myself. Stop staring, for Christ's sake. What sort of pie do you want?'

'I'm not hungry,' Ben said.

Ten minutes to go and they were one-nothing. Ben had been quiet through the game, he had been quiet all day really, nothing like his usual irritating self, droning on about how many orgasms his girl had had last night or how he'd just got a three-trillion-dollar bonus for basically doing bugger all.

Charlie sat there, watching his breath mist on the air, Ben sat beside him in his Jack Wolf jacket and his Arsenal scarf with the city slicker knot; he looked like one of the directors. Charlie couldn't help but feel like a total fraud. The old man would just wear his Arsenal shirt and a pair of knuckledusters, all weathers.

Ben was chewing his lip, worrying over something; couldn't be his love life, he'd just got back from a week in Antigua with an Amazon called Anastasia, the CEO of the catering company that hosted his firm's Christmas party. Like he said, he liked to eat his cake and have it too.

When Welbeck missed an absolute sitter, he didn't even stand up and scream abuse like everyone else, he just shook his head and muttered under his breath. The old man would be turning in his grave.

There were precious few chances after that. The stadium was half empty, and the game had settled into a listless stalemate, the players probably thinking about the game with Milan and how many Rolexes they were going to buy in duty-free on the way to Italy. 'How's the shoulder?' Ben said.

'It's all right,' Charlie said. 'Healed up nice.'

'How was your first couple of weeks back?'

'Total shite.'

'I thought you were going to ease back into it.'

'So did I.'

'That little kid that got murdered. They didn't give you that one?'

'I'm on the murder squad, Ben, they have to give it to someone.'

'Sounds rough.'

'Yeah I know, the boss was going to go easy on me, give me this twenty-year-old with his head blown off.'

'I don't know how you do it.'

'It's not the blood and guts that gets to me, Ben, it's the frustration. See, I know who did it, I just can't nail the bastard. He's going to do it to someone else if we don't get enough to bang him up. Can't sleep at night thinking about it. These kiddy-fiddlers, see, they can't help themselves. And every kid they do, they do damage. If they don't end up in the morgue, they top themselves when they grow up anyway, or end up on drugs. And so it goes on. Oh come on, Rambo, what are you doing?'

Ramsey shot from thirty yards out, it went sailing over the bar. At least it was a shot on goal.

'Saw a shrink during the week.'

'About time.'

'No, he was helping me profile.'

'Didn't think your lot went in for all that American psycho-babble.'

'Met him, social like. Offered him our tickets for the West Ham game for a bit of quid pro quo.'

'My quids, your quo, in this case.'

'Come on, you aren't going anyway, you're in Malden or somewhere.'

'Maldives.'

'Whatever. Just thought it would be interesting to pick his brains.'

'And?'

'He reckons, all of these blokes, it's their childhood that makes them like they are. Irreversible damage, he called it.'

'Well, they all say that, don't they? Some bloke offs some other bloke with a zombie knife, oh it's cos his dad didn't buy him any Lego when he was a kid. Pathetic, all that mumbo-jumbo.'

161

Look at us. It wasn't exactly Mary Poppins round our place but we turned out all right.'

'That's my point though, did we?'

'What do you mean?'

'Liam topped himself, Will's gone to live as far away as he possibly could without starting to come back, never worked an honest day in his life and is addicted to chemical substances. Jules married an Asbo. And Michael's a priest, say no more.'

'There's you and me.'

'No offence, but have you looked in the mirror lately?'

'What?'

'You can't form any long-lasting attachment to anything unless it's made by Apple.'

'You're just jealous.'

'Maybe I am. Because every morning when I have a shave, I find myself staring at a workaholic who spends all day looking at mutilated corpses, and who has gone out with more nut jobs than Broadmoor. Sorry, but I don't see any healthy adjustment going on here.'

Ben lapsed into moody silence, much like Arsène down there in the dugout, his head furrowed like one of those dogs, what were they, shar-peis. Every now and then he'd give a little twitch and look over his shoulder, perhaps looking for banners attached to airplanes – Wenger out! – or fistfights between season-ticket holders in front of the director's box.

'How's the love life? What's her name, your latest? Chelsea?'

'Not even close.'

'Remind me again.'

'Pippa. You think I'd seriously go out with a woman called after an opposing football team?'

'I'd go out with a girl called Accrington Stanley if she showed willing.'

'Yeah, but that's you, innit?'

'A rose by any other name, Charlie. You've been going out with her for a while now.'

162

'A few weeks. I know if it was you, you'd be going out to dinner to celebrate, but for the rest of us, that's not very long.'

'What does she do?'

'She's a teacher at some dodgy primary school in Croydon.'

'Sophisticated, then. Not like your usual.'

'Very funny, mate.'

'Blonde?'

'A bit.'

'As long as she's looking after you.'

Charlie shrugged.

'Groundhog day, Charlie.'

'I don't know where I am with her. One minute she's hot, the next minute cold.'

'Your usual type then. Neurotic and unstable. I don't know how you do it.'

Charlie looked at his watch. Three minutes to go. Barring a disaster, they could hold on for the three points; not an inspiring win, sure, one-nothing over a team of blokes only playing in the hope that they'd get picked up by a bigger club in the summer window, but it was something. It would keep them in the hunt.

'Heard from Will?'

'No news is good news.'

'Not necessarily. He could be lying dead in parkland somewhere and no one's found his body yet. Just saying.'

Ben leaned his elbows on his knees and pretended to watch the game. The intense frown of concentration gave the game away, really, because the football just wasn't that good.

'You all right?'

'What do you mean?'

'Don't mind me saying, but you don't seem yourself today. Like your mind's somewhere else. Problems at work?'

Ben seemed surprised at the question, like he didn't know how transparent he was.

'Work's fine. It's not that.'

163

'Come on, spit it out.'

'You know Uncle Pat's dying?'

'What? No. I didn't even know he was sick. What's wrong with him?'

'Lung cancer.'

'Shit. Poor bastard.'

Ben shrugged, like he couldn't care less.

'Haven't seen him since, Christ, he did my confirmation. Sorry to hear that. Where is he these days?'

'Just down the road.'

'I thought he was up north somewhere.'

'He was, till he got sick.'

'What hospital is he in? We should go and see him.'

'Why?'

'Well, he is our uncle and everything. I've no more time for religion than you have, but family is family.'

'Not that fussed to be honest.'

Southampton had the ball down the left wing, Arsenal had ten players behind the ball, there was absolutely no danger whatever. Their full-back shaped up for a speculative cross, no way they could score from this, all they had was their striker up there, some journeyman Slav they got for a song because his Italian club didn't want him. He had a great beard and that was the best you could say about him.

'Our Uncle Pat is a cunt,' Ben said.

'What?'

Čech was coming out for it. No, you tosser, Charlie muttered under his breath, stay on your line. He tried to focus, because that helped, that way terrible things did not happen. But, of course, that didn't always work, in fact it hardly ever worked. In the end, bad things always happened, and afterwards you blamed the team, but you also blamed yourself because if only you had prayed hard enough, shouted loud enough, somehow, by some supernatural football logic that no one had ever satisfactorily explained, you could have stopped it. That's why we all get so angry at football matches, Charlie thought, because when disaster happens, it's partly our fault.

'You know he interfered with Liam when he was a kid,' Ben said.

The ball floated in, Charlie held his breath, knew how this was going to come out.

'You fucking what?' Charlie said and turned around, but Ben wasn't looking at him, he was looking at Čech and Koscielny both going for the same ball and getting in each other's way. Why didn't they talk to each other?

'When he was six,' Ben said. 'Liam was Uncle Pat's altar boy.'

And there it was, Koscielny all in a tangle, a weak punch from the goalkeeper, the beard pounced on the loose ball, stabbed at it, and the ball dribbled over the line. Charlie felt his guts fall through his boots, thought he was going to be sick. The whole ground fell silent, as if the whole stand had turned their heads and looked at Ben in shocked silence. And there was Bellerín picking the ball out of the back of the net because no one else could be right bothered. In silence.

Liam and Uncle Pat. He couldn't believe it.

'Why didn't anyone tell me?'

'I'm telling you now.'

'Twenty-five years later.'

'Mate, I was four years old.'

'When did you find out about this?'

A shrug. 'I don't know. I was about twelve.'

The game had restarted, the fourth referee was holding up the sign, three minutes of extra time. Most of the crowd were drifting towards the exits anyway.

'Am I the only one in North London who didn't know about this?'

'Come on, Charlie, it was a long time ago.'

'You reckon you were eighteen when you found out. Why didn't you tell me then?'

'What was the point?'

'Hang on,' Charlie said, and he did his sums, you didn't have to be Einstein. 'You found out at Liam's funeral, didn't you?'

He didn't see Ben looking guilty very often, but this was one of those times.

'Mum told us.'

'Us?'

'Me and Jules and Will.'

'What about Michael?'

'I think he already knew. He was in the seminary by that stage. Didn't come to his own brother's funeral, you remember? Because suicides don't go to heaven.'

'Where was I?'

'You left early. Don't you remember? Never seen you so fucking angry. Anyway, Mum must have had a few too many sherries at the wake and that was when it all came out. Next day she swore us all to secrecy. She said, look it's all in the past, it does no good bringing it up. What will people think of us? That was her line and I guess we all bought it. She especially made us promise not to tell you.'

'And so you all kept quiet.'

'It was what Mum wanted. Besides, we were all afraid of what you might do.'

'So, you decided to protect poor Uncle Pat.'

'Not him, you. You would have done something to him, I know you would, and then you would have ended up in prison for it. There was one life already ruined, why make it two, what good would it have done, Charlie? You reckon you'd be where you are now if we'd told you about this when you were younger?'

'Maybe not.'

'Mum made us promise, swore us all to secrecy about it. She was sure you'd do something bad to him. She said anyway it was all in the past and she shouldn't have told us. We should all just forget about it, like she had.'

'And you believed her?'

'Maybe she was right.'

166

'So why are you telling me now?'

'Well, you can go and pull out his oxygen tubes if it makes you feel better, but he's dying now anyway, so it won't make any difference.'

The final whistle went. There were boos as the teams filed off and then what was left of the crowd poured out of the ground, Arsène looking more and more like an ageing classics professor who'd got one of his younger students pregnant, an intellectual with the weight of the world on his stooped shoulders.

'Why not us?'

'You were too ugly to be a choirboy, by all accounts, and by the time I was old enough, he'd gone up to Newcastle or Manchester or wherever it was he went to do the Lord's holy work.'

Charlie's hands balled into fists in his lap. Take a deep breath, Charlie my son, calm the fuck down. They were right, him and Jules, not to tell him. What they were saying was, you're too much like the old man, you would have sorted out the problem with your fists, like he did. The other night, that bloke with the spaniel had given me any more trouble, I would have done serious damage. Doesn't matter what he'd done, that is not the way to fix things.

'Let's go,' Ben said, and stood up.

Charlie stayed sitting. 'You reckon I'm like the old man?' he said.

'Get out, you're nothing like him,' Ben said, but there was a moment's hesitation before he said it, and they both knew it. They filed out. A bit different from the old Boleyn Ground days. They queued for the tube, smiled at the policemen on the horses, then headed for Covent Garden.

Ben said he knew a place that did great cocktails.

CHAPTER TWENTY

They hadn't reserved, and it was a Saturday, the place was rammed. Ben somehow managed to get in, a bubbly girl with a clipboard and a ponytail led them to a table. Charlie didn't see any money change hands but he supposed that was how it was done.

'You have to know one of the bar staff,' Ben said, 'or there's no chance of getting served in happy hour.'

'Have you slept with her?' Charlie said. 'And she's still friends with you? Or is it she doesn't know you've dumped her yet?'

'You make me sound so venal.'

'Do I?' Charlie said.

The place looked like a low-lit Victorian gentlemen's club. There were chequerboard floor tiles, pint-pot candle-holders on the tables, and black-and-white framed portraits on the walls, characters who looked as if they'd stepped straight out of the pages of a Charles Dickens novel. He looked at the menu; all the drinks were sprinkled with cumin and cane sugar and honey stolen from a forbidden Himalayan mountain.

He gave up, let Ben choose. A barmaid brought them two Flaming Zombies in a white skull glass with a flaming sugar cube on top.

'Three types of rum in this,' Ben said. 'You should have the Mexican Butterfly next. It's got agave nectar in it.'

'As long as they remember to take the pointy bits out.'

'The Illuminati used to meet in here, they reckon.'

'Well, they could probably afford to,' Charlie said, putting the cocktail menu back on the table.

'Proper banging in here later.'

'You thinking of hanging around?'

'We'll see what the night brings. Are you seeing Poppy?'

'Pippa. No, she says she's got a girls' night out.'

Ben raised his eyes, let him know what he thought about that.

'She's allowed.'

'Sure she is. What's she like?'

'A right looker.'

'But?'

'I didn't say "but".'

'Your expression did.'

Charlie tried his Zombie. 'How can you drink these? Proper knock your head off, this stuff.'

'Come on, Charlie, it'll put hairs on your chest.'

'It's put hairs on my eyeballs.'

'You were telling me about Poppy. Sorry, Pippa. Tell me she's not married like the last one.'

'Divorced.'

'Are you sure about that?'

'I've not asked to see the papers if that's what you mean.'

'Where is her ex these days?'

'He's at Her Majesty's pleasure.'

'Nice. What for?'

'She said it was fraud.'

'But being a good copper, you went straight on the PNC and found out for yourself.'

Charlie winced. 'GBH.'

'Nice.'

'A drug debt.'

'You sure can pick them, can't you?'

'You can't help who you fall for.'

'Of course you can, you silly bastard. You've just got a radar for damaged and useless women. It's uncanny. None of this is a coincidence, Charlie.'

'Pip's different, mate.'

'Doesn't sound like it to me. Bro, remember that time the old man took us all on holiday, it was Devon or somewhere.'

'How can I forget, it was the only time he ever took us anywhere.'

'Right, so remember you and me went off on our own.'

'We didn't go off anywhere. You were like, ten. You used to follow me around like a bad smell. I couldn't get shot of you.'

'Whatever. There was that old hotel a couple of bays along from where we were staying. They were demolishing it, remember. There was a bloke standing there with a red flag and you said something like, I'm not scared of red flags. And you went crawling past him in the long grass, and five minutes later they blew up the hotel and you came running back white as a sheet. You said you'd seen bits of roof the size of a phone box landing a few feet away from you in the grass.'

'Yeah, I remember.'

'The lesson was, you see a red flag, you run as fast as your little legs will go. It's about time you learned your lesson because if this Poppy—'

'Pippa.'

'Pippa married some bloke who has drug dealing and GBH on his rap sheet, that is a red flag. You hear that?' He put a hand to his ear. 'It's the sound of a bit of roof about to land right on your head.'

'But you should see her with the kids in her class, she's a real sweetheart, know what I mean?'

'Not really.'

'I don't want to stuff up another one. This is going good.'

'Oh Charlie, you don't know what going good looks like.'

'I'm supposed to be meeting her rents tomorrow.'

'What, Sunday lunch?'

'Something like that.'

170

'Take a food taster, bro.'

The place was getting louder, more parties crowding in, half a dozen girls shrieking in the corner. Ben ordered another round; at least these drinks weren't a fire risk.

'Is this the one with cactus juice in it?'

'Try it, you'll love it.'

Charlie took a long gulp at it. He tried to keep up with his younger brother but it was no good, he was gagging for a beer. 'I should have known about Liam,' he said.

'How could you have known? You were only eight yourself when it happened.'

'I was supposed to watch out for him.'

'Watching out for him was the old man's job.'

'The old man was a violent alcoholic, he was as much use as a parent as a chocolate fireguard.'

'You can't blame yourself for everything that happened in the George family. Uncle Pat was our freaking uncle, for Christ's sake. Back then people thought priests were decent people.'

'I can't help thinking what was going through his head that day, know what I mean? He walks on to a train track and lies down. Couldn't he have just come to me, or Mum, talked to one of us. Anything but that.'

'You had your own stuff you were getting through back then.'

'I was still his big brother. Sometimes I have this daydream, like, where I run on the tracks and pick him up and I get him clear just in time.'

'Let it go, Charlie. It's done. Wasn't for you back then, it would have been a lot worse. Come on, that's enough talking about that. Look over your shoulder.'

Charlie looked. There were two girls giving them looks, not bad sorts either.

'We could be in there,' Ben said.

'My life's complicated enough as it is. I'll leave you to it.'

'You leaving?'

Charlie finished his drink, stood up. 'Places to go, people to see.'

'What are you going to do about Uncle Pat?'

'What do you think I'm going to do?'

'Just don't smother him with a pillow or anything.'

'I'd rather pull out his toenails through his nose.'

'Dying slow. Maybe that's God's way.'

'Have a nice night,' Charlie said.

The cold air hit him like a heavyweight boxer; he even stopped to lean against the wall for a minute, pretended to be checking his phone. There was a cold drizzle drifting down, a mist around the orange sodium lights along the alley.

Uncle Pat.

He thought about Mayfield, what was it he said in that interview?

It's not the sex that messes children up. It's the fuss afterwards.

No one ever made a fuss about Liam, no one even knew. And then there were blokes like Norton: 'I'm the victim here.'

He had to find who it was killed Mariatu. He would do it for her, he would do it for the Okpotus, and he would do it for Liam.

CHAPTER TWENTY-ONE

There was a giant crucifix on the wall in the foyer and a statue of some saint Charlie didn't recognise, right outside the lifts. No mistaking the place, this was where the A-list Micks stopped off for the last time when afflicted by God's mysterious plan. He checked at reception then took the lift to the pulmonary ward.

The corridors were stark, all sick-coloured walls and strip lights, the patients four to a ward; they all had nasal prongs or oxygen masks. He heard some poor bastard gasping for breath behind a drawn curtain. A plump woman was pushing a trolley piled with dinners, a young nurse hurried past trailing a BP cuff and a clipboard.

If the nurse hadn't told him, yes, that's him, that's Father Patrick George, he wouldn't have recognised him. He had this vague memory of him, doling out the wine and biscuits in his white surplice when Charlie was a kid, his thinning black hair pulled across his skull like guitar strings. He wore thick black-rimmed glasses back then, but there wasn't much else he remembered, except the smell of him when he bent over to put the wafer in his hands, that tobacco stink that heavy smokers have. The bony claws that lay on the sheet were stained with nicotine, so he didn't suppose he'd stopped puffing away in the intervening years. The cancer had ravaged him, he was pretty much skeletal, modern medical science keeping him alive, nasal prongs feeding him oxygen, intravenous lines dripping in morphine and fluids, an ECG and a pulse oximeter to confirm the existence of life, at least in technical terms.

He had come to their house one Christmas, when Charlie was a kid. His mum had been anxious, almost giddy, like Jesus was coming to pay a visit, or George Graham. He had sat in the corner with his little glass of sherry and Ma had fluttered around him like he was royalty, would you like this, Father, would you like that?

Uncle Pat never said much but when he did Charlie remembered how the whole room fell silent, even his old man, who liked to shout everyone down with his own opinions. But even he wouldn't talk over the top of Uncle Pat, he always had the floor to himself. He tried to think how old Liam would have been when all this was going on. Ben was only just walking, so about then. Mum was so proud of Liam being the altar boy, helping with the Eucharist and all that carry-on, Charlie never had much time for it, even then. As soon as he was old enough to make his own decisions he said right, that's it for me, and he'd never set foot in a church since.

Uncle Pat had a private room with a nice view over the car park, no buildings to obstruct his view of heaven. He wasn't alone, there was a priest and two nuns sitting vigil with him, one of them was Michael. Loved this bit, they did, the dying. It was what they lived for.

He hadn't seen Michael in a while; he'd changed too, he looked plumper, redder in the face. He reminded Charlie a bit of the god he had when he went to Sunday school: smug, critical and hard to like.

At least a couple of years since he'd seen him, even though he came down to London every couple of months, by all accounts, to visit Ma. No one ever believed they were brothers, he didn't quite believe it himself. Michael was the good-looking one in the family, people said he looked like that old-time movie star, Cary Grant. He wore glasses, he was always pushing them further up his nose, and it gave him a thoughtful look. He had cultivated their father's Irish brogue, though the rest of them all spoke Cockney like their mum. And it was always Michael, never Mick or Mike. Father Michael.

He didn't look surprised or pleased when he saw Charlie. Instead there was an expression of mild irritation, or perhaps he just imagined it.

'Charlie,' he said and stood up.

'Hello, Michael.'

They shook hands, but only briefly.

'Have you brought Ben?'

'Why would I bring Ben?'

'No reason. This is Father Brian and Sister Josephine. They have come to share the vigil with me. A sad day. I was about to lead a prayer for Father Patrick's soul. Will you join us, Charlie?'

'Do you reckon that's likely or are you just having a laugh?'

'I never laugh about matters of the soul, you know that.'

'How long has he got, have the doctors said?'

'It's only our brother's mortal remains that are yet living. They say he will go to his reward tonight or early tomorrow.'

'His reward?'

'For a life of service.'

Ma had been so proud of Liam when he was asked to be an altar boy. He remembered hearing her telling one of the neighbours one day, they were sitting having a cup of tea in the front room, it was all she'd talk about: our Liam this, our Liam that. Liam would do anything to get himself noticed, even at that age; there was nothing he could have done that would have earned him more brownie points with Ma than getting hooked up with the religious. He was a funny little boy, their Liam, all red hair and freckles and weedy as all get-out. Charlie was forever sorting out kids who tried to bully him at school.

George, did you hit Ellis from the first form? He stole my little brother's lunch box, sir. They could still whack you with the cane in those days. Seemed like the dark ages now but it still went on as recently as that, especially in the Mick schools.

175

'Uncle Pat, remember me?' Charlie bent over the bed, hoping the old bastard would open an eye, something, let him know he was in there, that he understood. His breath was vile. He felt something touch his hand, he looked down, saw Uncle Pat's fingers close around his; there were liver spots stark against the parchment skin, you could make out all the bones and ligaments underneath. His lips moved, he mumbled something Charlie couldn't make out.

'He can't hear you, Charlie,' Michael said. 'Not now. His soul is with God.'

He snatched his hand away, worried that the old bastard was drawing comfort from it somehow. What had he hoped to achieve, coming here? It was too late anyway, Uncle Pat had managed a Jimmy Savile, he'd got away with it.

Had he been hoping to see some kind of remorse? That wouldn't happen; these blokes didn't know about things like that. Didn't he know enough about how their minds worked by now, criminals always made themselves out to be the victims somehow, you could never hold any of these bastards to account. That wasn't the way it worked. The only one who proper blamed himself for Liam dying was him and the train driver, and neither of us really had anything to do with it.

Charlie stepped back from the bed. 'You know he indecently assaulted our little brother?' he said to Michael.

Well, that did it. Michael shot out of his chair as if he'd been hit with a taser, Sister Josephine gave a little cry and crossed herself. Father Brian closed his eyes and started to whisper the Lord's Prayer.

'Charlie. The poor man is dying.'

'You knew, didn't you?' Charlie said.

'Please. Not here. This is not the time or the place.'

'When is the time or the place, Michael? Or were you going to work it into the eulogy?'

'We'll talk about this outside.'

'You're just as bad as he is,' Charlie said. 'You never spoke up. You never held him to account, did you?'

'Not now, Charlie. Please.'

A nursing sister put her head around the curtain to check if everything was all right. Charlie said there had been a vigil malfunction and walked out.

Charlie found the waiting room, bought a coffee from the machine, just for something to do, really. There was a mother in there with a four-year-old who was climbing on the plastic chairs and ripping up the *National Geographics*. She told him she wished she'd never had him, not the best kind of mothering he'd ever heard. He wasn't the best-behaved kid, no question, but then it might have been good if Liam had been more like that, instead of always being so eager to please.

Maybe there was something I could have done.

The plastic cup crumpled in his fist and he grunted as the hot coffee went all over his hand. The little kid stopped yelling and stared. Charlie threw the cup into the bin and went out. He found the men's, went in and held his hand under the cold tap.

When he came back out, Michael was standing in the corridor, looking agitated. 'Shall we take a walk?' he said.

It was freezing in the car park, the wind was bitter, but at least there were stars, a few of them anyway. Michael pulled a pack of crumpled B&H out of his jacket and lit up. No teaching some people. He stood under one of the sodium lamps, hunched and angry.

'You've put on a few pounds,' Charlie said.

'Our housekeeper's a grand cook.'

'Well that's nice for you. We don't get housekeepers in my job.'

'You don't need a housekeeper, just a barman and a barista. I see Arsenal are serving up the same old rubbish as last year. How's that going for you?'

'I have faith that things will get better one day. We all have to believe in something. Do you get along to games up there?'

A guilty puff on the fag. 'The local team. Tranmere Rovers.'

'You what? I thought they were in the Sunday League.'

'Back in Division Two now. I was at Wembley when they beat Boreham Wood in the play-offs. They play just down the road in Birkenhead and two of their first team come to the church. I even have a blue and white scarf. Are you still with the Met?'

'What else would I do with myself?'

'Hardly recognised you when you walked in, these fancy clothes and the shaved head. You look like you run the underworld, not police it.'

Charlie blew on his hands then shoved them back in his pockets, stamped his feet a bit.

'How's things with you? Saved many souls recently? Wouldn't expect there's too many Scousers in heaven, but I suppose you're paid to do your best.'

'You enjoy your own irreverence, Charlie, but you'll get no rise out of me. I lived with you half my life, I know how it goes with you.'

'Been to see Ma?'

'I have.'

'Brought her any more saintly pictures?'

'She asks for them, you know. They bring her comfort.'

'They give me nightmares.'

'Wouldn't have thought you had many of those, doing your job. How's Ben? Is he richer than Bill Gates yet?'

'He's working on it. His first goal is to sleep with more twenty-year-olds than Rod Stewart.'

'That will be a great deal harder to do, by all accounts.'

'He's got time on his side.'

'And Julia?'

'She's got her hands full with her chav husband and sick kid.'

'The one with the strange name.'

'Rom. It's short for Romeo.'

'Very Shakespearean.'

'Great kid though.'

'Is he any better these days?'

'Not really. Don't think he'll ever be better. He just has to live with it. One of God's little mysteries, this thing he's got. Very mysterious man, God.'

Charlie walked over to the statue of the saint that stood in the bushes outside the foyer. He read the plaque. 'Saint Jude,' he said. 'What's he good for?'

'Patron saint of the hopeless and the despaired.'

'They should put one of these outside the Emirates, next to Dennis Bergkamp. You heard about Will, did you?'

'Is he in trouble again?'

'Ben didn't tell you? Drug overdose.'

'Is he all right?'

'This time. He'll do for himself one day, it's just a matter of time, innit?'

'I shall pray for him.'

'I'll text him and tell him, he'll like that.'

'Are you mocking me again, Charlie?'

'No, I mean it, he will. He doesn't believe in it but he'll like that someone cares. Even if he pretends he doesn't.'

'Is he still in Australia?'

'Yeah, fits in right proper, they're all mad and stupid down there. No shortage of artificial stimulants either.'

'Shall we talk about what just happened up there?'

'What did happen? In your view.'

'You disgraced yourself and shamed a dying man.'

'I wonder if that's how Liam would have seen it?'

'This has nothing to do with poor Liam!'

'It has everything to do with our brother!'

'This does no good now, Charlie. What on earth do you hope to achieve with all this?'

'A measure of justice?'

'What's done is done. We are all sinners in our own way. We have only two choices, reconciliation with the Holy Spirit or damnation.'

'Or, the third choice, getting to the truth and laying it out on the table. See that's my religion, Michael, that's what I'm dedicated to. We all live our lives for something.'

'Father Patrick was a human being like you and me, he was prone to the sins of the flesh but he did a lot of good as well, later in his life. Tarnishing his reputation now will do no one any good.'

'Sorry, I don't agree. I'm just a tarnisher from way back, me.'

'You had no right to say what you did in front of our fellow religious up there. It was a cruel and spiteful thing to say over a man's deathbed. I cannot believe you did it.'

'You know what he did, don't you, you know what I'm talking about?'

'Perhaps.'

'And you kept this to yourself all these years. You're no better than he is.'

'It was not a choice, I was obliged by the vows I made as a priest to keep silent. The fact is, I was his confessor, and I could not break the sanctity of it. What he did or did not do is between him and God now.'

'He came to you to confess.'

'And why not? I was a fellow priest.'

'When?'

'It was a few years ago. I had not long been ordained.'

'Liam was our brother.'

'Whatever a man does, if he expresses remorse, true remorse, he may be absolved in the sight of God. It is one of the basic tenets of true belief.'

'What absolution did you give him: ten Hail Marys and do the washing-up in the presbytery for a month? And that makes up for everything, does it?'

'I understand that you have no sense of the sacred. But God and forgiveness are the same thing.'

'You do understand why our little brother lay down on the railway tracks in front of a train, don't you? You do get that?'

180

'You don't know that was why he did it.'

'I know that it's convenient for you to try and explain it away some other way.'

'No one is more sorry about what happened than I am.'

'No, that's not true. Do you wake up in a cold sweat some nights thinking that you should have done something? Thinking you should have *known*? No, you don't. You sleep like a baby. All this God-bothering hasn't made you more human, it's just made you smug. You haven't changed a bit.'

'Neither have you. You still think you can solve every problem with your fists. Don't you preach to me either.' He stubbed out his cigarette with his heel. 'I'd better be getting back. I take it we won't be seeing you at the funeral.'

'Only if you allow dancing on graves.'

Charlie watched him stalk away across the car park and back in through the sliding doors to the foyer. He thought about what one of their suspects said in his interview – who was it? Mayfield: none of us can help how we're born. Funny, but he agreed with that. Some people were just born wrong. You weeded them out, you didn't try to make them what they weren't or give them a place to hide.

CHAPTER TWENTY-TWO

'Hello Ma. How are you, all right then?'

She opened one eye, looked around as if she couldn't remember where she was, and perhaps she didn't. She was asleep in her chair, in front of her television, a cup of tea gone cold on the bedside table. She had her handbag on her lap, held in a death grip like always. The sound on the television was on full blast, he didn't know how anyone could sleep through that.

'Is your father home?'

'Mum, Dad's not here. He's gone.'

'Where's he gone, he didn't tell me he was going out.' She stared at him with her big, watery blue eyes and then it was like a light was switched on, and she remembered. 'I was dreaming again. I am a silly-billy, aren't I? Is Ben with you?'

'No, Mum, it's just me.'

'Oh well, never mind,' she said.

'You want a cup of tea?'

'I've got one right there.'

'No, it's cold. You want me to make you another one?'

'No, I don't like tea. What time is it?'

'It's ten o'clock.'

'Night or morning?'

'At night, Mum.'

'I thought it was a bit dark outside for morning. What day is it?'

'It's a Saturday, Ma.' She looked at him, trying to remember who he was, like she was at a party, and they'd been introduced, but she'd forgotten his name and didn't like to ask a second time.

There was a knock at the door. Charlie thought it was one of the nurses. The door was only ajar anyway, but when he got up to open it there was an old woman standing there in her dressing gown, holding a newspaper and a packet of crisps.

'What are you doing in my room?' she said.

Charlie checked the number on the door. 'This isn't your room. It's my mum's.'

'I'm going to call the police.'

'I think you've got the wrong room. What number is yours? I'll help you find it.'

She put a bony finger in his face. 'When my son gets home, I'm going to get him to smash your face in.'

One of the nurses came by and took her arm. 'Come on, love, you're at the wrong room.' She led her down the corridor. The old lady turned and looked back at him over her shoulder. 'Smash your face in,' she mouthed at him.

Charlie went back into the room and turned the sound down on the television.

'That's that Mrs Reeves,' Ma said. 'Silly as a two-bob watch, that one. Should be in the funny farm. The people they let in here, what kind of a hotel is this?'

'It's a nursing home, Ma, it's not a hotel.'

'All the money my Ben pays, you'd think you'd get better service. When am I going home, Charlie?'

'You can't go home, Ma. You keep getting lost.'

'Don't be silly. What are you talking about? I don't like it in here, the staff are rude.'

'They're not rude, Ma, they're really nice.'

Another tap on the door. Charlie thought it might be Mrs Reeves, or her son, come to smash his face in, but it was one of the nurses. She had a little paper pill cup and a glass of water. 'Here you are, Mrs George. Your medication.'

'What do I have to have medication for, Charlie? Tell her there's nothing wrong with me.'

'Just take your pills, Ma.'

'When's dinner?' she said to the nurse.

'You've had dinner, Mrs George, don't you remember? It was fish. You like fish.'

Ma looked at Charlie and when the nurse wasn't looking she tapped her head and made a face. This one's nuts as well.

'When's Liam coming to see me? He hasn't been to see me for months. After all I did for that boy.'

'I'm sure he'll come to see you soon,' the nurse said, and smiled at Charlie like, come on, get your family sorted out, will you, she won't be here much longer after all.

Ma took her pills and the nurse went out and Ma put on a theatrical whisper, they could have heard it in Cornwall. 'She stole my purse that one.'

'She didn't steal your purse, Ma.'

'She did. I don't trust her. Never liked darkies, me.'

'How can you say that?' Charlie said, and then reminded himself that it was useless railing against his mother's casual racism. He wasn't going to change her now, was he? But it jarred him, it did, and next thing he heard himself saying: 'Why didn't you tell me about Uncle Pat?'

She seemed to shrink in her chair. 'What about Uncle Pat?'

'You know what he did.'

The bag shifted on her lap, it was one of her tells; she knew what he was talking about. This is my chance to get at the truth, he thought.

'He's a good man, your Uncle Pat. A man of God.'

'Was he, Ma? Was he a good man?'

'A man of the cloth. You should never speak ill of a man of the cloth.' She clutched her bag a little tighter, everything she held dear in that bag. For a moment she looked up at him and he caught the look of fear in her eyes. She remembered. It hit him then; forgetting wasn't something that happened to you, it

184

was something you did, until one day it just wasn't your choice any more.

She had a tissue out of her bag, started tearing it up, letting the bits fall on the carpet at her feet, her little rain of memories. She looked up at him, imploring him to forget as well.

'Can you make me a cup of tea?' she said.

'Sure Ma,' Charlie said, and he picked up her cup and went to the door. What was the point, what was the bloody point?

'Mind out for that Mrs Reeves,' she called after him. 'She's lost her marbles. Doolally tap, she is!'

The clatter and echo of invisible footsteps, strip-lit corridors of white and oxblood-coloured tiles. He hated the tube at night. During the day, crowded with people, somehow it was all right, he could forget about the long airless tunnels and all that earth above his head, ready to crash down on him. Get a grip, Charlie. You have to get over this, my son.

A busker was playing bagpipes at the bottom of the escalators, 'Amazing Grace'; he remembered Ben had nicknamed one of his girlfriends that. A bloke in a suit was snoring on one of the benches, he'd had a big night by the look of it. The tube staff would kick him out at two after the last train, that wouldn't be quite as amazing.

A sudden rush of cold wind announced the arrival of a train, next came the roar and rattle of the carriages; frightened him when he was a kid, that noise, he never knew what might be coming out of the tunnel.

He thought about getting off at Monument, messaging Ben, seeing where he was, catching up for another drink. But Ben would probably be shagging his heart out by now, or else he'd try and line him up with the friend of some woman he'd just met, and he wasn't Ben, he couldn't do any of that thanks for a lovely night, I'll call you, business.

The carriage was empty except for a Goth couple down the other end of the carriage, they needed to get a room; he

185

wondered what they did with all those nose- and lip-rings when they were riding, did they ever get tangled up and have to call emergency services?

He ignored them and hunkered down into his coat. He thought about that old joke, if you get bored on the tube you can always look out of the window. He thought about the Christmas card Will had sent him, come right out of the blue that did: when was the last time anyone in his family had remembered him at Christmas?

It arrived late, he hadn't got it until after the New Year, and he'd been distracted by the Lucifer case so it was weeks before he opened it.

Dear Charlie, hope you have a good Christmas. You were a good brother to me. I'll never forget it.

He didn't even sign it. Maybe his counsellor wrote it.

He wondered if their dear Uncle Pat had had a go at him as well. It bothered him that no one had told him about that, that they'd managed to keep it a secret for so long. What other family secrets were there that he didn't know? And here he was, he was supposed to be a detective. He had bits of paper on the wall, saying that he was.

Ben was right, he would have put Uncle Pat in the hospital, or worse, if they had told him. Ben knew him better than himself. He supposed they all looked after each other, in their own way.

Perhaps too, they were all a little frightened of him. That was the sad thing, all his life he'd told himself he wouldn't be like his father. Everyone said that, though, didn't they? I'm not going to be like my father, not going to turn out like my mum. And whenever you did that, bingo, wait twenty or thirty years, and there you were, we all become what we hate.

CHAPTER TWENTY-THREE

Pippa's parents lived in Chelsea-tractor territory. 'I feel like a eunuch at a dick-waving contest,' he said to her as he drove along Fulham Road in his three-year-old Golf. 'You need at least a Beemer to come down here.'

'Don't be a prat, Charlie,' Pippa said.

Nice this, all the boutiques and designer shops, just have to close his eyes as he went past the Bridge and the underground, tossers in Chelsea shirts shopping for antiques with wives tottering along in Manolo Blahniks, get a life you mugs.

'Charlie, they're just people,' Pippa said, which showed him just how much she understood about football.

She pointed out to him where she went to school.

'You went to a girls' prep school?'

'Is that so surprising?'

'Not much like the school you teach at.'

'No Charlie, it's not. That's the whole point.'

Her phone pinged. She stared at it with an irritated look on her face then stuffed it back in her bag.

'Everything all right?'

She nodded.

'What's the matter?'

'He keeps messaging me.'

'Who? Your ex? I thought he was inside.'

'They get access to computers, don't they?'

'What does he want?'

'Nothing, Charlie. It's just on the right, down here.'

Her rents lived in one of the original terraced Victorian houses in Parsons Green, a modernised Lion house on a cherry-tree-lined street, within the Peterborough Estate.

The news came on the radio just as they pulled up outside, he leaned over and turned up the volume. 'Bugger me. The organic waste is going to proper hit the Mistral now.'

'What is it?' Pippa said.

'Another girl's gone missing.'

'So? You're not on duty, are you? You said it was your day off.'

'I think I know her. She's the sister of our sigwit in the Okpotu case.'

'You might as well be talking a foreign language, Charlie. What's a sigwit for Christ's sake?'

'Significant witness. This is going to throw FONC into a right knicker-twist.'

But it wasn't the DCI Charlie was worried about. He thought about his conversation with Mrs Williams a few nights before. What was it she'd said:

What will it take before you people do something? Some other poor girl getting killed?

He took his Nokia out of his jacket pocket and checked it. No missed calls. He would be hearing from the DCI sooner or later, no doubt about it, rostered on or not.

Pippa put her hand on his. 'Put the phone away, Charlie,' she said, not unkindly. 'Forget about work, for once.'

He slipped his mobile back into his pocket, on silent, but left the vibrate on. 'Right,' he said, 'let's go and meet the parents.'

Pippa's father looked like a retired bank manager, one of the old school types, back in the day, before all bankers turned into white-collar criminals. He wore a tie and had his glasses on a chain around his neck. He had a Home Counties accent and the vague air of a man who had mislaid his car keys.

His wife was bottle-blonde, well turned-out and formidable, and all over him like a cheap suit. She offered him both cheeks.

She was wearing fragrance, enough to stun a horse. They had heard all about him, she said. She was so glad to meet him at last. Call me Deborah.

Pippa only rated second place in the hugging ritual, Charlie noted. Her mother offered Pippa a cheek. Her father put his arms out, but Pippa seemed to back up, putting her arms on his shoulders to keep him at arm's length.

'Happy Birthday,' Pippa said, and handed him the gift-wrapped present she had brought with her, the card Sellotaped to the top of it. He leaned in for another kiss and she bent forward at the waist, like she was peering over the railing of a ship, and left a perfunctory smudge of red lip gloss on his cheek.

'Come in, come in,' Deborah said. 'Lunch is ready.'

Charlie thought, but remembered not to say aloud: fuck me. There was a double reception room, sunlit, with French doors that led out to a paved garden. It led through to a kitchen and breakfast room with bi-fold doors and skylights. There were Gaggenau appliances, moon-rock stone worktops, and even a wine wall with separate cooling areas for white and red wine.

Charlie asked if the tops were real moon rock, which Deborah thought very funny, possibly too funny, but he allowed for the fact that she was probably nervous too.

'Have you got a ballroom in the basement?' Charlie said, and Pippa scowled at him, but her father – Jonathan, not John – took the question seriously.

'No room. Only a gym, I'm afraid. Used to be the servants' quarters.'

'My great-grandmother probably slept there, then,' Charlie said.

There was a bit of a pause.

'I hope you like fish,' Deborah said. 'We're having fish because someone is a vegetarian.' She rolled her eyes and looked at Pippa.

'Mum, vegetarians don't eat fish.'

'Oh, for goodness' sake, of course you do,' Deborah said.

189

Charlie never found out how that conversation ended. Jonathan took him on a tour of the rest of the ground floor, explained how they had completely remodelled the house over the years, but had respected the Victorian aspects of the property by maintaining the cornicing and the ceiling roses. Two orange wooden giraffes looked startled in front of the ornamental fireplace.

'It's so much warmer now,' he said. 'We love how we can sit here in the family room and see right the way through those glass walls to the top floor.'

'Is this Pippa when she was a kid?' Charlie said, and nodded at the framed photographs on the mantel.

Jonathan picked one of them up, stared at it as if seeing it for the first time. 'She would have been about ten when this was taken. This is her brother, Daniel. Has she told you about Daniel? He's living in Singapore at the moment. Works for Standard Chartered, on the investment side. Clever boy. We're very proud of him.'

Charlie did a quick head-count of the photographs: six of Daniel, the clever one, two of Pippa. No surprise he had never come up in conversation, then.

'This used to be two rooms,' Jonathan said, turning around.

Charlie saw his reflection for a moment in the mirror; it was gilt-framed, bought for the cost of a football player at one of those antique shops they had passed on Fulham Road. It would have been considered overlarge at Versailles. He realised he actually looked the part, in his Aspesi blazer and polo shirt and blue chinos. No one would take you for a copper, my son. It's just you who can't forget you're from a family of bricklayers, drunks and downstairs maids.

Jonathan had just launched into a rant about the cost of getting a good tradesman when Deborah called them from the kitchen. Lunch was served.

'Has Philippa cooked you dinner yet?' Deborah said, as she brought bowls from the kitchen.

'I don't cook, Mum,' Pippa said.

Deborah raised her eyes, drawing him into her conspiracy. 'Thirty years old and she can't boil an egg.'

Pippa's smile had frozen on her face. She didn't even move like herself since they had walked in; she skulked around the house as if she thought she was going to get blackjacked any minute.

'You don't believe in this silly vegan business, do you, Charlie?'

Charlie was about to answer but Pippa cut across him for the second time. 'I'm vegetarian, not vegan.'

'All the same thing. It's melon soup,' she said to Charlie as he picked up his spoon. 'Just trying to do the right thing.'

'Philippa tells us you're a police detective,' Jonathan said.

'I'm with one of the major incident teams, at Essex Road.'

'You must see some terrible things,' Deborah said.

'Not as much gratuitous violence in my job as there is teaching at a primary school.'

It was a joke, or he thought it was, but no one smiled.

'Some other poor girl's gone missing last night,' Deborah said.

'Let's not talk about it now, Mum.'

'Is that the sort of thing you have to deal with, Charlie?'

'Something like that.'

'They say she lived near that other girl who got murdered, the black one.'

'Does it matter what colour she was, Mum?'

'I'm just saying. She was black, wasn't she?' She did the thing with her eyes again. 'Can't eat meat, can't say black. Poor Charlie. How do you put up with her?'

Pippa pushed her soup away. 'What's for lunch, really?'

'I told you, I bought some lovely pieces of Cornish cod, and there's courgettes and finger carrots to go with it.'

'You're serious?' Pippa said, and threw her napkin on the table. She picked up her soup plate and went back to the kitchen. Charlie heard her throw it in the sink. Deborah got up and followed her out. He heard them arguing through the French doors.

'Would you like some more wine?' Jonathan said, and the bottle of Chassagne-Montrachet hovered over his glass. Charlie held up a hand: thanks but no thanks. He needed to keep his wits about him this afternoon.

'So, Pip tells me you're a professor,' Charlie said, doing the right thing and trying to pour oil on troubled waters.

'These days I work as a consultant to the petroleum industry. I'm part of a team helping to develop new laser Raman techniques to assess the maturity of organic matter in petroleum basins. I have a particular interest in carboniferous shale gas plays.'

'That sounds interesting,' Charlie said.

'Deborah and I are going to New York next month for a conference of the International Subcommission on Cretaceous Stratigraphy. We're staying at the Plaza on Central Park. Quite looking forward it.'

'Get in,' Charlie said, and felt himself sweat. I have to get out of here. He quickly checked his Nokia. No calls yet.

Jonathan leaned in, bringing Charlie into his confidence. 'There's a position for a junior researcher coming up at Kingston University soon. I am hoping Philippa will apply. She's bright enough if she's willing to apply herself.'

He heard Pippa and her mother whispering in the kitchen. A truce had been agreed, he hoped. Deborah reappeared with two plates. Pippa followed her in, looking hunched and pale. '*Bon appétit*,' Deborah said and raised her glass. They started eating. Pippa, he noticed, just had some courgettes and a few carrots, which she was pushing around her plate as if they were markers on a tactics board.

'What have you two been talking about?' she said.

'I was just telling Charlie, there's an opening for a researcher coming up at Kingston. I was hoping you'd apply. I'll make sure you have the inside running.'

'I've got a job.'

192

'Not much of one, though, is it?'

'I think it's a great job,' Charlie said. 'We don't have enough good teachers.'

'But there's no money in it, is there darling?' Jonathan said. 'This could lead to much bigger and better things. No matter what people say, private enterprise is where the money is. God knows you could do with it, that waster you were with left you with practically nothing.'

'Did she tell you about him?' Deborah said to Charlie.

'Can we talk about something else?' Pippa said.

'We never liked him. Absolutely covered in tattoos.' She leaned towards Charlie so that she could confide in him. 'He's in prison now.' She dissected a piece of cod. 'Don't know what she's thinking half the time. Do we, darling?'

Charlie watched Pippa's face. Been to a lot of murders, he thought, never actually seen one happen in front of me. But there's always a first time.

There was a long silence and then Jonathan leaned across the table with the Montrachet. 'Who'd like some more wine?'

They drove back along the Fulham Road. Pippa didn't speak until they were almost at the Victoria and Albert. She sat curled up in the seat, half turned away from him, a tight ball of rage. 'Did you see him try and hug me?' she said.

'Your old man?'

'I can't stand him touching me,' she said, and that threw Charlie off balance, after the stick she'd just copped from her mother.

'Is it always like that?'

She shrugged but didn't say anything. Charlie imagined the Brompton Road lined with a hundred thousand Bens, and every one of them was waving a red flag.

'Can we go and get a drink?' Pippa said.

Just then he felt the Nokia vibrate in his jacket pocket. He pulled over to take the call.

'Who was that?' she said, when he hung up.

'My boss. The red flare's gone up over that missing girl.'

'Nothing to do with you though, is it?'

'I have to go in to work for a couple of hours.'

'Fuck me, Charlie.'

'Haven't got time,' he said, trying to make a joke of it, but none of his humour seemed to be hitting the mark this afternoon.

'Just drop me home,' she said.

She didn't say another word on the way to her flat in Walthamstow, didn't even look back and wave after she got out.

Well, that was fun.

CHAPTER TWENTY-FOUR

As he drove into Essex Road, Charlie saw that he wasn't the only one called in to work on a Sunday. Opposite the entrance to the nick were a few dozen press and TV vans, a handful of journalists on the steps, rehearsing their updates. Charlie couldn't help but wonder why Mariatu Okpotu hadn't received quite the same amount of attention. The idea of a serial offender on the loose always got the newsroom bosses hot to trot.

The DCI was already in the Incident Room, sitting on the corner of the desk with his jacket off, sleeves rolled up, almost looking like a real copper. Charlie felt a rush as he walked in, what he'd been waiting for, this was their chance. There were HOLMES people at all the terminals, the phones were ringing, and the DI from the rostered incident team, Brady, had her whole intel team there.

He recognised the girl on the whiteboard, though he hadn't taken much notice of her the first time they met. The close-up had come from a family portrait, they would have to pixelate the rest of the family when they gave this to the media. Brooklyn Williams was fourteen going on eighteen, scowling at the camera like she'd just been booked for possession, and way too much make-up.

Brady had scrawled a rough timeline on the board. She'd been missing for twenty-four hours. Statistics said they'd better find her soon if they wanted a happy ending.

'Charlie,' the DCI said. Charlie nodded at Brady. I wonder

if she'll be pissed off if FONC takes this one away from her. I would be.

'All right then?' Charlie said.

'Where have you been?' the DCI said, looking him up and down.

'I was at lunch.'

'At Buckingham Palace, by the look of you,' he said, and handed him a sheaf of witness statements, the Williamses' version of events.

'When was she last seen?'

'The parents went to a barbecue on Saturday about twelve,' Brady said. 'They left Brooklyn at home in charge of her two younger siblings, they got home at about five o'clock and she was gone.'

'When did she go out?'

'The boy . . . what's his name?' She pulled out her notebook.

'Reuben,' Charlie said.

'Reuben. He said it was about four o'clock. He thought she got in a car down the bottom of the street.'

'What sort of car?' Charlie said, and thought about the rusted heap of crap he'd seen sitting on blocks in Norton's shed.

'He doesn't know. He didn't actually see the car, he said he just heard one driving off soon after she went out.'

'Where did she say she was going?'

'Just out.'

'But she was supposed to be in charge of them.'

'That's what he said.'

'What about her phone?'

She picked up a typewritten sheet off her desk. 'She was talking to one of her schoolmates for almost two hours, as schoolgirls do. The call finished . . .' She checked the printout. 'The call finished at 15.53. That was it. One further call, from her father's phone, just after they got home, at 17.11.'

'She didn't pick up?'

'She didn't have it with her. It was upstairs in her bedroom.'

'How many fourteen-year-old girls would go anywhere, even to the loo, without their phone? Doesn't happen.'

'Struck me as a bit strange, too.'

'Strange? It's impossible.'

'We're running intel on her phone, all her social media, nothing so far to explain why she would leave the house without any explanation.'

'Fourteen-year-old girls don't talk to their little brothers,' the DCI said.

'But they do talk to their friends,' Charlie said. 'They break a nail, it's all over Twitter. She has to have been meeting a friend, and if she was meeting a bloke, she'll have bragged about it to her little circle.'

Brady shrugged.

'When did the Williamses report this?'

'As soon as they got home,' Brady said. 'Normally, the stations wait twenty-four hours on something like this, but this was elevated to a Level 1 Missing Person pretty much straight away.'

'Because of the murder,' Charlie said.

'Yeah, because of the murder.'

'There has to be some way we can trace her. What about money? Has she got her old man's credit card?'

'Apparently not. He says there's nothing gone missing.'

'Is she definitely gone? What about the house? Have they checked the garden shed, looked under the bed. I mean, proper.'

'Of course they have. Come on, Charlie. Besides, her brother saw her go out.'

The DCI looked at his watch, seemed to be making up his mind. 'I've got to go downstairs, talk to the gentlemen of the press. We're putting a live-to-air appeal on this evening's news.'

'Why am I here, sir?'

'Because, Charlie, I'm thinking of handing this case over to you. I've talked to Brady here, and she agrees you're better placed to expedite things.'

'You hit the ground running,' Brady said. 'You already know the Williamses and you know our prime suspect.'

'It may have nothing to do with him. Teenagers go missing every day. Twenty thousand last year just in London. Just because she lives close to the girl that got murdered doesn't make it the same case. It may not even be an MIT job.'

'But it is, Charlie. And you know why.'

'We can't let the media run our cases.'

'Don't be naïve. I'm putting you in charge of this. Go and find Norton, bring him in here for questioning.'

'Don't we still have him under surveillance?'

'If we did, do you think we'd be here now? Surveillance costs money, Charlie, I had to pull the team off after we let him go.'

'Hasn't anyone interviewed him?'

'We can't find him,' Brady said.

'You are joking.'

'Don't joke about things like that,' the DCI said. He stood up and put his jacket on, ready to head downstairs.

'Are you making this a category A inquiry, sir?'

The DCI smoothed down his hair, straightened his tie, ready for the cameras. This was his classic swan manoeuvre, Charlie thought, unruffled on the surface, paddling like fuck out of sight. Once he called in the cavalry – the search teams and the helicopters and the divers – it was an open cheque. Still, he was the one had to balance the books at the end of the day. If Brooklyn was in mortal danger and he didn't do it, the press would eat him alive; if she'd gone to Brighton with her boyfriend, the commissioner would call him in for a Please Explain, and there goes his career. The Tory government was already squeezing their budget.

All that bollocks about saving money on Brexit. They had the best forensics in the world at Lambeth, they were getting privatised, they were closing nicks all over London. If people knew the real cost ratio they put on human life, would they still vote for the bastards?

'Sir?'

'Charlie, I'll make that call first thing in the morning. Meantime, eliminate Norton from this inquiry.'

'If it isn't him?'

'Then your lot will get their time off when this is sorted.'

The DCI turned towards the door.

'Sir.'

'What, Charlie?'

'It's not that I don't want the case, I do, but . . . this isn't even Norton's MO. She's fourteen.'

'The murdered girl was only eleven.'

'But Brooklyn looks like twenty. Norton likes them young.'

'Charlie, that's your headache now,' he said and walked out.

Brady shrugged. 'I'll bring you up to speed,' she said.

Charlie had the on-duty sergeant, Barlow, start calling his team, told Parm and Joe to turn off *Inspector Morse* and refreeze their TV dinners and get themselves in to the nick, the rest of them to be in the IR at seven in the morning latest. Meanwhile, he grabbed a decision log and called down for a squad of uniforms to come with him to find Norton.

As he rode down in the lift he went through the possible scenarios in his head: one, it had nothing to do with their inquiry, and he was being dragged into something that should have gone to DI Brady's team; or two, somehow the two cases were linked and the DCI's gut instinct was right, for once.

Scenario two just didn't make sense. Norton was only interested in pre-pubescent girls and Brooklyn was everything but. What troubled him was the notion of a teenager without a mobile phone that hadn't been surgically amputated from her right hand. No way would a girl that age go anywhere without access to social media.

And that led him to the third scenario, that the Okpotu and Williams cases were linked but Norton wasn't the common denominator. There was a third person lurking, that they had missed, and they had followed Mariatu along the disused railway line and been in the car that picked Brooklyn up from her street yesterday afternoon.

It was dark when he got down to the car park. There were four uniforms in stab vests waiting for him with their sergeant, all likely lads eager to be at it. He had a quick word with their sergeant and they blue-lighted their way through the gates.

On the way, Charlie's Nokia went off in its cradle. It was Barlow, back at the nick. 'Guv, are you on the way to Norton's house?'

'Yeah, is there a problem?'

'You could say that. We've just had a call from the inspector at Crouch End. Someone's torched Norton's workshop. They're having a bit of a street party down there.'

'Have the emergency services been called?'

'The fire brigade and the TSG are in attendance.'

'Oh brilliant,' Charlie said and hung up.

CHAPTER TWENTY-FIVE

The street reeked of smoke, it was hard to breathe, and the heat coming off the fire was intense. There were four fire units trying to get hold of the blaze. He saw two yellow-helmeted firefighters retreating from the backdraught, the fire had spread to the house behind the shed, there were flames belching out of a ground-floor window. He heard a crack as the shed roof caved in: that's my evidence in there, Charlie thought.

There were still people at both ends of the street, not just casual bystanders; he saw a squad of TSG, visors down, heard the crack of their batons on their glass riot shields as they pushed people back. It looked hellish in the flashing strobe of the emergency vehicles. Oh, they'd had a proper laugh, this lot. Hackney all over again, if they weren't careful.

The street was half flooded, there were fire hoses snaking all over the road. He saw Mansell standing by one of the patrol cars, his mobile glued to his ear. He must have seen Charlie but didn't seem in any hurry to end the call; he could have been talking to the commissioner or perhaps he was just telling his wife he was going to be late home.

He hung up abruptly and dropped the phone into his coat pocket. 'Right cock-up, this,' he said.

'What happened?'

'I'd just started my shift when we got a call that there was a mob down here, they were trying to beat that bloke Norton's gate down. I sent some squad cars down here, but it was already getting out of hand, my lads had people throwing half-bricks and all sorts at them, and then someone set light to the yard. Molotov cocktails, my fellas reckon. That's when I called in the TSG.'

'What set this off?'

'They've all heard about the girl that's gone missing. Apparently this was all organised on Facebook. That Mark Zuckerberg needs his arse kicked.'

Charlie saw someone coming towards him out of the corner of his eye. He didn't recognise him at first, not in the dark; he wore a brown leather jacket over his pyjamas, and his hair hung in strips down one side of his face like peeling wallpaper.

'Detective, detective,' he kept repeating.

'Sir, can you stand back behind the cordon, please sir.'

'No, I won't stand back,' he shouted, and actually stamped his foot. 'I live here!'

His wife ran up behind him, her pink satin slippers speckled with mud.

'This is your fault, detective, you should have provided protection for us.'

'Where is he?' Charlie said.

'We don't know where he is,' Mrs Bahremi said over her husband's shoulder, 'we threw him out. We don't want people like that on our property.'

'You threw him out. When?'

'When he came back from the police station, we told him, we told him he had to go.'

'When did he leave?'

'He left last night,' Mr Bahremi said. 'He came and asked us for his rent money back, he threatened us, why should we give it back to him? We rented him the property in good faith.'

'My husband was frightened,' Mrs Bahremi said. 'We had to give it to him.'

'I wasn't frightened, I was being fair. I was protecting you!'

'What time last night did he leave?'

'I don't know, we were watching television. Eight o'clock perhaps.'

'Was he driving that motor car, the one he had on the blocks?'

'I don't know. Perhaps. No. I don't know.'

'Did he say where he was going?'

'We didn't care where he was going, why do we care about such things, what are you going to do about all this? We are ruined!'

'You didn't tell the insurance company you had sub-let, did you?'

'That has nothing to do with it! This is all because you didn't do your job. Why didn't you arrest him after what he did to that little girl? I am going to sue, yes that is what I am going to do, I am going to sue you and the Metropolitan Police!'

Charlie turned back to the fire. It looked like they finally had it under control; what he was worried about now was his evidence, all those big burly firemen in boots trampling all over his forensics.

'That bastard fixed the car,' he said aloud, 'he came back here and fixed the car, put the wheels back on and drove it away, he planned to do that all along.' He had the horrible feeling that he'd been outsmarted, that the whole bad hygiene thing was a disguise, to put them off the scent, literally. That scrote had put one over on him.

Charlie turned his back on the Bahremis, found the crew commander, he was standing by one of the units conferring with two of his firefighters. He looked up when Charlie came over. Charlie flashed his warrant badge.

He held up his hand, listened to the tinny chatter on his radio, gave a couple of short commands and then looked back at Charlie. 'Problem?'

'Any bodies in there?' Charlie said.

'Were you expecting some?'

'Possibly.'

'No, my guys say it's all clear. We stopped it spreading to the top storey of the house, but the shed is pretty much burned out, not much left for your CS boys to pick over. The fire had a hold before we arrived.'

Charlie could see as much for himself. The workshed had been reduced to a black sludge with a few charred and smoking timbers.

His Nokia rang.

'Sir.'

'This is just what I was hoping to avoid,' the DCI said, made it sound as if he held Charlie personally responsible.

'No sign of the girl,' Charlie said. 'That's good news.'

'A PR disaster is never good news. Where's Norton?'

'It looks like he got away in that old motor he had in the shed.'

'Shouldn't be hard to find, then.'

'Except the car didn't have plates. He's not that stupid. I'm starting to think he's as stupid as a fox.'

'Just find him, Charlie.'

'His landlord said he came to see them four hours after the girl went missing.'

'Maybe he's got her in the boot, maybe he did for her before he left. There's still a chance she's alive. I'm making Norton our prime suspect on this. Just find him,' he repeated, and hung up.

Charlie had only spoken to them the week before, but he barely recognised the Williams family. Brooklyn's father looked as if he had been hollowed out with a blunt spoon; he sat on the leather sofa next to his wife, hunched over, barely speaking. His wife was animated with anger and fear; she wouldn't stop talking, asking him question after question and barely waiting for the answers. Have you arrested that creep who killed the little girl? Have you searched his house? Why is this taking so long? Why do we have to answer more questions, we told the other detectives everything we know?

Why haven't you found our little girl?

Reuben and Lucee sat at the other end, the little girl eerily placid, Reuben staring at him with the same affected street cool he remembered from last time.

Charlie told her about the fire, and that Norton was missing, but that he was not their only suspect. No, the fire services found no bodies in the house. No, we did not have Mr Norton under surveillance, we can't put a twenty-four-hour watch on every sex offender in London.

'Why are you here?' Mrs Williams said. 'Why aren't you out looking for my Brooklyn?'

'Mrs Williams, my superiors have given this investigation the highest priority. That is why I am here. I need to go through your statements again, to make sure I am absolutely clear what happened yesterday afternoon.'

'We've told you everything we know,' Mr Williams said, still staring at the carpet.

'I have to ask you this. Are you sure she doesn't have a boyfriend? Could she have been seeing someone you might not have known about?'

'She's only fourteen years old, Inspector,' Mr Williams said.

Charlie looked at Mrs Williams. 'Well, nothing serious,' she said. She copped a look. Clearly, Brooklyn's father knew nothing about this.

'She was seeing someone or she wasn't?' Charlie said.

'Well, she was always talking about boys, like girls that age do. But I don't think she'd . . . you know.'

Charlie waited.

'They were just teenage crushes. I don't think she'd actually done anything about it.'

'You would know better than us, wouldn't you?' Mr Williams said to him. 'You've got her phone and her iPad. Have you talked to her friends?'

'I'll be sending a team to the school tomorrow to talk to her friends.'

'This is not like her,' Mrs Williams said. 'She would never just go off without telling us.'

205

Charlie nodded sympathetically and thought, that's not my experience of teenagers. But let's not compound the anguish.

He turned to Reuben, who was sporting some faux silver bling thick as an anchor chain, and a hoodie with a skull motif. 'Reuben, you told Inspector Brady that she left the house suddenly, without saying anything.'

A nod.

'No idea where she went?'

A shrug.

'You don't seem very upset.'

'It's peak but I'm not going to get moist. Manz had beef with her every day.'

'Can you talk English, son?' Mr Williams said. His wife nudged him. Not now, the look said, let's not do this now.

'I'll have one of my team come to see you in the morning, so they can keep you up to date with the investigation,' Charlie said. 'Meanwhile, you have my number. You can call me any time.'

'Just find this Norton,' Mr Williams said. 'We want our daughter back.'

His voice broke and his shoulders started to shake. Mrs Williams put her arms around him, then she looked up at Charlie. I told you this would happen, her eyes said. What if you're too late?

He wasn't expecting any of his DCs before first thing in the morning, but when he got back to the nick he found Lovejoy was already there, sitting at her desk, reading the intel reports, a printout of the Williamses' witness statements dumped on her keyboard. Almost nine at night and she looked bright and perky, as if she'd just come back from a fortnight in Bora Bora.

'Haven't you got a life?' Charlie said.

'Not really, guv. Sad, isn't it? You reek of smoke. Thought you'd given up.'

'The locals went and torched Norton's shed, innit? Don't you watch the news? What are you doing here, you didn't have to come till the morning.'

'Wanted to get a head start. This doesn't make sense to me.'

'What doesn't, Lovejoy?'

'Spends all day on Snapchat and on the phone to her girl-friend and not once does she say anything about going out. Teenage girls don't do that, they tell each other everything.'

'Perhaps this was a secret.'

'I don't buy it. There's something off about this.'

Charlie pulled up a chair and slumped into it. 'Got any theories?'

'Not yet. What about you, guv?'

'I think FONC has run the panic flag up the pole too soon. I'm not sure these two cases are connected.'

'Once people start setting fire to sheds in North London, it puts a bit of pressure on.'

'We cannot let the hoi-polloi mess with our judgement, Lovejoy. That way lies madness. And that bloody Reuben, he's fair giving me the yips. Thirteen years old and he's carrying on like he's Soulja Boy. And there's something else, can't put my finger on it. But he's not telling us the gospel.'

'You don't think it's Norton?'

'Mariatu, yes, I'm bloody sure of it. But not Brooklyn Williams. Not the right age, not the right look, not his MO. It's a waste of our time. I'll bet you London to a brick she's a run-away. My guess, she's going to show up on Instagram tomorrow with a selfie of her and some twenty-five-year-old standing in front of the London Eye.'

'So why did Norton take off?'

'I don't know. Maybe he's just shitting himself because he thinks we're getting close on the Mariatu case. Maybe he knew the locals would go vigilante on him. We won't know until we find him.'

Lovejoy had on a navy-blue trouser suit, all business as

usual, her streaked ash-blonde hair perfect, even this time of the day. It was only the little crow's feet at the corner of her eyes that betrayed how tired she was, how many hours she must have worked in CID to get this gig so fast. She perched herself on the edge of the desk, holding her decision log like it was the Holy Bible. Her eagerness inspired him.

'So, what's the plan, guv?'

'We do what the DCI tells us to do. Tomorrow first thing we'll have sniffer dogs, divers, helicopters, all out looking for her. You know how much a helicopter costs? It's two grand just to whizz the propeller around a couple of times. God knows how many volunteers will show up. We're checking the wetlands, the reservoirs, all God's little acre.'

'What about his car?'

'You saw that heap of crap he had on the blocks; it was unregistered, which means he must have stolen plates for it. Parm's checking it now.'

'But you don't think she was abducted?'

'No, I don't. But I'm covering my bets all the same. Parm's looking at all the local cab drivers, in case she flagged one down last night. She's checking if any of the local drivers have criminal records we should be aware of. We'll check all the CCTV from the local tube stations and buses – she can't have vanished into thin air.'

'I still think it's Norton,' Lovejoy said.

On cue, Parm came over, holding a sheaf of printouts, threw them on the desk. 'Set of plates stolen yesterday morning from outside a house two streets from where Norton lived. I've got some pings on the ANPR, both on the A11. The vehicle is headed north, towards Cambridge.'

'Good work, Parm.'

'We've got him,' Lovejoy said.

'We can't be sure, but it's as good a lead as we've got.'

'But why Cambridge?'

Charlie pulled up Norton's file on the screen. 'His father

lives out in the wilds of Suffolk. He's headed back to hearth and home.'

'Do we pay him a visit?'

'Not tonight. I'll call the local Bill and they can do it. If that's where he is, we'll talk to him in the morning.'

'What if you're wrong, guv?'

'About Norton?'

'He might still have her. She could be in imminent danger.'

'We'll soon find out. I won't rest until we find him, Lovejoy, but we have to keep our minds open to all possibilities, know what I mean? Now why don't you go home and get some sleep. It's going to be a very long day tomorrow.'

'What about you, guv?'

'I've got a camp bed in the office. I'll use that.'

'I only live in Camden. My dad's got a big bowl of his ham and pea soup and some crusty bread waiting for me when I get home. You're welcome to some. You can kip at our place and we can still be back here for an early start.'

Charlie didn't know if he should be seen leaving late at night with one of his team. How would that look?

'Bloody love ham and pea soup, me.'

'Settled then,' she said.

He wondered for a minute if Lovejoy had an ulterior motive. No, he was flattering himself, wasn't he? Besides, she batted for the other team.

As they left, he took one guilty look back at the HOLMES team still at their desks, still hard at it. He reminded himself there were still staffers in the POD van down the high street where Mariatu disappeared, coppers all over Suffolk out looking for their prime suspect. They hadn't given up.

'Come on, guv,' Lovejoy said. 'You need some rest.'

He followed her out.

CHAPTER TWENTY-SIX

Lovejoy's dad lived in a three-bedroom end-of-terrace Victorian house in Belsize Park, not far from the heath and the Royal Free. It wasn't what he had been expecting. It all looked very neat from the outside, in a moneyed but offbeat area; he expected to bump into Helena Bonham-Carter or Morrissey as he got out of her car.

'This must have cost,' Charlie said.

'You thought I grew up on an estate, didn't you?'

'Course not,' Charlie said, but that was what he had thought.

'Dad used to be in a band, back in the day.' She told him the name of the band and a couple of singles they'd had, but he'd never heard of them, they were before his time. 'The rest of them all died of sex and drugs and rock 'n' roll.'

'I didn't know it was an actual medical condition.'

'You don't get out enough.'

The outside of the house was A-list; once they were inside there was another shock. It looked like one of those antique stores he'd been in in Paris or Brussels, everything just piled up everywhere, a giant Jenga game of newspapers, paperback books, plastic bags of old clothes and vinyl LPs. There was an old dishwasher rusting in the hallway and a television, possibly black-and-white, propping open the door to the living room.

'Nice doorstop,' Charlie said. 'It could trend.'

A spaniel came bounding out and leaped at Lovejoy, it had a stuffed teddy bear in its mouth. It gave Charlie the same treatment, ran around the hallway three or four times, then ran back into the living room.

'Recognise him?'

'Is that him?' Charlie said. 'Looks like a different dog.'

'Doesn't take much.' He followed her inside. There was a grey-haired man in a black t-shirt sitting on a red leather arm-chair in front of a plasma television, surrounded by the same clutter that Charlie had seen in the hallway. There was a pet bed in front of the gas fire, with a blanket, a few soft toys and a pillow that said: RESERVED.

'This is my dad,' Lovejoy said. 'Dad, this is my boss, Inspector George.'

'Charlie.' He held out his hand.

Mr Lovejoy peered up at him through a pair of magenta-tinted glasses. He had on distressed jeans and a pair of pink slippers. He could have been Keith Richards, without the rings and the headband.

'You remember. He's the one who gave me Charlie.'

'He's not come to take him back, has he? Only I took him to the vet and he said he hadn't been looked after. He had worms and his anal glands needed squeezing. Not cheap getting anal glands squeezed.'

'I wouldn't do it for quids,' Charlie said, but no one laughed.

'The thing with spaniels,' Mr Lovejoy said, 'is they need their anal glands squeezed every six weeks or there's a build-up. Nasty.'

'Can't imagine.'

'And he was starved, he was. You weren't feeding him.'

'Charlie didn't do it, Dad.'

'Well someone did it to him. He didn't do it to himself. Vet said he had cracked ribs. Like someone had kicked him.' He gave Charlie a wild stare. 'Can't understand how someone could be cruel to an animal – heartless, that is.'

Charlie the spaniel was still running in circles with the soft toy in its mouth. 'What did you give him to fatten him up,' Charlie said. 'Cocaine?'

'He's pleased to see you.'

'He's trying to shag my leg.'

'He wants some more of your biscuits.'

'Looks like he wants more than that. Get off, you dirty bugger.' Charlie bent down to pull him off and the dog leaped at him, he had to catch him.

'He does like you,' Lovejoy said.

'Dogs can be very forgiving,' her father said.

'Is that his bed?' Charlie said.

'That's for the day. He sleeps on Dad's bed at night.'

'Is he a cop?'

'Yes, Dad. I told you, I work with him. He's my guv'nor.'

'You haven't told him about, you know?'

'I don't think he's worried about your stash, Dad. He's got more important things to worry about.'

'Just don't give any to the dog,' Charlie said. 'I don't want him to grow up doing drugs.'

Charlie and Lovejoy sat in the kitchen, eating soup. Charlie checked the date of one of the yellowed newspapers in the pile beside him: 1995.

'I spoke to one of his shrinks this one time. He said that people like Dad feel empty inside so they try to fill up their lives with things.'

'He has a very full life.'

'No, it's sad, Charlie. I try to make light of it, too, but I know how it looks. And you're right, it's mad. Every day when I go to work I take out four plastic bin liners of rubbish. I swear when I get home he's managed to smuggle them back in again. When nothing is important, everything is important, see.'

'The shrinks can't help him?'

'You have, a bit.'

'Me? You told him about the mess in my office, so he didn't feel so bad?'

'No, Charlie. The dog.'

'How do you mean like?'

'I was really worried about him when Archie died.'

'Who's Archie?'

'His old black Lab. He was ancient, seventeen or something when he died. He was heartbroken, swore he'd never get another one. So Charlie was a godsend. I knew he couldn't resist. I told him he was just helping out for a couple of days. Been good for him, gets him out of the house taking Charlie for walks, otherwise he just sits there playing on his iPad and listening to vinyl.'

'Well, that's good then, innit? Taking him to the vet would have cost a fortune, mind.'

'He's not short of a quid.'

'From the band?'

'God, no. Their manager stole half of it, the rest went on drugs. No, he went into IT after he gave up music. Very clever man, my old dad. Doesn't look it, I know. He made this program they use for scans, don't ask me what it's for, but he flogged it to the NHS for seven figures. It will keep Charlie in worming tablets for the rest of his natural. Did the owner ever come looking for him?'

'No, not seen anyone,' Charlie said.

'Good. Both got a clear conscience then.'

'My conscience is always clear.'

'He's a good dog, that one,' Lovejoy said. 'Miracle really, the way he'd been treated.'

'Like people, innit? You can make a good dog bad, but you can never make a bad dog good. This soup is the proper business. Did you make it?'

'I make a gallon at a time, so Dad's always got something when I'm working late, which is pretty much most of the time. Otherwise he'd live on toast and tea.'

'When did you move in?'

'After my last relationship broke up last year. I wanted company and he needed someone to look out for him. He gets sort of weird at times and he's been a bit lost, ever since Mum left.'

'He can't be that old.'

'It's not his age. Partly it's the drugs and also, well, you know, he was a drummer, and you know what they say about drummers.'

'No, what do they say?'

'Like the old joke: "How do you tell if the stage is level? The drummer is drooling from both sides of his mouth".'

Charlie laughed. 'You must have had quite a life when you were a kid.'

'No, I had a very normal life. When I came along his drumming days were well over.' She went to the stove and refilled the bowls. Charlie tore off another piece of bread. 'Can I ask you something, guv?'

'That depends, Lovejoy. Ask me, and I'll decide whether I want to answer.'

'Do you ever get used to looking at dead bodies?'

'Some of them, yeah, to be honest, it's just evidence. But kids, no I don't ever yawn and say next. I hope to God you never will either, if that's any help.'

'What does bother you, then, about the job?'

'Well Lovejoy, I'll tell you, when I was a little kid I used to lie awake at night in winter worrying about all the dogs that had been left out in the back yard in the rain. These days I still worry, I worry about all the kids that are out there, who I'll never be able to save.'

'How do you mean?'

'Your teacher ever read you that story, "Little Red Riding Hood"?'

She nodded.

'My teacher did. I loved that story. One day I asked her, is there such a thing as the big bad wolf? And she said, well yes, I suppose there is, Charlie. And I said, do they get in disguise then, so no one knows they're really a wolf? Is that how they do it? And she said, yes Charlie, they do. So I said, so how do you know if someone's a wolf or a good person? Know what she

214

said? She said, you'll have to ask your mum. But I couldn't ask her because she didn't know. I knew she didn't, because she'd married a monster herself.'

'So why was it your favourite story?'

'I liked the ending.'

'The ending?'

'The woodcutter doesn't try and rehabilitate the fucking wolf. He doesn't give him twenty years and then parole him. Know what he does? He chops the bastard up. That to me was a happy ending when I was a kid.'

The spaniel trotted in, holding a chunk of bread. 'Oh God, Dad's fallen asleep,' Lovejoy said. She got up. 'Charlie,' she said to the dog, 'give me the bread.'

He wasn't about to do that, having waited patiently for its original owner to doze off and give him his opportunity. He squeezed between two mountains of *Guardian*s and *Daily Mirror*s to eat it in peace.

Charlie could hear Lovejoy's dad snoring in the other room.

'Time for bed,' he said.

'The spare room's through there,' Lovejoy said, pointing to a door. Charlie imagined a mattress balanced on top of five feet of second-hand furniture, but what the hell. Anything was better than that camp bed. Better get some sleep.

Big day tomorrow.

CHAPTER TWENTY-SEVEN

'Nice,' Charlie said as they drove through the double gates.

The gravelled driveway was bordered by a white post-and-rail fence; it led to a wide sweep of lawn dotted with copper beech and ash trees. There was a pond, with ducks. Charlie liked ducks. In another life, one where he wasn't born in Walthamstow, he could have lived here.

Blaxland House was a faux Tudor manor with a clay-tiled roof and lattice windows, straight out of *Horse and Hound*. The blue and yellow patrol car parked outside spoiled the effect.

Charlie and Lovejoy showed their warrant cards to the uniform at the door and went in. There were two plainclothes CID in the sitting room, talking to an elderly man who Charlie took to be Norton's father.

'Here's Inspector Morse now,' he heard one of the CID say to his partner, then they came over all smiles and shook his hand. They didn't know he'd heard but he let them have that one. They were, after all, from Ipswich.

'You've caused quite a stir up here,' one of them said. 'Your DCI made it sound like we have Hannibal Lecter on the loose.'

'It may not be quite that bad. Have you found him?'

'He's not here, but he has been, according to the old boy.'

'When?'

'Yesterday morning. He didn't stay. Didn't tell Mr Norton where he was headed, and apparently he didn't ask. We've organised a search, but there's nothing to say he's still around here.'

'Thanks.'

'Anything to help you fellas out,' he said, a flicker of the eyebrows at his offsider, showboating.

'Mind if we have a word?' Charlie said, and nodded at the grey-haired gentleman who was watching them with an expression of *noblesse oblige* from the Chesterfield next to the inglenook fireplace.

'Knock yourselves out,' the detective said. Charlie couldn't remember the CID man's name even five seconds after he had introduced himself, and didn't care to.

He and Lovejoy went over and Charlie told him who they were and why they were there, observing the formalities, which he thought he'd appreciate. They sat.

Norton studied them down the length of his nose. He was one of those men who, even in their eighties, looked as though they wouldn't mind a fight. His thick silver hair was parted with military precision. He had large hands, a farmer's hands, though now they were stained with liver spots and the knuckles were distorted by arthritis. He wore a grey cardigan and a spotted bow tie.

'These gentlemen said you are looking for my son,' he said.

'We believe he may be able to assist us with our enquiries.'

'I'm sure he could assist you with any number of enquiries. What is it you think he has done?'

'At this stage your son is just a person of interest.'

'Into what, may I ask?'

'Into the disappearance of a teenage girl.'

He raised an eyebrow. 'Uncharted territory for him. You are familiar, of course, with his criminal record? I cannot tell you the degree of shame he has brought to our family.'

'I can't imagine,' Charlie said.

'You want to know where he is. As I have told your colleagues, he showed up here yesterday, wanting to know if he could stay here, gave me this sob story about having nowhere else to go. Whose fault is that? Everything anyone ever gave him he just pissed in their hand.'

'What did you tell him?'

'I said I keep some pigs behind the barn and he was welcome to get in the sty with them, but if that was not to his liking, there was nothing else I could do for him.'

'I see.'

'Your colleague looks shocked,' he said, looking at Lovejoy.

'Not that shocked. We have met Timothy.'

Mr Norton grimaced, as if he had bitten down on something foul. 'It gave me no pleasure to do it. But I won't have him in my house, not any more. I have fulfilled my obligations as a father, and more.'

'How long since you'd seen him?' Lovejoy asked.

A shake of the head. 'No idea. Ten years. Perhaps more. He was in prison for some of that, as you know. I didn't visit.'

'How did he get here?'

'He was in a car. It looked like he'd got it from a scrapyard.'

'How did he react when you told him he couldn't stay here?'

'The usual way. He screamed abuse at me and said he would stab me in the throat. It's not the first time he has threatened me, of course. I told him to do it or to fuck orf.'

'What did he do?'

'He fucked orf.'

'In the car.'

'Eventually. It was slow to start. I thought we might have to call the RAC.'

'Do you know where he is likely to have gone?' Lovejoy said.

A shake of the head.

'He gave you no indication?'

'None. I didn't ask. I don't know where he's gone, and I care even less. He ruined my life, that little bastard. I spent more time and money on him than all my other children combined and what do I have to show for it?'

'Have you any idea where he might be?' Charlie asked him.

'He told us he had no family left,' Lovejoy said.

'Is that what he said? I suppose, in a way, it's true. He

218

doesn't. His brothers wouldn't give him the time of day. They're all family men, got good jobs. I put them all through university: one of them works for Rolls-Royce, another one's a paediatrician. One asks oneself where one went wrong. I didn't treat any of them any differently to how I treated Timothy. So why did he turn out like he did?'

Not going to get anywhere here, Charlie thought. He was about to leave.

'What did he tell you people?'

'Sir?'

'What did he say, about me? You can be honest, Inspector. You look like a forthright chap.'

'He said you abused him.'

'Did he now? Well, I suppose he would say that. I was strict, I admit. Of course, for years I went over and over it, in my head. It's natural, I suppose. Perhaps I was tougher on him than the other boys. But then my other sons weren't like him.'

'In what way?'

'For one thing they weren't cruel.'

'Cruel?'

'I found him once in the garden, just standing there. There was a bird's nest lying at his feet. He had this most curious look on his face. There were these dead fledglings at his feet, in the grass. I said, what have you done? He just looked at me. Do you know what he'd done? He'd brought down the nest and he'd stamped on them all, in his boots, all the chicks. The mother bird was flying around and around the garden, making this terrible plaintive cry. I kept saying to him, why, Timothy, why.'

'How old was he?'

'He was ten, Inspector. Ten years old.'

'Did he ever tell you why he did it?' Lovejoy asked him.

'He said he wanted to know what it felt like.' He paused to clear his throat. 'Some days I don't even think about him and those are the good days.'

'Can I ask where Mrs Norton is?' Charlie said.

219

'She died a few years ago, cancer. I still say he was to blame, everything he put her through. He was expelled from three different private schools. I gave him a job in my factory and the lazy little sod upset the rest of my workers; they were going to walk out if I didn't sack him. He was always doing something, always killing things, animals and small birds. Sick little bastard. Do you know what I think, Inspector? I think some people are just born evil.'

'Have you any idea, any idea at all, where we might find him? Would he have gone to any of his brothers for help?'

'I told you, they haven't spoken to him since they were children. They all hate him.' He sighed, thought about it. 'He liked camping, sleeping rough. He particularly liked caves, tunnels. I don't know why. Not that you'll find many caves around here, I'm afraid. But that's all I can think of, Inspector.'

One of the CID came into the sitting room. He nodded to Charlie and he followed him back outside. 'Well, we've found your lad for you,' he said.

'Nice one, where is he?'

He lowered his voice, though Charlie doubted that Mr Norton could hear them out here. 'He's hanging from a tree not two miles away.' He scribbled something in his notebook. 'That's the nearest crossroads, put that in your GPS, it will take you there. They've put up a cordon, the pathologist is on his way from Ipswich.'

'How did they find him?'

'I'd like to say it was fancy police work, but it was a bloke out walking his dog.'

Charlie nodded. 'Them and joggers,' he said. 'They have all the fun.'

Charlie liked being out in the country, he wished he could stay longer. They drove along narrow country lanes, past hedgerows and muddy footpaths with stiles, brown bare fields full of shivering wet sheep. Lovejoy switched on the wipers as they drove through a sun shower. This is the life, he thought. Think I'll ask for a transfer to Major Incident Team, Little Offingham.

They could make out the flashing blue lights from a quarter of a mile away through the drizzle. They turned down a no-through lane; there was a copse of skeletal trees just on the rise, he could see the uniforms in their high-viz jackets searching the grass in there. Lovejoy pulled up behind a patrol car and they got out.

A freezing March day, Charlie was glad of his Stone Island jacket. There was yellow tape strung through the trees, he saw the cop at the cordon frown, thinking they were rubberneckers. Charlie pulled the coveralls and overshoes out of the boot, gave his spare set to Lovejoy. He showed the constable his warrant card and signed in.

'The sergeant's over there,' the uniform said. 'They've just cut the bloke down.'

'Didn't have to do that,' Charlie said, 'they fall naturally when they're ripe.'

They made their way up the hill.

'Did you see the look he gave you?' Lovejoy said.

'Some of these young blokes need to grow a sense of humour if they're going to last.'

The ground was frozen rock hard underfoot and, although the drizzle had stopped, the branches were dripping; he felt something cold slide down the back of his neck. The high-viz jackets were the only colour anywhere.

Charlie stood with his hands in his pockets, clocked the scene. A sergeant and a uniform were standing over the body. There was a grocer's crate lying on its side against the trunk, which could have been what Norton had stood on when he was fixing the rope. The uniform had cut the rope a few inches down from the branch.

He looked around. There was an army-green one-man hiking tent, a couple of empty tins lying around it. He heard the plaintive cry of a crow; he always thought that was the loneliest sound God ever made.

'I wonder if this bastard's taken all his secrets with him,' Charlie said to Lovejoy.

He spared him only a cursory glance, looking for anything unusual. He'd seen a lot of hangings in his career, and he never cared for them. Norton's lips were swollen purple, but his jaw had clenched tight, he had bitten through his tongue. There was blood and saliva all down the front of his Batman t-shirt. Had he ever taken that thing off? There was a large stain around the crotch. He stank worse than he usually did.

'Any chance this wasn't what it looks like?' Lovejoy asked.

'We'll soon find out,' Charlie said.

Charlie looked at the empty tins, baked beans in barbecue sauce, the other one some sort of stewed meat. 'The condemned man ate a hearty breakfast,' he muttered.

He hadn't lit a fire. How long had he been dead? Charlie bent down and tried to move Norton's arm; it wouldn't bend, he was in full rigor. He was no pathologist, but he would guess more than twelve hours then. He couldn't see a torch lying around, and he would have needed light to tie the rope, so some time yesterday then.

The sergeant was watching him, he looked old school, thought the murder squad all had brollies and pinstripe suits, he supposed.

'Sergeant. DI George, this is DC Lovejoy. Murder Squad.'

'Sir.'

'We've been looking for this bloke in relation to a case involving a missing schoolgirl. Have you got a CS team on the way?'

He nodded.

'Have you checked the car?' Charlie asked, and nodded at the Corsa that was parked half in the ditch down by the road.

'Empty.'

'And the boot?'

The sergeant gave him a look. I'm still in uniform but I'm not stupid, son.

Fair play, Charlie thought. 'All right, I don't want anyone to go near it until the SOCOs have been through it.'

'It's a right piece of shite, only got one seat in it, bare metal on the floor, not even carpet.'

'Bet it hasn't even got a reversing sensor. No sign of anyone else?'

'I've got my boys doing a sweep of the area, so far, nothing. I've rung the super in Ipswich, asked for more resources. It will take a while.'

'Good job.'

Charlie saw a half-dozen uniforms heading slowly in a line down through the trees. Not many places here to hide a body.

'Why would he bring her here?' Lovejoy said. 'That means he would have had her in the car somewhere when he showed up at his father's place.'

Charlie didn't see any sense in it either.

He put on a pair of blue latex gloves and crawled inside the tent, gagging at the smell. 'This is the glamour of working in the murder squad, Lovejoy, rooting around among some paedo's soiled underwear.'

'Only reason I joined.'

There was a sleeping bag, rank, and a plastic HMV shopping bag filled with unwashed clothes, tracksuit bottoms, a few t-shirts – they stank of motor grease and old sweat. He found a cheap blue daypack and dragged it outside into the fresh air. He unzipped it and looked inside; a torch, more tins of food, a bottle of water. There was a side pocket, a piece of paper jammed into it. He unfolded it. It was a crudely drawn map, the biro ink partially smudged by rain.

'What is it, guv?'

'Looks like a treasure map,' Charlie said. 'X marks the spot. Where's Marketborough?'

Lovejoy took out her phone and googled it. 'There's a Market

Harborough in Leicestershire. No, here it is, Marketborough. It's in Oxfordshire.'

'Where did that little girl go missing?' Charlie said. 'What was her name, Tiffany. Tiffany Strong.'

'Duddington.'

'How far is that from Marketborough?'

She checked on her phone. 'Less than five miles.'

He showed Lovejoy the map. 'Look. Here it is. He's marked the church and a roundabout. The road leads off the roundabout, away from the church, down here to a crossroads. He's inked a cross right here, next to some trees.'

'What do you think it means?'

'I think this is the final confession of Timothy Norton. This is where he buried Tiffany Strong.'

Charlie told Lovejoy to get an evidence bag from the boot of the car and popped it inside, labelled it and took it with him. 'One last thing,' he said to her. He put on another pair of latex gloves, leaned inside Norton's car and started the engine. He gunned the engine with his hand. 'Hole in the exhaust,' he said to Lovejoy.

'Is that significant?' she said.

'Could be,' he told her. 'Come on, let's get going. We have to scan this and send it to Oxford.'

CHAPTER TWENTY-EIGHT

Two uniformed police from the local nick stood outside the Williamses' gate. There were a dozen TV news vans parked up and down the street, they turned their cameras on Charlie as he went. Jesus, he thought, they must be desperate, that's not going to keep the punters from switching channels. Lovejoy followed.

He showed his ID to the officer and they went up the path. Malik opened the door and let them in. 'They're in there,' he said.

The Maltese was jumping up at him, wagging her tail. 'Hello Molly,' he said, and bent down to give her a pat before they went in.

The Williamses were sitting on the Chesterfield, at opposite ends. Only Mrs Williams looked up; she gave him the thousand-yard stare. 'Have you found her?' she said.

She looked as if she'd stepped off the set of a horror film: her skin had the pallor of wet cement and her eyes were rimmed red; he had seen ice addicts under the bright lights of an interview cell looking better than this. Her husband sat slumped beside her like he'd been filleted.

'Not yet.'

'I heard on the news that you found him. It said he was dead.'

'Yes. He took his own life. He was found in Suffolk, near his father's home. He hung himself. But there was no sign of Brooklyn, I'm afraid.'

'What do you think he's done with her? She could be some-where tied up, or something.'

'Mrs Williams, there is still no evidence that he had anything at all to do with your daughter's disappearance.'

She didn't believe him, of course. He supposed in an odd way it gave her hope.

'Maybe he's hidden her. She could be just tied up in the dark somewhere.'

'There's something else I think you should know, and I'd rather you hear this from us before you see it on the television. When we found Mr Norton, we also found among his effects a hand-drawn map. Using this map, our colleagues in the Oxfordshire police have uncovered some human remains. They were not recent. We believe they are those of a young girl who had been missing for eight years. We believe Norton was responsible for her murder and he meant the map to be found after his death.'

'What has this got to do with my Brooklyn?'

'Clearly, nothing. In fact, there is no evidence at all linking him with your daughter's disappearance.'

'So that's it? That's all you're going to do?'

Perhaps Lovejoy could see his exasperation. She leaned forward. 'Mrs Williams, police divers and sniffer dogs have been deployed to search for her, there are almost three hundred volunteers helping our police officers scour the wetlands around the reservoir. We have even used a police helicopter. We are doing all we can.'

'I will get back to you the moment we have any news,' Charlie said. 'Perhaps the doctor could give you something to help you sleep.'

'I don't want to sleep. I'm not going to sleep until you find her.'

Molly started scratching at the glass on the French windows to go out. Reuben and his little sister were outside, Lucee was playing on the plastic swing. Reuben was sitting on the garden bench, watching her.

The swing went creak-creak-creak.

'Do you mind if we have a minute with Reuben?' Charlie asked.

'He's already told you everything,' Mr Williams said.

'Still,' Charlie said. 'If it would be all right.'

Mrs Williams nodded. Charlie opened the door and Molly raced out, barking, licking Reuben's hand. Charlie and Lovejoy went out too. The Williamses made no attempt to follow them.

Reuben looked up. 'You banged up that rude boi yet?'

'I'm afraid Mr Norton won't be able to help us find your sister, Reuben. He's gone to rude-boi heaven, if there is such a place.'

'What, you mean he's dead, like?'

'Yes, that's what I mean.'

'Did you shoot him with tasers?'

'No Reuben. He did it to himself.'

Reuben looked impressed, then pleased. 'You still reckon he did for my sister?'

'We don't know.'

'Never find her now, hey?'

'We're not giving up hope yet, Reuben,' Lovejoy said. 'It does make things a bit more difficult for us. Unless you can think of something.'

'Me?'

'You are still the last one to see her, Reuben. You are sure it was him, in the car?'

'Just saw a motor, that's all, I didn't say it was him, did I? I heard the door slam, looked out of the window, tried to see where she was going, hard to see anything from that window in there, innit?'

Charlie smiled at little Lucee on the swing. She didn't smile back. 'In your statement you said you didn't see a car. Just then, you said you did.'

Reuben laughed and pointed a finger. 'I saw what you did. Proper clever, you are.'

'Well?'

227

'I told you everything, all right?'

'Reuben, this is not a game. You hear that? It's a helicopter with heat sensors, it's searching for your sister. Costs a right proper quid, that does. There are hundreds of people out there looking for her, police divers scouring the bottom of the lake. It's wet and it's cold and dark as a bear's bum down there. Now if you know something, and all those people are wasting their time, you are going to get yourself into more trouble than you can possibly imagine.'

Reuben stared at his feet, picked some imaginary lint off his Nikes. He took off his baseball cap, ran a hand through his oily mat of hair.

'Reuben?'

'She made me promise not to say.'

'Say what?'

'All right, I never saw a motor. I said I did, but I never. Not really. Heard one though, taking off, just after she got to the corner.'

'We don't care about the motor, Reuben,' Lovejoy said. 'What we want to know is, what was it your sister made you promise not to say?'

He slapped his baseball cap against his thigh.

'Reuben, this is important.'

'She'll be back. All this fuss. She be just loving it, man.'

'Just tell me what you know.'

'She a skank, my sister, real talk. The rents don't know half what she's done.'

'What has she done?'

Charlie waited. Come on, you little toerag, spit it out.

'She had a boyfriend in training, didn't she? He chirpsed her one Saturday down at the Westfield.'

'What's his name?'

'You think she'd tell me?'

'How old was he?'

'Old, man.'

'Twenty? Thirty? Five hundred and eight?'

'I don't know, man. She said he was like ancient. He had a job, real talk, a car and everything. She said he was, I don't know, twenty-five, some shit.'

Charlie looked at Lovejoy. Stop me from killing this kid.

'How often did they meet?'

'Two, three times. She got scared, wanted to cancel him, he got real mad about it, she said.'

'Did she say anything more about him?' Lovejoy said. 'What did he look like?'

A shrug.

'Did she tell you where he lived?'

'I don't know. He didn't live in our manor, maybe down Stratford somewhere. Don't tell me rents I know all about this, I want to be excluded from this narrative know what I mean?'

'Why didn't you tell us this before?' Charlie said.

'I told you. Brooklyn made me promise, right?'

'What were her words exactly?'

'She said she was going out to meet someone, I knew what she meant. She said she would be back before the rents came home, right?'

'So it was him in the car?'

'Like I told the other bacon, I heard her go out, I saw her at the corner. I thought maybe I heard a motor, then she was gone. Couldn't clock that, could I? You see for yourself, go to the window and see. Cannot see the corner from there.'

Charlie went back inside, went to the window. The kid was right. The view was obscured by the street trees and a postbox. He went back out. Reuben was still sitting on the bench, scuffing the ground with his 110s.

'What did this motor sound like?' Charlie asked him.

'Didn't sound like anything. Just like a motor.'

Charlie nodded, apparently satisfied. 'I wish you'd told us this before. You could have saved us all a lot of time and trouble.'

'She made me promise, man.'

Lovejoy sat on the swing next to Lucee. 'I thought you didn't like your sister.'

'I don't.'

'So why are you covering for her?'

'Still my sister, man. You're going to find her, right?'

And Charlie couldn't be sure, but for a moment he thought their little roadman was about to tear up. He could have imagined it, though.

CHAPTER TWENTY-NINE

The DCI stared at the whiteboard, a symbol now of the team's confusion. Two arrows linked the photographs of Mariatu and Brooklyn. The two lines converged under Norton's mug shot, taken in the custody suite a couple of weeks before. He snatched it down from the board, crumpled it in his fist, and dropped it on the floor. He was the one who decided to link the two investigations, Charlie thought, he can't blame me for this cock-up.

The DCI picked up a red marker pen and drew a question mark on the whiteboard where Norton's picture had been.

'What if it's not one question mark,' Charlie said, 'what if there should be two question marks up there?'

The DCI didn't turn around. He just stood there, with his hands on his hips, staring at the whiteboard. No one said anything. Then he rubbed out the question mark he had just drawn and tossed the marker at Charlie. 'Brief me in my office when you're done,' he said and walked out.

Not like the DCI to throw a tantrum, Charlie thought. Must be getting heat from upstairs. The team sat there, sprawled in their chairs, or leaning against desks, all looking at each other, waiting for someone to come up with an idea. Charlie would have liked to have given them one, but he was all out.

'So, what happened up in Suffolk then?' McCullough said.

'We sent a scan of the map we found in Norton's tent up to their serious crimes division. They sent a SOC team to the location, where they found the skeletonised remains of what their

231

pathologist believes to be a young female between seven and ten years old. The remains included fragments of a school blazer; the crime officer told me that the school badge was reasonably intact, that it belonged to the same school Tiffany Strong attended before her abduction and disappearance in 2010. We obviously don't have a positive identification as yet, from dental records, but I am certain that the remains are hers.'

'So this was like, his deathbed confession?' Malik said.

'I suppose.'

'Sick bastard,' the skipper said.

'And there was no sign of Brooklyn?' Wes said.

'Forensics will go through it, but that could take weeks. But no, Wes, unless they find something, it seems unlikely that he had anything to do with Brooklyn's disappearance.'

'He didn't ping the ANPR on the A11 until after nine on the night she disappeared. That gives him four hours to grab her, get his stuff and get out of London.'

'Wasn't him. If that was his car at the bottom of her street, Reuben would have heard it. Anyway, makes no sense. We're trying to ram a square peg into a round hole here, just because it's the only peg we have. Right?'

'So now FONC has stuck us with two separate investigations instead of one,' the skipper said. 'Bloody brilliant.'

'It seems that way.'

'So now what?'

'The Okpotu file stays open, but at this stage we have no new leads. We have to give priority to Brooklyn Williams, in the hope that she may still be alive somewhere and counting on us to find her.'

They nodded along with him, but he knew what they were all thinking. He was thinking the same thing: the statistics said that there was, on average, six hours between abduction and murder. Brooklyn Williams had been gone over forty-eight hours; if she had been taken, the chances of finding her alive were fading fast.

But they couldn't afford to think like that. They had to give her every chance. 'Let's go through this again,' he said. 'Parm?'

'We've been through everything on her iPad and her phone, just the usual shit, no evidence that she was being groomed, no evidence of a boyfriend, casual or serious. No sexting, her Twitter feed was crap; a bit of bullying but she was the instigator not the victim.'

'See, that's what I do not get,' Wes said. 'If she arranged to meet this bloke, how did she do it? They would have to have messaged each other somehow.'

'Perhaps she had a burner phone,' Lovejoy said.

'A fourteen-year-old with a burner? How would she know about things like that?'

'Like they know everything. Movies and the internet.'

'But why go to all that trouble?'

'Maybe this bloke gave her the phone,' Rupe said. 'It would be the smart move.'

'Possible,' Charlie said.

'Nothing on her feed since Saturday?' Malik asked.

'Just her friends posting messages. Her last log-in was three forty-one on Saturday, just before she went missing.'

Charlie looked at Lubanski. 'How did you and Mac go at the school?'

She shook her head. 'We spoke to every kid in her class, her teachers, nothing.'

'There was one thing,' McCullough said. 'It's a long shot.'

'Any shot will do, Mac.'

'One of her mates reckoned she'd met this bloke down the Turkish takeaway, and she told her she sort of liked him, but he said he was sleeping rough so that put her off.'

'Amazing that,' Lovejoy said.

'Brooklyn said he'd asked her for her number but she wouldn't give it to him.'

'And?'

'Well, get this. She reckoned Brooklyn told her that one night

233

this character followed her home and hung around outside her house, only took off when her parents came home.'

'When was this?'

'A couple of weeks ago.'

'Before Mariatu was murdered,' Charlie said, thinking aloud. 'Anything else?'

'That was it. Said she never mentioned the geezer again.'

'A good-looking gutter-nutter,' White said. 'That'd be a first.'

'Two weeks,' the skipper said. 'Even if we could find a camera near the kebab shop, it would have been wiped by now.'

'Lube, you and Mac get down there and see if the owners remember this bloke.'

'Bring us back a couple of chicken skewers and a *pide*, would you?' the skipper said. 'Nowt for Wes – he's a vegetarian.'

'They have vegetarian in kebab shops,' Wes said.

'Anything else?' Charlie said.

'I still don't buy this,' Lovejoy said. 'Mrs Williams says none of her stuff is missing from her room. A girl doesn't run off like that and not take anything with her.'

'Maybe she didn't intend to run off,' Joe said. 'Maybe it wasn't this bootsie she was away tae meet, maybe it was this other fella, the one her brother talked about, from the Westfield. Maybe she thought she was just away for a little ride in his motor, a bit of a tumble in his back seat.'

Charlie nodded. 'If she took nothing with her, we have to assume that wherever she is now, she did not go there willingly.' He looked back at Parm. 'How did you go with the local taxi drivers?'

Parm shook her head. 'Nothing so far.'

'Let's stay on that one,' Charlie said. Despite all the background checks, two thousand cab drivers had been charged with criminal offences in the last five years in London. What if she had flagged down a cab to go and meet her boyfriend somewhere, and that was the motor Reuben thought he heard at the end of the street?

'Talk to Cab Enforcement as well,' Charlie said. 'I want to put a line through the possibility that she jumped in a cab.'

'Even if she did,' the skipper said, 'he could have had his tracking system turned off.'

'Let's do it anyway. What about the phones?'

'Still running hot, mostly bloody time-wasters. Half a dozen people saw her getting in a bloody UFO in Finsbury Park.'

'Guv.'

He looked up. It was Gale. He looked terrible.

'Ty. What are you doing here, mate? Everything all right? How's your daughter?'

'Better. Can I talk to you?'

'Sure.'

Charlie was going to take him down to the canteen but Gale said he needed a smoke, so they stood down in the yard, stamping their feet against the cold. Three patrol cars blue-lighted out through the gate.

'Gave these things up three times since I've been doing this job,' he said, grinding out the butt with his heel. 'I fucking hate them.'

'Not easy,' Charlie said.

'I need a transfer,' he said.

'All right. Sorry to lose you.'

'I just can't do this any more, guv. The hours. The stress. I was looking at my daughter in the hospital this last few days, thinking about how I've always thought, one day I'll have more time to spend with her. But I won't, will I?'

'Murder rate is on the rise, you know that, Ty. Economy is up the shit, but the murder business is bloody brilliant. We're only going to get busier.'

'I don't know how you do it, day in, day out.'

'Maybe because I don't have as much to lose as you do. What are you going to do?'

'I'll probably get out, soon as I can. It's a single man's job, this.'

235

It occurred to Charlie that Gale was a couple of years younger than he was, but he preferred not to think too deeply about that.

CHAPTER THIRTY

The next day was bright and cold. He felt like he had a hang-over, though he hadn't had a drink in days. He stared at the whiteboard, hoping something would jump out at him. A sure sign of desperation, that.

His Nokia rang. It was the sergeant in charge of the dive team, out at the wetlands. This could be good news or bad news; if it was a body, it would be both. Charlie listened, said thanks, we'll be right over, and hung up.

The dive team stood on the cement path next to the lake, in their distinctive blue jackets and beanies. There were weight belts slung over the low railings, among the spools of red and yellow safety lines. The police dive sergeant was helping one of his team out of their gear. Their breath formed little clouds on the evening air, it was freezing. Dry suits or not, he wouldn't have their job for quids; all that rummaging around in cold, muddy water among the weeds and traffic cones and Tesco trolleys and used needles.

Two of the off-duty divers were standing behind the screen, staring at the body. One of them was eating a sausage roll.

'All right, fellas?' Charlie said.

One of them, Collins, recognised him from a previous job. 'Hello, Charlie. This one of yours, you reckon?'

Charlie had a bit of a look. He heard Lovejoy gag and excuse herself. 'New, is she?' Collins said.

'Relatively,' Charlie said.

A waxy, grey adipocere had formed on large parts of the body, where the fatty tissue under the skin had saponified. The skin had turned a greenish black, and was peeling off. Fish and lice had been at work on the face, not much of it left that was recognisable as human. The belly had bloated with gas. The fingers looked like boned, boiled beef.

'That who you were looking for?' Collins asked. His mate finished his sausage roll and licked the tomato sauce off his fingers.

Charlie shook his head.

'How can you tell?'

'Well, number one, unless I am greatly mistaken, that is a wedding ring on the finger there, or what is left of the finger. Number two, that shoe is not something a teenage girl would wear on her feet. Three, this body has been in the water for a long time, my MisPer hasn't been gone more than seventy-two hours.'

'Sorry, Charlie.'

'Don't apologise. I'm still hoping I'll find her alive. You never know your luck in the big city.'

He found Lovejoy who had her hands on her knees, taking in deep breaths.

'It's not Brooklyn Williams,' he said.

'So now what, guv?'

'Now it's someone else's problem. I've got enough of my own.' He nodded to the sergeant and the other diver, who had peeled his dry suit down to his waist, and pulled a beanie down over his ears; that's the way lad, your nipples can freeze and drop off in this weather, but as long as your ears are warm.

'So it's not her, are you sorry, or are you pleased?'

'What I am is hungry, Lovejoy. I need a coffee and something to eat. I haven't had anything since the bacon sarnie I had at the service station on the way up to Suffolk this morning. Bugger me, do you see that?'

'What guv?'

'That duck with the green head. That's a northern shoveler, you don't see many of those in London. Come on. Let's go back to the car. I'll drive, you update the decision log. I'm ravenous.'

As they drove under the bridge, Charlie clocked the yellow and red lettering of a large sign at the bottom of the embankment:

WITNESS APPEAL MURDER:

ON THURSDAY 1 MARCH 2018, THE BODY OF A YOUNG GIRL WAS FOUND AT THE TOP OF THIS EMBANKMENT. HER NAME WAS MARIATU OKPOTU, AGED 11 YEARS. SHE WAS DRESSED IN A SCHOOL BLAZER AND GREY SKIRT.

DID YOU SEE OR HEAR ANYTHING?
CAN YOU HELP?

IN STRICTEST CONFIDENCE.

The Crimestoppers and Incident Room numbers were printed underneath.

As they drove up the high street, Lovejoy pointed out a bagel place opposite the station.

'Bagels? Really, Lovejoy?'

'Better for you than sausage rolls, guv.'

'Who eats bagels? Even the ducks won't eat them. Ever fed bagels to a duck, Lovejoy? They sink. You can get done by the RSPCA for giving a duck a bagel. Bagels are for people who wear scarves indoors.'

'OK, it was just a suggestion.'

'What about that place over there? They look like they do a decent coffee.'

'How can you tell that from here?'

'It's called Gino's. Italians know about coffee.'

'I bet the owner's called Jason.'

Lovejoy pulled in to the Tesco car park. Another day, Charlie thought, and still no closer to finding Brooklyn Williams. A clear sky for once, the vapour trails turning pink, looked pretty, even though they were stuffing up the environment.

There was a kebab shop next door to the café. Wasn't that where Brooklyn had met that bootsie? He stopped and looked down the lane that ran down the side of it, but there were no homeless, and no one even vaguely good looking.

He went in the café, ordered his usual flat white with an extra shot and a latte for Lovejoy. The almond croissants looked tasty, so he bought two of those as well. The TV was on and there were half a dozen people sitting at the tables, staring at it.

It was by-the-numbers reporting, a body bag being loaded into a coroner's vehicle, crime-scene officers in white coveralls clustered around a police vehicle, holding clipboards, some yellow police tape strung between the trees, an interview with the man with the dog, the one who had found the body. A head shot of Norton, and then two minutes of replaying old footage from the previous week, how he had been helping police with their enquiries into the death of schoolgirl Mariatu Okpotu and the disappearance of Brooklyn Williams. They used some screen grabs of Mariatu from the CCTV outside the betting shop, a family portrait of the Williamses; Charlie recognised it from the table in the entrance hall, the other children's faces pixelated out.

The bulletin cut to a replay of the Williamses' live TV appeal, from last night; he saw FONC sitting with the press officer, the Williamses next to them, Mrs Williams sobbing her way through the prepared statement, her husband beside her, stony-faced.

'Someone out there must know where she is, we beg you, please come forward and contact the police ... we just want her home, safe and well ... please, it's breaking our hearts not to know ...'

She couldn't go on. The DCI finished with a personal appeal

for the abductor to call him directly, setting a deadline for Brooklyn's return.

'What are the cops doing?' someone said. 'Did this Norton geezer do it or didn't he?'

'They wouldn't have a clue,' a woman said. 'I reckon the real murderer's at home havin' a laugh.'

'Typical of the Old Bill,' another man said. 'They couldn't catch a cold in a flu epidemic.'

Charlie smiled. He'd never heard that one before.

He got his coffees and went back to the car. He tore open the paper bag, took a bite out of one of the croissants.

'Get in. Lovely, that is. Food of the gods, Lovejoy.'

'Only if the gods are overweight and have a cholesterol problem.'

'So you don't want yours, then?'

He watched her as she ate the croissant, wondered about the Gaelic ring on the third finger of her left hand that she never took off, the tattoo on the inside of her right arm; she always kept her sleeve pulled down so he couldn't quite make out what it said. He supposed she was quite pretty, when you thought about, just not in the girly-girl sort of way, not what Ben would have called his type.

'It was on the telly in the café,' he said. 'About us finding Norton. They followed it up with the Williamses' appeal.'

'Nothing about the little girl in Oxford?'

'They haven't joined the dots yet.'

'Were they talking about it? In there?'

'A bit. There was a consensus on how useless we are. Don't take it personally. Then some bloke started on how all paedos should be castrated at birth. The logic of the thing seemed to escape him. I mean, all males fantasise about eleven-year-old girls. When they're eleven. It's just some blokes never grow out of it.'

'That's what that bloke Mayfield said, wasn't it?'

'Well he was right, Lovejoy. That's the scary thing about

geezers like Mayfield; the educated ones are always the worst, because of how they justify things. All that crap about the Greeks he was yapping about. What really does my crust, was he was sort of right, about the art and stuff. Like that statue in Florence. David. People have remarked how he isn't particularly well endowed.'

'Not a Goliath.'

'Exactly. Also, he isn't circumcised, even though he was Jewish. That is because the Greeks liked young boys, just like Mayfield said. But equating aberrant and destructive sexual deviancy with the works of Pythagoras is stretching a point, in my opinion.'

'So it's not new, then?'

'How do you mean?'

'Men these days, they've all got something going on. There's blokes who like other blokes, blokes who like kids, blokes who like robots. It's getting harder to find blokes who like women.'

'And there's women who like women,' Charlie said, testing the waters.

'Some, but I reckon the odds are still in your favour.'

'Not lately, Lovejoy.'

'Really? I heard you had a very active social life.'

'Where did you hear that?' Charlie said.

'People talk.'

'Well, it's active, just not very functional.'

'You still going out with that teacher?' She saw his expression. 'Don't mind me asking.'

'Doesn't anyone have anything better to talk about?'

'Your romantic life is a subject of great fascination for everyone, I'm afraid.'

'Time for everyone to get a life.'

'Is she nice?'

Charlie thought about that. Was she nice? Pippa was sexy, unpredictable, troubled, spontaneous and interesting.

But was she nice?

242

'My little brother says she's got a lot of red flags.'

'What does that mean?'

'I think he means I am generally unlucky in love.'

'I don't believe in luck, guv. No such thing.'

Her phone pinged. She looked at her WhatsApp and smiled. 'Your boyfriend?'

'My dad,' she said. 'He's sent me a picture of Charlie.'

She showed him her phone. It was Charlie the spaniel eating yoghurt off a spoon; it was all over his face, even around his eyes.

'You want the rest of that croissant?' Charlie said.

'No, you have it, I'd like to at least live till I'm forty.' She started the engine. 'I wonder if she's still alive. Brooklyn.'

'Who knows? I'd like to think we'll close this one, but after that first forty-eight hours, things get tough. Sometimes cases don't ever get solved, it's not always like it is on *Broadchurch*. Other times, like that Paula Fields murder, it takes ten years to bang up the psycho that did it. Look at it this way: we did solve one crime, that poor little girl Norton killed. At least her family will know what happened to her now, they have a body to bury. Cold comfort I suppose, but that's the way it goes in this job. Perhaps ten years from now one of us will get a call, and we'll pull up the Brooklyn Williams file on the computer, or on a hologram, or whatever we've got then, they'll say we found her for you. Just like we did with Tiffany Strong. And for all the work we put in, sometimes it just comes down to luck.'

'So what now, guv?'

'Well now, I've had my coffee, we'll go back to the nick and hope we catch a break. We've got an unsolved murder, a missing girl, and my DCI is pissed off and looking for someone to blame. What else could possibly go wrong?'

His iPhone rang.

CHAPTER THIRTY-ONE

'The Ride of the Valkyries' ringtone during working hours could be the nursing home telling him his ma had had a funny turn, or it was Ben with some gossip on one of the Arsenal players that he reckoned just couldn't wait. Ben got a lot of inside running from one of the girls in his office who was besties with one of the Arsenal WAGS.

He was surprised to see Pippa's ID come up.

She was hysterical, carrying on so badly he couldn't make out everything she was saying. He was at the door, she said, trying to get in. Who's at the door, he said, but she wasn't making any sense. He told her to hang up and ring 999. 'We'll be right there,' he said. He clipped the blue light to the roof and gave Lovejoy the address.

'Is this MIT business, guv?'

'Just do what it says on the tin, Lovejoy,' he said. 'Who's the guvnor around here?'

The Stow was one of the coolest places to live in London these days; not so cool you couldn't get shot at the railway station, but it was comforting to know things hadn't changed that much. He'd hung out with her down there quite a bit, there were a few too many pound shops and halal butchers in the high street for his liking, and he was suspicious of any place that had shops selling beard oil, but the Queen's was a proper East End boozer and he had found a place down at the markets to buy bacon jam.

It was a lot safer than it used to be when he was a kid, as long as you stayed out of the tower-block estates. Back in the day he had learned to swim launching himself off the five-metre diving board at Walthamstow Pool and Track. It was the Waltham Forest Feel Good Centre now. There was even an industrial park with microbreweries.

So he wasn't surprised when they got there to find that Pippa's trouble wasn't local but imported.

Pippa had rented a flat, the downstairs of a Victorian terrace in one of those gentrified streets where advertising executives lived next door to cocaine dealers and drove the same model Saabs. It had a black door with leadlights and heavy enamel paint. No damage, as far as he could see.

There were two patrol cars and an ambulance parked in the street outside, beacons flashing, the usual rubberneckers. Charlie knew one of the attending uniforms, he'd been at the Essex Road nick for a while. When Charlie arrived he was standing on the pavement, looking slightly bored, taking a statement from one of the neighbours.

'Hello Sangram. How's it going then, all right?'

'What are you doing here, no one's been murdered yet.'

'What happened?'

Sangram thanked the neighbour for his help and took Charlie aside. 'A domestic, usual shite, it was still going on when we got here.'

'Is she all right?'

'She's in the ambulance; she's a bit knocked around but nothing for you blokes to worry about.'

'Actually, I'm here as a private citizen really.'

'Then I'll have to ask you to get back behind the cordon,' Sangram said with a straight face and Charlie assumed he was joking.

Sangram's partner was standing by the patrol car, talking into the radio. Charlie got a glimpse of the bloke they had arrested, Pippa's ex, sitting in the back, his hands cuffed behind

245

him. He had a bull head, a tracksuit top, and a tattoo on the side of the neck.

He gave Charlie the stare, looking proper hard, as blokes did when they were in that situation.

'Well there goes your parole, my son,' Charlie thought. So much for freedom; a quick visit to the ex, then back playing mum to a Hell's Angel doing fifteen years for GBH. Hope he oils it.

'Did he give you much trouble?' he said to the uniform.

'A bit. Took four of us. Lively young lad. Broke my sergeant's nose. We had to taser him.'

'That was bad luck. Did he say anything?'

'Not after we tasered him.'

He'd done plenty of these, when he was in uniform; he always felt a visceral reaction to it that went way beyond the job. He still did domestics, but these days they were the ones that ended with a female body in the back of the coroner's van and a bloody hammer or knife lying on the floor of the kitchen. Pippa was the last person this should happen to, a classy and well-educated girl with well-to-do parents. Most of his work turned up in council estates and tower blocks, and it wasn't hard to figure out why.

She was sitting on the stretcher in the back of the ambulance, a silver blanket around her shoulders. She had on a short dressing gown over the top of her t-shirt, not much else. Funny, that. The paramedics had patched her up, she was holding an ice pack to the side of her face and her lip was cut. One of the ambulance crew was taking her blood pressure.

'Are you all right?' Charlie said.

She nodded, but didn't look up at him. 'It's my fault,' she said and he thought he couldn't have heard her right.

'How did he get in?'

'I let him in. I had to. He was going to bust the door in.'

'You let him in?'

'I thought I could calm him down.'

'What's he doing here? Did you know he was getting out?'

'Yeah, he rang me.'

'He rang you from prison? You never told me about that.'

'I don't have to tell you everything.'

'I would have stayed over, if I'd known. I could have protected you.'

'You're always at work,' she said, and the look in her eyes surprised him, she was so angry. 'You wouldn't have been here anyway.'

'You still should have told me.'

'You should have seen the cops, took four of them to take him down.' She said it as if it was a good thing. He didn't know what to make of it.

He got out of the ambulance, the other paramedic was packing up the gear, getting ready to leave. 'Is she going to be all right?'

'One of the cops reckons she was unconscious for about thirty seconds when we got here. We'll have to get that checked.'

'Which hospital are you going to?'

'The Free.'

'Right. Thanks.'

Charlie went back to the car. Lovejoy gave him a look.

'Another red flag,' she said.

'Just drive, Lovejoy.'

'Back to the nick?'

'Via the Free.'

'Is she all right?'

'She'll live. They're taking her to hospital for scans.'

'And the bloke in the patrol car is?'

'Her ex-husband.'

'Divorced?'

'Separated.'

'Her husband then.'

He looked at her and she just shrugged. She had a point,

he had to stop this, hanging around with other blokes' wives, separated or not.

A&E was doing a brisk trade: there was a geezer with a bandage around his finger and blood all over his shirt, another one lying on the floor with his knees drawn up to his chest, groaning. Someone else was shouting at the coffee machine. He couldn't make out if they were angry or just in pain. He showed his ID to the triage nurse and she buzzed them through.

Pippa was sitting on a bed behind a curtain in one of the A&E cubicles. He told Lovejoy to wait on the other side of the curtain. 'Sure guv,' she said. He knew what she was thinking, and he wished she would just stop it.

'How are you then, all right?' he said to Pippa.

That was quite a shiner she had there; she looked like Quasimodo. She gave him a look, cold as you like, as if he was the one that did it. There was a bandage over the line they'd put in her arm.

'I'm fine, Charlie. Why don't you go home?'

'Wanted to make sure you were OK.'

'I'm fine. Just go.'

'You should have told me he was getting out.'

'Thought you knew. You are a cop. Anyway, this isn't all about you.'

'The uniform outside says you're not going to press charges.'

'I don't need this right now.'

'I mean, he just beat you up, put you in hospital. And you're not going to throw the book at him?'

'You don't understand. He doesn't mean to be like this. He needs my help right now.'

'If those patrol cars hadn't got there fast as they did, he could have killed you. They reckon he was off his nut.'

'How would you feel if you found another bloke's gear in your wife's bedroom? It was a shock. He just lost it for a minute. It was my fault, I hadn't had the chance to tell him.'

Charlie took a moment with that. Sangram had confirmed for him that the front door was undamaged, there was no sign of forced entry anywhere. So it wasn't quite like she was telling it, was it?

Sangram's partner was taking photographs of her injuries, show us your arm, turn your head a bit to the left, matter-of-fact, she must do a couple of these every day, he supposed. Nurses came in and out, checking her blood pressure and pulse.

'What was he doing in the bedroom?'

'He's still my husband.'

'What does that mean?'

'I can't deal with this right now, Charlie.'

A porter came in, said he had to take her upstairs for X-rays. He flipped the brakes on the trolley and wheeled her out. Charlie stared after her. Should have listened to my brother, he thought.

Sangram's offsider started bagging her clothes, they were looking at section 20 GBH, she said, but if she wouldn't lay charges, her husband would be home in time for dinner.

'Know her, do you?' she said, casual.

'A friend,' Charlie said.

He nodded to Lovejoy, and she followed him outside. The electronic doors at the end of the corridor slid open and he went out, took a deep breath of cold air. The red and blue lights of an ambulance flashed as it pulled into the forecourt.

'We done here, guv?'

'Yes, Lovejoy, we are done here. We are definitely done here.'

He got in the car, let Lovejoy drive, didn't say a word all the way back to the nick. He thought about what Ben had called him once: Crusader Rabbit. 'You spend all day every day out there, righting wrongs, locking up the bad guys, saving princesses from dragons. Where does it get you, Charlie? Where does it ever get you?'

The only victms are in fairy tales. The rest of the time, people brought it on their bloody selves.

CHAPTER THIRTY-TWO

Four days, and still nothing. The search had been scaled back. It was as if Brooklyn Williams had disappeared into thin air. No one had seen her after she left the Williamses' house that Saturday afternoon; White had logged a hundred hours of CCTV footage from the high street, from every possible camera in a one-mile radius; they had checked the records of every cab company in North London, scoured the wetlands, searched any area of wasteland that might have concealed a body. The DCI was now enamoured of the theory that Brooklyn Williams had gone off with the man she had met at Stratford shopping centre. But who was he? They had nothing, absolutely no lead to investigate. They had received hundreds of calls on Crimestoppers and into the IR hotline, there was still nothing substantive.

He had pulled Malik after twenty-four hours at Mrs Williams' request. Malik hadn't been unhappy about it either; white collar racists, he had muttered under his breath.

This is going to play out just the way I told Lovejoy it would, he thought. The DCI is going to invest fewer and fewer resources, Mariatu will be forgotten, so will Brooklyn Williams, except in the minds of their families, and perhaps blokes like me.

The Williamses had organised a vigil at the local church. The place was packed, half the locals had turned out, Charlie and Lovejoy parked outside in her Sierra. The DCI had signed off on a surveillance van to record everyone going in, but he didn't really expect much to come of it.

'We've got a positive on the body they found in the lake,'

250

Charlie said. 'There was an old-timer went missing from an old folk's home down the road about a month ago. Poor old bastard must have fallen in.'

'Well, that's two mysteries we've solved then. But we still haven't found who we're looking for.'

'I'm starting to think we might not.'

He waited until everyone had finished filing in, then he and Lovejoy crossed the street, went in, stood at the back, near the door. The DCI had told them to be careful. Tensions are running high, he'd said, people are blaming us for what's happened around there.

It was hushed inside, the church lit by dozens of candles. The Williamses sat at the front, their heads all in a row, Lucee's barely visible over the back of the pew. There were photographs of Brooklyn on the altar, one of her when she was much younger, in a school uniform, smiling. Her friends were in the congregation, some of them crying hysterically. Mariatu's family was there as well, Raymond Okpotu and his wife and their two daughters, all of them united in their shared loss.

Raymond Okpotu saw Charlie and gave him a long, cold stare before turning away. Blames me for not getting him justice, Charlie thought. That is my job, isn't it? He probably thought they had been forgotten in all the hysteria surrounding Brooklyn Williams's disappearance and he supposed, to a point, he was right. Perhaps that was one of the reasons he was here, to remind everyone they were grieving too.

The minister came out of the vestry and welcomed everyone. He said they were there to pray for Brooklyn and ask God for her safe return to her family. There were prayers, a few hymns. Then Mrs Williams got up and stood on the bottom step of the altar and took out the little speech she had written on the piece of paper she held crumpled in her fist.

'Our Brooklyn,' she said. 'She's such a good girl, only fourteen, her life hasn't even started yet. I know she's out there somewhere, I know she is. If someone's got her, I just want us all to pray that God can speak to him somehow, make him see the kind of girl she is and let her go. All I want is for her to come back to us, so we can be a family again.'

That was as far as she got. She broke down. Mr Williams just sat there not moving, it was the minister who had to step forward and grab her before she fell on her knees, and help her back to her seat.

There was a long silence then someone yelled out, he couldn't make out who it was: 'What are the police doing?'

There was a shocked silence, then the same voice yelled out: 'They should have found her by now.'

Someone turned around and yelled at them to hush, that wasn't what they were there for. Charlie thought it was going to get ugly, these things did sometimes, but the minister was on to it, he stood up and talked over them, calmed them all down, said they shouldn't focus on blame, instead they should keep the family in their prayers and to trust in God.

He led them all outside. The verger was waiting on the fore-court with a large net bag full of balloons. The minister turned and addressed everyone, over the roar of the buses on the high street, said they were releasing the balloons as a sign of letting go of all worry surrounding Brooklyn Williams in the sure knowl-edge that she would soon be returned to her family safe and well.

The verger tugged the string on the net bag and on the second attempt it opened, and the balloons floated up in a ragged red and blue cloud to a lowering sky.

Brooklyn's father was the first to leave, trudging home with-out a word to anyone; he left his children and his wife staring up at the darkening sky, following the flight of the balloons until they disappeared. One by one, people came up and hugged her or shook her hand. Some even bent over the two children, gave Lucee an encouraging pat on the head, most of the women in tears, the men grim-faced.

Raymond Okpotu came over, his hands folded in front of him; a tall man, he looked down on Charlie with mournful eyes. 'So, Inspector, there is still no further progress on finding the man responsible for murdering our daughter.'

'I'm afraid there isn't.'

'We all seem to have become distracted by the missing girl. As much as I pray for their family, I also pray for my own, and hope to receive some justice for what happened to Mariatu.'

'We have not been distracted. Far from it, I assure you. We are still hoping that our forensic department will provide us with further leads we can investigate. Unfortunately, these things can take time.'

He nodded, unimpressed by Charlie's rehearsed speech. 'Poor Mr Williams. Everyone feels sorry for him, his family, as they do for us. But until it has happened to you, you can't really know what it's like. Please find him, Inspector.' He put one large hand over his heart. 'I implore you, please find him. Just give us justice.'

And he walked away.

'So, how's your work, then?' Ma said.

He looked at her out of the corner of his eye, not quite sure if she was serious. 'It's all right.'

'What is it you do again?'

'I'm a police officer, Ma.'

'That's right. Got a head like a sieve, I have.'

She looked so tiny there in the passenger seat, smelled like an old lady, she did, he sort of wondered when that had happened. Once she used to wear too much perfume, it would make his head ache; these days she didn't wear any and smelled faintly of boiled vegetables. She was her but not her in so many ways.

'Look at all this building going on,' she said. 'I don't understand how it all stands up.'

'How do you mean, Ma?'

'It must be so heavy. How can the ground hold it all up? You'd think it would all fall through to the other side. No wonder our rates are so high.'

'You don't pay rates any more, Ma.'

'You haven't answered my question.'

'I don't know why the houses don't all fall through to Australia. That's like asking me why the sky is blue.'

'I'm not talking about the sky, I'm talking about buildings, trust you to make it all confusing.'

'Well, I don't know, all right. They just don't.'

'I'll ask Ben, he'll know. Where are you taking me?'

'Just thought we'd go for a drive, give you a change of scenery.'

'I don't know how you remember all these streets, if it was me, I'd get lost.'

'I've got GPS, everyone does these days.'

'I don't understand all that new-fangled stuff. Gives me a headache. Where are we?'

'Don't you remember? We used to live just down that street over there.'

'Did we?'

He thought about their old two-up one-down, couldn't even rent there now, never mind buy it; last time he looked it had sold for over half a million quid.

'It all looks different to what I remember. Everything's changed. You got a lot of darkies around here these days, why can't they all go back where they came from?'

'If everyone went back where they came from, we wouldn't be here either. We'd be on a potato farm in Ireland.'

'What are you talking about, your grandfather was from Bethnal Green.'

'And my other grandfather was from Kilkenny.'

'Oh, I don't remember that.'

Charlie found a park, went around to help her out of the front seat. She was still lively enough, she was off before he had even got his pay-and-display ticket. It was only her mind had gone; the rest of her could still finish the London Marathon, he reckoned.

'What you taking me to a nightclub for? It's the middle of the day.'

'It's not a nightclub, it's a café.'

'Looks like a nightclub to me. Are you sure?'

'Ma, just take a seat. What do you want?'

'What's that?'

'It's a waterfall. It's like art.'

'Look at all these lights. That's Jesus, that is. What have they got Jesus all lit up like that for? You sure this is a café?'

Charlie ordered her a cream tea, extra jam, and a flat white for himself. The rain had set in again and they sat in the tea shed and watched it drip from the eaves on to the gravelled terrace.

'So why are you looking so worried?'

'I'm not worried.'

'Yes, you are. Written all over your face, it is. Like that time Liam drew all over your homework when he was little.'

'Just work.'

'What about work? All you have to do is direct traffic all day.'

'Mum, I'm a detective now.'

'Are you? You should have told me. What are you worried about then?'

He used to tell her things once, he remembered, when he was eleven or twelve. She was different then, she couldn't help him with his homework, but she was streetwise, in her way. She was on it, too, didn't forget things back then, knew just what grades all of her boys had and knew all of their teachers' names, and what position each of them played in their football teams, and how many goals they had scored.

But that was then.

'You always were a worrier.'

'Was I?'

'When you were a kid.' She heaped several inches of cream on half a scone and shovelled it in. 'This is your fault. I shouldn't be eating cream, it's not good for you.'

'A bit won't hurt,' he said.

'Always had to do things your way, that was your trouble. Always had to work things out for yourself.'

'How do you mean?'

'You remember when you had that science homework, and your uncle Bill came down from South Shields for the day, and he was a science teacher, and I said, show your uncle Bill, and you wouldn't, you said you had to do it yourself. Only twelve you were. Just like you. People would tell you things and you wouldn't listen.'

He didn't remember Uncle Bill very well, wasn't even sure whatever incident she was talking about had ever happened. It startled him sometimes, her memory for things that happened a long time ago, most of the time she was right. Whether she was right or not, it certainly sounded like him.

'What are you suggesting?'

'Whatever's bothering you, you should ask for help.'

'I've got a whole team of people helping me.'

The other scone went in. She said, through a mouthful of crumbs: 'No, I know you, if you can't work it out yourself, you don't like to listen.'

'You've got a bit of cream,' Charlie said, 'right here.' He picked up a napkin and dabbed at her lip.

'Lovely this is,' she said. 'It's like a proper café.'

Charlie dropped her off back at the home, instead of going home himself he went in to the nick, even though it was his day off, logged into the HOLMES, checked back through the calls that the skipper had logged for that week, most of them time-wasters, a few that should have been sectioned under the Mental Health Act. There was a woman in Barnet, said she knew what had happened to Brooklyn; he drove out there but, as he suspected, she turned out to be a clairvoyant offering to track her vibrations if he would take her to the crime scene. There was another man, lived in the Ladder north of Finsbury Park, left his name, the skipper had checked the file, a history

256

of schizophrenia. Possible, he supposed. Charlie went to talk to him as well; over a cup of tea in his kitchenette he confessed to murdering her, but couldn't even describe what she looked like.

The other name turned out to be Lucee Williams's teacher, a Julie Anderson. The reason for calling the IR room seemed vague, and no one had been actioned to see her yet. It was late, and he'd wasted the whole afternoon on this, he would talk to the skipper about Anderson in the morning. The flat was cold and empty when he got home. He reminded himself to get the key back off Pippa tomorrow.

Of course Lucee's teacher would be worried about her. That didn't seem like a good enough reason to call the Incident Room.

He wished he had a dog.

CHAPTER THIRTY-THREE

The problem in some cases wasn't that they didn't have enough information, it was that they had too much. There were messages posted on all of Brooklyn's social media, and since the TV appeal there were thousands and thousands of messages, some from friends and family, most of them from complete strangers. They all had to be monitored.

Hundreds of telephone calls, thousands of posts and tweets and emails; the skipper had drafted in extra warm bodies to try and stay on top of it. Now here was Charlie, leaning over his shoulder, wanting to go back through the HOLMES files of the Okpotu case, as if he didn't have enough to do already.

The skipper tapped a finger on the monitor screen. 'Now then. Here she is. Anderson, Julie Anderson. I told you about this one.'

'Didn't anyone go and see her?'

'I sent Mac to talk to her. She was off sick, I was going to action it again but I suppose it got lost in the system. She didn't make it sound very important. Is it?'

'I don't know. Maybe not. I just don't want to miss anything.'

'Is that why you went to see them bloody time-wasters yesterday? Don't know why you bothered. I could have told you it would come to nowt.'

'Give me her number, I'll give her a call.'

'As long as it's nowt to do with tarot cards,' the skipper said, and made a face. He went to make himself a cup of tea.

Julie Anderson reminded him of his old infant-school teacher,

Mrs Taylor, a kindly soul with a big bosom. He had liked her, she hadn't laughed at him when he told her he wanted to be a policeman when he grew up. The only time she had ever got angry at him was when he had hit some kid for trying to steal his lunch. She told him it was not the way to solve problems; when he told his dad about it, he had patted him on the back and said, next time son, put the slipper in as well.

'Thanks for coming in, Mrs Anderson.'

'Well, I was glad to get your call. I wondered why no one had been out to see me.'

'We did send out a couple of detectives to speak to you, but the school said you were away.'

'I had flu. You know what it's like, working in a school. I thought they'd come back, if they thought it was important.'

'They probably should have done, but in all fairness, we have all been a little overworked lately, and sometimes things get overlooked.'

Julie Anderson smiled and nodded. She clutched a manila folder to her, two-handed, as though she was afraid someone was going to snatch it away.

'You rang our hotline, saying you had information for us regarding the murder of Mariatu Okpotu?'

'Well, I don't know if you would call it information. I thought a long time before calling you. It might not be anything. But it's been all over the news, of course, the school has just been in turmoil. I remember little Mariatu. I never met her, but I remember her from the school choir. She was a lovely girl.'

Charlie tried not to let his impatience show. Beside him, he could see that Lovejoy was as eager as he was to see what was in the manila folder. 'This may be nothing. I could be wasting your time. I'm quite embarrassed now I'm here.'

'Well you never know,' Charlie said. 'Any information at all is always gratefully received.'

'Lucee Williams is in my class. She's been away, of course, poor thing. Ever since her sister disappeared.'

Charlie waited.

'I was tidying up the classroom on the Friday before, and I knocked over her tray. I found some drawings in among her work. I'd never seen them before, I have no idea when she did them. I didn't know what to think. I still don't. It may be nothing.'

'What may be nothing?' Lovejoy asked her.

Finally, she put the manila folder on the desk and opened it. She took out three drawings, clearly made by a small child. They were all very similar; three stick figures, one with a brown face, and a red splotch on the back of her head. Another figure had a baseball cap and was holding an orange oblong. The third figure had yellow hair and a skirt and was smaller, half the size of the other two figures.

'I'm sure this is just something she's seen on television. She's a very sensitive child. I'm probably wasting your time.'

Charlie heard Lovejoy take a deep breath.

'She definitely drew these?'

'They were in her tray.'

'And you're worried that this might not be just her . . . imagination?'

'I hope it is. But it's not like her to draw things like this. It's, well, worrying.'

They had not made the manner of Mariatu's death public. A lot of people in the local community still believed she had been strangled. How could a five-year-old girl know that Mariatu had died from a blow to the back of her head unless she had been there and witnessed it?

Charlie tapped his index finger on the square brick building at the bottom of all three of the drawings.

'Would you say, looking at these drawings, that this boy here, with the cap back to front on his head, has just hit the little girl with the brick?'

'I don't see how you can read it any other way, guv,' Lovejoy said.

'Do you mind if we keep these?' he said.

'Of course not,' Mrs Anderson said. 'If you think they're important.'

'I'll go and get evidence bags,' Lovejoy said.

She went out. Mrs Anderson frowned. 'You think she saw something?'

'Possibly. Did you ask her why she drew these?'

'As I said, I only found them the Friday before her sister disappeared. She hasn't been back to school since.'

'Have you ever taught her brother, Reuben?'

'I'm reasonably new at the school. I wasn't here when he was in the first year. I hear the other teachers talk about him sometimes.'

'And what do they say?'

'Well, he doesn't have a very good reputation.'

'In what way?'

'The talk in the staff room is that he's very . . . aggressive. I've seen him myself in the playground hitting other boys, smaller boys. He has been suspended twice for hurting other children in his class.'

'Hurting them how?'

'You should really talk to our headmaster about this.'

'I will. But to save me time?'

'I believe he cut another boy with a pair of scissors. He swore it was an accident, but the cut needed stitches. There have been other complaints. None of the other parents let their children play with him. I believe they are all quite scared of him.'

'And what about Lucee?'

'You've met her?'

'I've interviewed the family on several occasions.'

'Well then, you've seen for yourself, she's a quiet little girl. Never says much.'

'Ever in trouble?'

'Never. She's a very smart little girl, but she doesn't have much interaction with the other kids. At break times she mostly just walks around with her brother, they don't even play, sometimes they even hold hands.'

'She doesn't have friends?'

She shook her head. 'To be honest, I think it's a little unhealthy. I spoke to the Williamses about it at their last parent interview a month or so ago, but they don't seem much interested. They seem to like the fact he takes such an interest in her, if anything. Built-in babysitter, I suppose.'

Lovejoy came back. They put the three drawings in separate evidence bags and labelled them. Charlie thanked the teacher for her time. 'You have been very helpful,' he said. 'Very.'

They went back upstairs, gave Mrs Anderson's statement to the skipper and Charlie went to get his car keys. When they got outside, Charlie stopped and looked up at the clouds. 'We all long for the sky,' he said. 'We do not wish to think on that which lies below, in the dark of the ground.'

'Guv?'

'Sorry. It was something this psychologist bloke said to me recently. He was explaining why people are scared of the dark.'

'Because there really are monsters.'

'Yeah, something like that.'

'Shall we go and see the principal?'

'Not right now, we can get to that later. I think first we pay a visit to the Williamses'. Our little friend Reuben has some explaining to do.'

CHAPTER THIRTY-FOUR

Mother keeps saying what's that smell, she keeps saying it over and over. It has been there for days and days but now I suppose the essence of her is so strong that even she knows now. I say to her, I can't smell anything, like I do not know, but Brooklyn is spreading everywhere, through the ceiling, through the walls.

Mother goes around the house sniffing, like a dog, looking in things, she is making a face, I do not like it.

She goes outside to check the gas, then she comes back in, thinks it is something behind the refrigerator. She pulls it out and looks behind it, sniffs in the freezer. She goes up the stairs and pulls down the ladder to the attic and she says I think it is coming from up here. I wish she would stop but she keeps saying to me over and over, can't you smell it? I tell her please Mum stop, stop, and she looks down the ladder at me and she says I think there is a dead rat. I try to stop her, I don't want her to get herself murdered, but she has put me in a difficult position. I tell Lucee, go and get your coat we are going out, and she says where are we going, and I say, just out.

Mother comes down from the attic and I think perhaps now she will stop and wait until Father comes home but that is when I see it, I look up and there is a stain in the ceiling and I watch it spread. It gets bigger, like clouds changing all the time. I try to concentrate, thinking what different shapes I can see. At first it looks like a tiger then it looks like a horse but then it just looks like Brooklyn. There is a teardrop, a small one at first, and it lands drip, drip, on the tiles in the kitchen floor.

And then Mother comes in, she says that smell is definitely coming from upstairs somewhere and then she looks at me and then what is dripping on the floor. I know straight away by the look on her face what is going to happen and there is nothing I can do to stop it.

I can't stop it happening and it is all going to be her fault.

There is a funny look on her face and I don't like it and it makes me feel really funny inside. What is that? she says, and she comes closer like she wants to know but she doesn't, not really. And there is another drip, drip, and the stain on the ceiling is a browny colour and the puddle on the floor gets a little bit bigger. She gets down on all fours and puts her hand over her mouth, and she puts her fingers in the puddle and sniffs and says, what is that?

She looks up at the ceiling again, and she is working out which room it is up there, and she looks at me, and she says, what have you done, and I try to warn her, I do, I try, but now it is too late, it is all her fault.

I say, don't go in my room and her face goes all white but she doesn't look angry she looks scared. She goes up the stairs and I turn to Lucee, what is it Reuben, Lucee says. She has her coat on, just like I told her. So now I know what I have to do.

I say to her, go and play in the garden, and she turns and runs out because she knows when I use that voice I mean it. I run up the stairs after Mother and I stand in front of my bedroom door, and I tell her, don't go in my room, no one is allowed to go in my room, not ever. Because if no one goes in my room it didn't happen, it was just something I thought of, not something I did, not really.

Don't go in my room, Mother, I told you.

What have you done Reuben? she keeps saying, over and over, and I think she is going to shake me, like she used to do when I was a little kid. She takes a step towards me and then stops.

There is a banging at the front door, it is the policeman who has been standing outside, I can see him standing there through

264

the frosted glass. Mother goes really quiet and stands there not moving like she cannot make up her mind what to do. She looks at me then back at the door. The policeman knocks again, a bit harder this time.

She goes to the door and I hear the policeman ask her, is everything all right in there, and she looks back at me and then she says, yes everything is fine, thank you officer.

I heard a lot of screaming, he says to her, I was worried, and Mother says, no it's fine, everything's fine and she shuts the door.

And then she looks at me and I know she knows, really she knows, but she doesn't want to tell him, she needs time to be sure, needs time to think about it.

I tell her again, don't go in my room.

When people will not listen, it is not my fault. Brooklyn would not listen, and that monkey, she would not listen either, she just kept laughing and teasing me, I told her to stop, but she just kept on.

Lucee listens to me. Lucee never laughs.

My room is dark, my room is always dark, there is just my computer, the screen glowing, warm and safe, a green glow, like seeing the world through my night vision. Mother goes to the window and pulls open the curtains and she lets in all this horrible light, it ruins everything, everything. There is my bed, which I never make, with all its nice smells, and my clothes and food things on the floor, and in the dark I know just where they are and in the light she has taken away everything that makes them special and nice. I cannot believe what she has done, and I yell at her and I grab at her arm but she is stronger than I think and she shouts at me and she pushes me away and then she hits me. She has never hit me. It doesn't hurt, I just cannot believe she has done it.

She is still shouting but I cannot make out the words, because she has her hand over her face. She keeps pointing to the sleeping bag under the bed, the red nylon leaking sleeping bag.

She sways on her feet and I think she is going to faint, but she doesn't. She grabs me by the shoulder and she shakes me, and she stares into my face. I turn my head, I don't like it, but she grabs my chin and makes me look at her. What have you done, what have you done, she is yelling, but she knows what I have done, I think she knows all along what I have done.

She stamps her foot and gives a little scream. Then she kneels down and reaches out a hand to the sleeping bag, she wants to look but she doesn't want to look, all at once. There is a puddle on the carpet, she touches it and rubs her fingers together and sniffs them, and then her eyes go really wide and she makes this gagging noise, in her throat, like our dog when it is being sick on a fur ball.

She touches the tuck of the sleeping bag, peels it back. Brooklyn's skin is starting to turn purply-black, like I have seen in the pictures on the internet. My mother starts to cry. I don't like it when she cries so I hit her with the cricket bat I keep behind the door. It still has bits of Brooklyn's hair on it.

I don't like people coming in my room. I don't like people teasing me. If they didn't come in my room, they wouldn't get themselves murdered. It is their fault.

After I finish killing her, I look at my watch. It has taken one minute and thirty-five seconds. When Brooklyn got herself murdered it took one minute and fifty-five seconds. That made me laugh. I remember Father always used to tap her on the head and say you're dense you are. You have got a thick head. So there, I have proved it.

I go downstairs, I don't know what I should do now, so I make some popcorn in the microwave for me and Lucee. While I eat the popcorn, I watch Lucee playing on the swing in the garden; it is raining but she does not seem to mind. Molly is barking and trying to catch her feet with her teeth. It's funny.

I cannot decide the colour of the sky. Over there, where the clouds are thickest, it is the kind of grey called elephant's breath. Yes, that is it. Elephant's breath.

She sees me watching her through the window and she holds out her hand and says come and push me. I give her the bag of popcorn and then I push her on the swing, and while I push her I think about what I should do. I cannot hide Mother in the sleeping bag, I will have to do something else. I am not ready to go to my other dark place, I have not got enough traps or enough food, but Mother has ruined everything.

Did Mummy go in your room, Lucee says, and I say yes, she went in my room, and Lucee says, but no one is allowed to go in your room.

No, no one, I tell her, and I give her another push on the swing.

When is Daddy coming home, she says, and then I remember he has gone out for his walk. I say soon, soon he is coming home. I say, wait here to Lucee and I get the cricket bat from upstairs and I eat the popcorn and stand by the window and wait for him. I have made up my mind what we will do.

CHAPTER THIRTY-FIVE

The house was quiet but both the Williamses' cars were in the carport. There was just one patrol car outside, a uniform with his hands folded in front of him, standing by the gate, looking miserable in the drizzle.

'Looks like the media have lost interest,' Charlie said. Just a couple of vans, neither of them from the BBC.

'Need a brolly?' Lovejoy said to the constable as they went in.

He glanced at her and said, 'I'm all right, ma'am. I've stood out in worse.'

'Anyone been in and out this morning?' Charlie said.

'Just Mr Williams, he went out about eight o'clock, said he wanted to go for a walk, looked proper shocking he did. Poor bastard. Came back about half an hour ago.'

'Anything been happening?'

'A bit of yelling and screaming going on, don't know what that was all about, I knocked on the door, Mrs Williams said everything was all right. It's quietened down again now. I think she was just having a row with the boy. I don't know, suppose they're a bit fraught with all that's going on.'

'Suppose they are,' Charlie said.

Charlie knocked on the front door and waited and then he knocked again and when no one answered he nodded at Lovejoy and she went to the window and peered in and shrugged and shook her head. 'According to the uniform outside, they're all home,' she said. 'You reckon something's going on?'

'Well they weren't shouting and screaming for nothing.'

'Should we try and break in?'

Charlie thought about bending down and looking through the letterbox but he had on his blue Ted Baker overcheck so he nodded at Lovejoy and she was eager enough.

'Oh, Jesus.'

'What have you got?'

'I can see a foot.'

'Just a foot or is it attached to a body?'

'It's attached to a body but it's not moving. Looks like a man's shoe.'

'We're in then,' Charlie said, and he went back to the uniform and asked him for his Maglite, went up to the door, and smashed it against the frosted glass. He reached inside and unfastened the latch and opened the door.

Mr Williams lay face down on the carpet, halfway between the hall and the living room. The uniform stood on the step behind them, the blood draining out of his face; fuck me, he said. Charlie could hear him thinking, there goes my promotion. Another five years of standing around in worse than this, without an umbrella.

'Can't you hear the dog?' Charlie said.

'The dog?' he said.

'Round the back. It's been yapping the whole time.'

'I'll call for back-up,' the constable said.

'Too right my son,' Charlie said, 'you call for the cavalry. I'm going to check inside, see what's what.'

The constable waited on the step, whispering into the radio on the collar of his stab vest. Lovejoy went to follow Charlie inside, he put a hand on her arm to stop her. 'It's a crime scene, Lovejoy, I'll call you if I need you.'

'But the boy,' she said.

He gave her a look. 'I do not need back-up for a thirteen-year-old.'

Charlie looked across the road at the two news crew drinking coffee in front of one of the vans; they had started to take an interest, he reckoned they were about to get the scoop of their lives.

'Make sure those buggers don't get a view of this,' Charlie said to Lovejoy. 'Get a cordon up. Five minutes and this street is going to turn into the Notting Hill Carnival.'

Charlie turned away but he didn't just barrel in, his first duty was to preserve life and that meant preserving his own first of all. He didn't know who was responsible for Mr Williams lying there on the living-room carpet, he didn't know anything yet, so he hefted the Maglite in his right hand and checked three-sixty before he stepped all the way in.

It only needed a cursory glance to tell him that Mr Williams was dead, he didn't bother bending down to look for a pulse, the poor bastard's brains were all over the shagpile. There was a chair behind the door, it seemed odd for a moment and then he pictured a thirteen-year-old standing on it, just to give himself enough height for a good swing.

A cricket bat lay on the carpet, the end of it covered with matted blood and hair. It was a Puma, coral and black, nice grip, not cheap, good bit of gear. Some of the hair was blonde and Williams had dark hair, so Charlie supposed it had been used more than once.

If the constable on duty outside hadn't heard anything, Reuben must have put him down with the first hit; the rest of it was just – what was it the pathologist had called it? – frenzy.

Charlie backed out of the room, cautious now, don't go through any doors without checking first, my son, not now you know how this works. Don't want to get yourself hooked to the boundary. There was a master bedroom downstairs, he swung the door right back, made sure there was no one behind it, then step by step to the en-suite, the SCO19 boys would have laughed if they'd seen him, ready to do a hard stop with a torch.

The bedroom was a mess, sheets half on the floor and dirty underwear everywhere, as you'd expect, he supposed, from people living in distress. He went up the stairs, nice and slow, heard Lovejoy shouting at the news crew outside. He stopped on the landing, took a deep breath to steady himself. His mouth was dry and had a nasty taste.

There were smears of blood on the carpet.

He hesitated, there were three doors, two bedrooms and a toilet; choose your poison, Charlie.

There was a smell, he knew it straight away, there was a body up here, not a fresh one. But there might be someone still alive, he had to check, couldn't wait for the back-up. He took the nearest door, turned the handle, kicked it open, he was a bit too enthusiastic, it flew off its hinge, cracked against the wall.

Nothing, just a cistern with a nice pink knitted cover on it.

Two doors left. Which one is it going to be, Charlie? He threw back the first door, stood with his back against the wall, feeling like a total prat, but he didn't want some dwarf in a Nike baseball cap coming up behind him and sconing him with an item of sports equipment.

But it was just a little girl's bedroom, it said 'Lucee' over the bed in giant pink cut-out letters with two giant pink plastic butterflies either side. Everything was pink; the coverlet, the lace pillowcases, even the antique bed frame and drawers.

He crossed the landing, well, process of deduction, this is it.

He turned the handle, kicked open the door and stood back. Holy Christ.

No one in here needed their pulse checking either. Mrs Williams, or what was left of her, lay prone on the carpet. Messy. The smell coming from the bed was rank, nothing he hadn't smelled before, but only at crime scenes where the body hadn't been found straight away.

There was something wrapped in a sleeping bag under the bed by the looks, he supposed that was where the smell was coming from. He could guess who that was. So only Reuben and the little girl still not accounted for. Lovely.

He took two steps into the room, careful not to tread in

anything nasty, checked the wardrobe for any more surprises. He took a look out of the window and down into the back garden, the Maltese terrier was going off its nut, trying to scale the back fence. There was a gate that opened onto a lane at the back, just the other side of the garden shed. So that must be how he got out; had he taken his little sister with him? No sign of another body, so they had to hope for the best, even now.

The carpet was littered with empty packets of spicy Doritos and McDonald's wrappers, empty smoothie cups. The walls were stark, most teenage boys he knew had posters of pop stars or footballers, but not Reuben. Charlie looked for his phone, a quick clock of the desk and the bedside table. He couldn't be the only thirteen-year-old in London who didn't have one. There it was. So he hadn't taken it with him, he'd thought about this, which was smart.

There was a tin of luminous paint and a garden trowel in the corner, next to the bed. God alone knew what that was about.

He heard sirens, the local Bill on their way. The news crews wouldn't be far behind.

Lovejoy was waiting for him on the step when he got outside.

'What have you got, guv?'

'It's *Macbeth* in there,' Charlie said. 'Been doing this job a long time but I've never seen anything quite like it.'

'Reuben?'

'He's not there, neither is the little girl. The rest of them are dead.'

'Not Brooklyn as well?'

Charlie made a face.

'You are kidding me, guv.'

'I wish.'

Two police units arrived almost at the same time, lights and sirens on; a TV van turned the corner at the bottom of the street, Charlie heard more sirens in the distance.

'Party time,' he said.

'What do we do?'

'Once our crime scene is secure, we have to go looking for young Master Williams.'

'How did he get away?'

'There's a gate at the back, leads to a lane. That's why the dog's going nuts, they went without it.'

Another patrol car pulled up, he saw curtains moving in windows up and down the street, people came out to their front gardens, never mind the bit of rain. There was a camera pointed at them, a journalist had his microphone out, his sound man was standing right behind him, he was looking for someone to ambush with questions.

'Smile, you're going to be on tonight's news,' Charlie said.

He saw Mansell get out of one of the patrol cars, that was quick; he could see him looking around at the circus gathering and it wasn't hard to work out what he was thinking, what every line manager would be thinking right now, who is going to take the fall for this?

Charlie went over, saw Mansell's face drop even further when he recognised him. Every nightmare the poor bastard had ever had, all happening at once.

'What the hell is going on?' he said.

'There are three deceased in there.'

'But I had a man posted.'

'Not his fault, I don't think. One of the bodies is Brooklyn Williams, the same Brooklyn Williams we've been searching for, for four days.'

'You can't blame my boys for this.'

'Yes I can, I can blame your boys, I do blame your boys. I said it, didn't I, have they checked every room in the house, and you assured me they had.'

'Where was she?'

'Under her brother's bed. Gone to her reward several days ago.'

'Well, fair play, who would have thought to find a teenage girl in her little brother's room?'

'It is not our business to make assumptions,' Charlie said, and then he thought about the assumptions he had made at the beginning of the investigation, the assumptions they had all made.

'Want a job done right, you have to do it yourself,' someone said over his shoulder. It was Lovejoy.

'And you are?' Mansell said, sticking out his chin.

Charlie was about to rein her in but then he thought, no to hell with it, there are two people dead now who didn't need to be.

'DC Lesley Lovejoy, sir. I worked uniform in Croydon, we had a few MisPers when I was there, and our sergeant always told us, don't start a search until you've turned the residence upside down, top to bottom. We found one missing six-year-old hiding in an upstairs airing cupboard.'

'Well this little girl was a teenager and she wasn't going to fit in no airing cupboard,' Mansell said, and Charlie thought, he's defending his troops, no harm in that. He knows this is going to come back on him eventually anyway.

'What's done is done,' Charlie said. 'This is a crime scene now, no one is to go in or out till the crime unit and the pathologist get here. We also need to find these two.' He showed him the framed family portrait that he had taken off the hall stand. 'This is Reuben and this is Lucee. They're both missing.'

'The deceased in there,' Mansell said. 'How did they die?'

'Two were bludgeoned to death with a blunt instrument within the last hour. I believe this boy here is the person of interest.'

'What, the kid?'

'They are on foot so they can't have got very far. Do what you can.' Charlie walked away. He wouldn't want to be in his shoes after the commissioner had finished with him.

Charlie nodded to Lovejoy, she followed him back to the house.

'Don't go doing that,' he said.

'Doing what, guv?'

274

'Winding up a police inspector. Bad enough you do it to me, I have a kind and understanding nature; do it to blokes like that and you'll get yourself in trouble.'

'I don't wind you up, do I guv?'

He led her through the crowd of uniforms at the front gate and around the side of the house. He reached over the fence and unhitched the latch, told her to follow him.

'Where are we going?' she said.

There was a shed, a swing, a packet of microwave popcorn lying on the paving stones.

Charlie went to the shed, there was a latch but no padlock, he threw it open and took a quick step back, imagined junior roadman running at him with a garden fork, but there was no one inside, no dead little girls.

'Should we wait for back-up?' Lovejoy asked.

'I am the back-up.'

The Maltese was still scratching at the gate. 'Didn't he say he always takes the dog with him everywhere?' Lovejoy said.

'Not this time.' Charlie took a look through the kitchen door, saw a lead hanging up on a hook next to the refrigerator. 'Grab that,' he said, 'it's time this little girl went walkies.'

The Maltese almost choked itself pulling him down the lane. She knew the way, or she thought she did, and she was in a hurry to get there. When they got to the road, Charlie told Lovejoy to go back and tell Mansell to have a couple of uniforms follow them in the car.

When he got to the high street, people stopped what they were doing and stared at the geezer in the sharp-looking suit chasing a fluffball on a lead. A few likely lads in hoodies had a bit of a laugh at his expense, he ignored them. He supposed they must look pretty funny, if they didn't know there was a little girl's life on the line.

It wasn't until he almost got to the betting shop that Lovejoy caught him up again, Tottenham vs Arsenal in the front window offering 2/1 on Harry Kane getting the first goal; bloody annoyed him, that did, even though he had more important things on his mind.

He knew where they were headed, knew it from the moment they took off through the gate. They were headed down to where Mariatu took her last walk.

'Are they behind us?' he shouted at Lovejoy.

'Just coming now, guv.'

The Maltese pulled them down the cul-de-sac to the disused railway line, through the wire fence, not many people about, a jogger heading home for his shower, Lucozade and healthy salad. The Maltese was still straining at the leash, for a little dog she had a lot of stamina, proper eager to get to where she was going.

CHAPTER THIRTY-SIX

'Look at this,' Charlie said. 'Someone's picked the lock.'

The dog was already inside, circling the ladder.

'You want to wait, guv? I can see the uniform, there's two of them, they've seen us. There's more on the way.'

'Wait? It's a thirteen-year-old kid.'

'Who's murdered four people already.'

'I'm not bottling it going after a school kid. Every second we wait, the little girl is in danger.'

For all that, she was right. He needed something to defend himself. He still had the Maglite in his pocket, it would have to do.

'Remember what happened the last time you went in without back-up?'

'Yeah, I remember, I saved this woman's life, because if I'd waited Dr Lucifer was about to use her as a human kebab.'

'All right, let's do it then.'

'Not you, just me.'

He peered down the shaft, a series of alternating ladders inside a vertical metal cage. There was sweat like cold grease all over him; he felt suddenly hot and sick, like that time he was on Ben's boat, rocking at anchor, breathing diesel fumes. He leaned against the wall and threw up, not a lot, just a bit.

'You all right?' Lovejoy said.

'Claustrophobia,' he said. He started down the hole. 'You don't tell anyone about this, not anyone.'

Force yourself, Charlie, just think about the kid, nothing

else. As he went down he kept one hand on the ladder, gripped the Maglite in the other, kept the beam swinging around, searching the dark below him, his shoes clanging on the metal rungs. He heard Lovejoy coming down after him, he knew she'd ignore the order to stay where she was, that was what he would have done as well.

He had to keep going, can't stop to think about this, Charlie, you know what will happen, your muscles will freeze, got to keep moving. There's a six-year-old girl just come down this ladder, if she can do it, so can you.

He shone the torch around, the beam picked out the bent metal ribs of an old tunnel, a grimy brick wall with gridded gaps for ventilation, the platform of a station no one had ever used. There was a huge mound of spoil – clay, sleepers and brick – blocking off that end of the tunnel, he couldn't climb over that.

He heard Lovejoy jump down on to the ground beside him. 'Can you see them?'

He shone the Maglite the other way, saw something moving down there, fixed the beam on them. 'There they are,' he said. He couldn't judge the distance in the torchlight, a hundred yards he supposed.

'Come on,' Lovejoy said, and she tugged on his arm and pulled him with her; he couldn't let her go ahead, so he made himself keep moving. It was muddy underfoot, there was rain streaming down the walls, it was just the surface that was slippery, the ground felt rock hard underneath.

He heard squeaking, something fluttering from the light, there were bats down here. They had had this place to themselves for so long, they must be proper pissed off lately. He heard the Maltese still barking, the noise magnified and echoed in the tunnel, then the uniforms, shouting down the hole, just get yourselves down here, lads.

'Are you OK, guv?' he heard Lovejoy say behind him.

He couldn't get his breath to answer her. Where were they? He swung the torch again.

'Did you tie that dog up?' he said. 'I don't want it hurling itself down the hole.'

'Do I look like someone who doesn't care about dogs, guv?'

The Maglite beam started to flicker.

'Fuck,' Charlie said, 'the battery is running out.'

'Why are they running to one side like that?' Lovejoy said.

He could just make them out with the torch, they had darted to the left, were hugging the left-hand wall of the tunnel, single file. It didn't make sense, why weren't they running down the middle, it was easier down the middle.

'Wait a minute,' Charlie said, but Lovejoy didn't hear him, and he tried to grab her arm to stop her but he was too late. He heard her stumble. There was a sickening thud and then a sound came out of her, it chilled him, he hadn't heard anything like that since he was in uniform and had to attend car smashes with people trapped inside.

The Maglite went out.

He banged it against his knee, switched it on and off a couple of times; it flickered on again. He looked around. Lovejoy was gone. He called her name, the torch beam found her, he thought she was on her knees but then he saw her foot had gone down a hole where the rail tracks were supposed to have been.

'Is it your ankle?' he said and shone the light on her face. Her eyes were wide, and she was trying to say something but no sound would come out, just a horrible, choking noise. She's broken her ankle, he thought, and knelt down beside her and grabbed her and started to pull her out of the hole but she shrieked and pushed him away, kept saying fuck and Jesus over and over, he couldn't figure out what was wrong with her.

He shone his torch down the hole and saw what it was, there were three nails through her left shoe, blood leaking everywhere, a puddle of it down the bottom of the hole. Oh Charlie, Charlie, Lovejoy said, and she grabbed his arm in a death grip and made a long, keening sound that echoed up and down the tunnel.

He got it, finally, a booby trap; he helped her ease her weight on to her other knee. Her whole body was rigid with pain, like trying to move a marble statue.

The torch beam flickered and turned yellow, and he thought, well, that's it then, it's too dangerous to keep going, anyway, I can't leave Lovejoy; and then he heard Lucee scream.

'You've got to,' Lovejoy said. 'Go after her.' She was still panting, getting control of it, the blood coming back into his arm as she relaxed her grip.

'Where are those coppers?' Charlie said. This new breed, he thought, it's right what they say, young blokes now, they're soft and they're slow.

'They're not the SAS, guv.' Lovejoy gasped as another spasm hit her. 'Oh fuck, oh fuck, this is fucking unbelievable, I think I'm going to faint.'

Another scream. What was he doing to her? The Maglite flared and he shone it down the length of the tunnel, a boy and a little girl with monstrous shadows.

'Go after them Charlie.'

'I can't leave you.'

'The others will be here in a minute. If anything happens to that little girl, it's on us.'

He let go of her, stood up.

'If you stay to one side of the tunnel you'll be all right.'

He heard voices behind them.

'Down here quick!' he shouted. 'We need urgent assistance, we have a man down, man down!' Straight away he thought: I'm going to pay for that later, she is going to have a go at me for using sexist language.

She pushed him away, get the girl, she said, just get the girl.

He picked his way to the edge of the tunnel, testing each step, his blood pounding in his ears, he just wanted to get out but he was stuck down here now, and there were only two ways out: one way was with Lucee in his arms, the other was like Lovejoy, bleeding and sweating with pain in the back of an ambulance.

280

He heard something scrabbling in the dark, rats he supposed; the torch beam caught a cockroach scuttling up the wall, it froze in the light.

'Come on, you can do it, Charlie son, you did it when you went into the tunnel that day with Pippa and the shrink, you can do it again now. He could see the light shaking all over the place; man up, Charlie.

The torch beam turned from white to yellow, he was getting close now, he could see the little girl struggling with her brother, he was only maybe fifty yards away, and then the torch flickered again and went out. He banged it against his thigh. Nothing.

Just him and the dark now.

CHAPTER THIRTY-SEVEN

I can hear them behind me, I can smell them, more strangers in my special place. I don't like it. They should not bring light down here, I will make them all get murdered, I will.

I don't know how they found me, until I hear Molly barking, a long way back in the tunnel. Lucee is the problem, and now I wonder if I should have brought her. She cannot go as fast as I want, she keeps crying, if she keeps crying like this she will make herself get murdered. I do not know if I will like it if I do not have Lucee, it will be like not having a shadow.

I don't like this thing, Lucee says, and she takes off her night-vision goggles and throws them on the ground and I look around for them, but even with my night-vision lens I cannot see them, there are just shapes, and the torch he is shining at me makes it hard to see. I do not have a torch, just the knife I took from Mother's kitchen. When he gets close I am going to stab him and stab him until he stops running after me and the light goes out.

Lucee starts crying again, I shake her hard to make her stop, but it only makes it worse, she screams and the noise echoes around and around inside my head until I can't stand it. I have to slap her, slap her really hard, to make her stop. She stops screaming and instead she makes these gasping noises, like she is drowning. I never thought she would be like this, she always liked it before when we came down here, or when I cut up dead birds, and when that girl got herself murdered, she was the one shouting hit her, hit her, dirty little monkey.

They have all come into my world now and I don't like it, this place was meant to be just for me, me and Lucee. This is all that monkey's fault, she is the one that started this, with her smirking and her laughing and saying her nasty things. If she had not seen us come out of the brick house that day, everything would be all right. She was just a monkey girl and her mum has no hands, so I don't know why everyone cared about her getting herself murdered.

Lucee tries to pull away from me when I grab her hand, and I think, I had better stab her now, but then I feel her go limp. There are these others in the dark now, I can hear them calling out and then there is just a woman's voice, screaming and moaning. She has stepped on my booby trap, I know she has, and I am excited because it has worked and I wonder what it looks like, her foot. I wish he had stepped on it; I wait for him to scream too, but I can see him now, still following, the bright light of his torch, he is close to the edge of the tunnel, he is clever.

I can hear a train announcer's voice, all that muffled and metallic sound, I can smell the bodies and the grease from the track. There is a wall blocking the entrance to the underground station on the other side, a part of it has been knocked down; once I tried to scramble over the top over the bricks and rubble, but then I found another way through.

There is a gate, a metal one with bars, and I know where it goes, it goes into the tunnel at the end of the platform. There was a lock on the gate, it was a really old one, and the chain was all rusted, it had been there a long time. But I opened the lock, months and months ago when I first came down here; it was easy, I learned how to do it on the internet. Lucee and I, we will go through the gate and wait until there are no trains and we will get up on the platform. And when a train comes along we will get on, and we will stay on the tube until it gets to the very last station. We can get through the barriers, it is easy, I have seen people do it lots of times, the guards do lots of shouting, but the people just laugh and run away.

He is very close now, the policeman. I am sure now the others will not catch me, only him. I have on my NVG, sometimes if I am down here a long time I can see even without them but I have not been nearly long enough out of the light. That policeman's torch makes everything blur, like looking through broken glass, and if I move my head too fast I lose track of him.

There is an alcove in the tunnel wall and I press into it. I can smell dust and mould and rats and other nice comforting smells. I can hear him behind us, he is panting hard, like he is scared, like he can't get his breath, he must be really unfit. I grab Lucee's hand, it is cold and damp and I put my hand over her mouth because I do not want her to scream again, I do not want him to know where I am. We have to keep really still.

His torch goes on-off, on-off, and now the light is turning yellow. Then everything goes black and I hear him say bad words, a lot of them. Now what will he do? If he comes past us now I will be able to see him and he will not be able to see me. I will stab him with my knife, stab him and stab him, it will be fun, and Lucee and me, we will run away down to the end of the tunnel to the trains.

I feel Lucee wriggle so I hold her really tight and pinch her nose so she cannot make any other sound. I think perhaps if I hold her like this she will die and then I will not have to worry about her and perhaps it will be better for her too, because then she will not be scared any more.

He is still coming up the tunnel, he is mad, he is, he has no torch. I can see him through the NVG, just a green shadow, like seeing underwater. He stops, leans against the tunnel wall. Just a few more steps, please. Lucee makes a noise, trying to breathe, she kicks and kicks, he can hear her, she is kicking me, she won't be still. I squeeze her nose tighter, I think maybe the only way is to stab her too with the knife. I have never stabbed anyone. I wonder what it will feel like. It might be fun.

Lucee bites my hand, really hard, and wriggles free and so I cannot stab her properly, I just swing with the knife and I

284

hear her scream. But then I know he is really close and I turn my head to look, but I turn around too fast, and it is like when you get off a fairground ride, suddenly I feel really giddy like I am going to fall over, and I have to put out a hand to the wall. I cannot see him any more, I do not know where he has gone, I can smell him though, very close, he has on cologne, like my father wears, a smoky citrus smell. And I smell sweat, a fear smell.

Where is he? The goggles are no good, I panic and want to rip them off. Instead I take a deep breath and steady myself against the wall. The shadows settle like shapes. I see Lucee now, she is right there, and he is there too, right in front of me, he cannot see me, so I raise the knife and choose where I will stab first.

CHAPTER THIRTY-EIGHT

Charlie slapped the torch against his thigh, it flared back, the beam was weak, yellow. It's not going to last, Charlie, you know that, it's going to die any minute and you'll be left alone in the dark with Psycho Boy, and remember, Psycho Boy has serious form. Wonder what kind of weapon he has with him, sure and certain he has come down here prepared.

Lucee was screaming again, there was something going on. Why would he kill her now, why didn't he do for her at the house like the others?

'Reuben. Can you hear me, Reuben? Take it easy now son, come on boy, it's all right, whatever you've done, we can work this out.'

Even as the words came out of his mouth, he thought, this is crazy, there's no point talking to this kid. This is proper mad. How does he know where he is going?

The torch went out again, he stopped and slammed it against the wall, but this time nothing. It started then, the panic. Suddenly he was back in the coal shed, he could hear his father laughing as he turned the key in the padlock, that'll teach you, you little gobshite. How old was he? Three, four?

He heard rumbling, felt the ground shaking under him as a tube train pulled in to the station somewhere at the end of the tunnel. He could make out a flickering light down there, the lights of a carriage, just near the end of the tunnel loop, then the ghostly howl of the backdraught. The muffled voice of the train announcer made as much sense from fifty yards away as it did if you were standing right there on the platform.

Charlie crouched down, tried to make himself a small target. It was pitch black, except for the flicker of torches at the end of the tunnel, but the uniforms were too far away to help him. The kid was muttering to himself, he was close, couldn't be more than a few feet away. And Lovejoy was screaming, Charlie where are you, where are you, what's happening, talk to me.

He needed a light. He fumbled in his pocket for his iPhone, and dropped the Maglite; the phone wasn't in his pocket, he remembered now, he'd left it on charge in Lovejoy's Sierra. The Nokia was a piece of crap, it didn't have a torch. Shouldn't have dropped the Maglite. At least it was a weapon, of sorts. He scrabbled in the dirt, couldn't find it, it must have rolled off into the dark somewhere.

No, wait a minute, there it was, he felt his fingers close around it, and the heft of it was somehow reassuring. Scone the little sod with that, he'd know about it.

Then a flash of light, the whole tunnel illuminated for just a moment. He had to put a hand over his eyes to shield them, it was the two uniforms on their way, you took your time boys. One light, then two, they swung their Maglites from side to side trying to figure out what was happening. Lovejoy was screaming at them, this way, this way, and they were both shouting at once and yelling into their stab vests, good luck with that fellas, your radios aren't going to work down here.

One of the torches flicked around the walls and stopped, rested on Lucee, slumped down against the wall, blood all over her. Another flicker and arc and there was Reuben, standing not a few feet away, stock still. He was lit up for just a moment in the torch beam, he was wearing night vision goggles, the image intensifier pulled down over one eye, making him look like a cockroach, a giant fucking cockroach holding a kitchen knife.

Then the light went off, the uniforms were shining their

torches back on Lovejoy, she was shouting at them, Not me, leave me, help Charlie, help my guv'nor.

'You shouldn't have come down here,' Reuben said, 'you've ruined everything. It's not my fault.'

Charlie got to his feet, stumbled backwards through the dark; have to keep to the edge, Charlie, stay away from this little sod's traps. He couldn't see the knife but he heard it, heard it cutting through the dark. Charlie kept retreating, one hand on the tunnel wall for balance, Reuben slashed again and the blade caught in his jacket. Charlie kept scrambling back, another slash, and then his foot tangled in something, and he went down. He put up his hands, instinctively, imagined himself lying in the Haringey morgue and the pathologist pointing out the defence wounds to some other detective.

He couldn't see Reuben, where had he gone, where the hell was he?

One of the uniforms shone his torch towards them; Charlie saw Reuben standing over him with the knife raised, but the light blinded him, magnified through the intensifier on his night vision glasses. He yelled and threw up his hands.

Charlie scrambled to his feet, struck out with the Maglite, missed by a country mile. The torch beam swung away again. That was it then, he was in the dark, off balance, he knew what was coming.

He couldn't see Reuben, but he could hear him, the bloody kid was laughing at him. He tried to ready himself, but how do you get ready for a knife going in you?

Then he heard a shriek, panicked, desperate, so loud it hurt his ears. The noise went on and on. And even though he knew straight away it was Reuben making the noise, he sounded so agonised he almost wanted to comfort him. He knew what it was, of course, knew what he'd done.

He'd put his foot right down on one of his nail traps. All this crying and sobbing, Charlie thought; this is what poetic justice sounds like.

CHAPTER THIRTY-NINE

Lovejoy's father was trying to teach Charlie to fetch a ball without much success. It was a brilliant day, the leaves back on the trees, vapour trails criss-crossing a blue sky. It would be summer soon. He liked summer, no football to watch, no hopes to be crushed on a weekly basis, three months to imagine all the great players Arsenal might buy before the start of the next season, even though they never did.

Mr Lovejoy threw the ball and Charlie hurtled after it, ears and tongue flapping. He caught up with it, and Mr Lovejoy shouted, Come on Charlie, bring it back. It looked to him like Charlie saw no point in bringing it back after he had gone to the trouble of catching it, so he lay down in the long grass at the edge of the park and started to chew it.

'He doesn't get the point of the game yet,' he said.

Lovejoy had crutches and a moonboot. The doctors said it would be months yet before she would be fit enough to go back to work, but in other ways the experience had done her a bit of good. She wouldn't want to make a habit of it, but in the eyes of the team she had gone from the newbie try-hard sucking up to her boss to a hero in her own right. All it had taken was one misstep.

She had been in surgery for three hours, and in hospital for over a week.

'How's the foot?' Charlie asked her.

'Healing slowly. My surgeon says I'm never going to be a sock model.'

'That's bad luck.'

'And I always wanted to be a sock model. Another dream come crashing down. How are things at Essex Road?'

'The usual. Wes is talking about becoming a vegan. FONC is doing everyone's head in. We're all missing you, Lovejoy.'

'Be a while before you see me in there again. That bastard did quite a bit of damage with his little toys.'

'You did all right.'

'All I did was step in a bear trap.'

'No, you went down the ladder after me. Not in your job description.'

'Not in yours either.'

'Doesn't do me any good, know what I mean, like? I nearly get filleted by a fidget-spinner in a baseball cap, and what have I got to show? Insult to injury, the DCI knocked back my claim for expenses – that was a four-hundred-quid suit got ruined, plus the shirt was quality, too. Try and get one of those at the regular price on my salary. FONC said I should be buying shirts from Primark, I mean who does that?'

'Well you're my hero, guv, any consolation. No one else I'd rather step into a bear trap with.' Charlie the spaniel had found something particularly gross to roll in. Lovejoy smiled as she watched her dad pursue him round the trees.

'What's going to happen to the kid?'

Reuben.

The last time he had seen him, he was cuffed to a trolley with his foot in a bloodied bandage, his steely blue eyes watching him with the same disinterest as that first time he had interviewed him. We own you now, man, Charlie had whispered to him. What you did to your foot, that was bare jokes.

He looked so small with the oxygen mask on his face, lying under the silver thermal blanket, just his head sticking out. He didn't look evil, which was why evil got away with so much.

The paramedics had put a line in, but the nails were still in his foot; it would need a surgeon to get them out, the paramedics said, try and do it here we could rip half his foot away with it.

He almost said: yeah, but it's worth a try, isn't it?

'He's thirteen, Lovejoy, perhaps they'll try and rehabilitate him, give him a new identity and a hundred hours' community service, like Venables and that other scrote who murdered James Bulger. Or maybe they'll see him for what he is and he'll spend the rest of his natural in a secure facility doing finger painting so the rest of us can sleep at night. I know what I'd vote for.'

'Clever little shit, wasn't he? He gave us Norton, then he told us about some boyfriend of Brooklyn's that never existed. He led us round by the nose.'

'I should have seen it,' Charlie said. 'If I had, three people would still be alive.'

'You saved the spaniel. And the little girl.'

Charlie smiled. Yeah, he did something right.

Lucee had needed a lot of stitches, she would always have a scar, but that was the least of her problems. Charlie tried to imagine what her life would be like, how many years ahead sitting in a room with a shrink. Still, you never knew, like Mrs Okpotu, some people lost their hands and their whole families, they still got on with things somehow. It wasn't what happened to you, it was what you were made of.

'How's your girlfriend?'

'I don't have a girlfriend.'

'Ah. That was a smart move.'

'That's what Ben said, as well. He reckons I should go dry for a bit, sort myself out.'

'And will you?'

'I doubt that very much. I mean, you have enough tries, you have to get it right eventually, don't you?'

He had gone back to see Raymond Okpotu, just briefly. He wanted to tell him personally what had happened to his daughter and that they had caught the person responsible for it. The man had said he wanted justice and Charlie had been able to give it to him. He didn't think it would be consolation for immeasurable loss but, in his experience, justice was what counted with most people.

You see, he had wanted to say to him, we did not forget Mariatu. This time the boy soldier was held to account for what he did.

Raymond Okpotu had not said much. He shook Charlie's hand and thanked him, and for Charlie, that was enough.

He wished he could have done the same for Liam, and for Will. It was like he had told Michael: people don't want you banging on about absolution and God's mysteries. They just want to know someone down here has done what's right.

'Well, you take it easy, Lovejoy. I'll save your place back at Essex Road.'

'Thanks, guv.'

'Looks like Charlie will need a bath when he gets home,' he said.

He walked back to his car, left her and her step playing with the dog. He watched them for a bit from his car before he drove off. Made his heart glad, it did. Couldn't call it a happy conclusion, exactly; four people dead, two of them children, and God alone knew what would happen to the little girl. Still, he had plugged a hole in the dam for another day, saved some other poor sod from the same misery; it was the best you could ever do.

He thought about Reuben, about the boy soldiers in Sierra Leone, chopping off people's hands. How old were they when they lost their innocence? Or is innocence just some fairy story we tell ourselves, that doesn't really exist outside our imaginations, like Bambi, like Father Christmas?

He thought about Pippa: what did she mean that afternoon, *I can't stand him touching me.* He supposed he would never find out about that now. Wasn't his business. Like Ben said, his job wasn't to ask why the red flags were there, his job was just to run before a bit of roof came down on him.

292

Then he thought about his bastard of an uncle rotting in hallowed ground, what he had done to Liam, perhaps what he had done to Will. So much lies beneath, rustling and hissing down there in the dark, behind people's eyes. Nothing is ever quite what it seems, is it?

He shrugged the dark thoughts aside. Had no more time for them on this bright spring afternoon with mare's tails brushed across the sky and a spaniel yapping, chasing a tennis ball on the grass. Bright side: he'd made it through another week intact, had a chance to have another shot at things. He looked back at Lovejoy and her dad and had to smile. Sometimes people should just spend more time playing with their dog, he thought: there'd be a lot less trouble in the world.

ACKNOWLEDGEMENTS

A big thank you to my wonderful editor at Little, Brown, Krystyna Green, for having faith in me and in Charlie George. Thank you again to Kelly Falconer at Asia Literary Agency for getting me the gig, and to Penelope Isaac and Rebecca Sheppard at Little, Brown for their patience during the long editing process. And last but not least: to Lisa, for the long hours reading and re-reading, and re-reading again, and for pushing me to do better. Couldn't have done it without you, babe.